"*R*and," she whispered, too thunderstruck to move. Her heart fluttered. Pain and pleasure joined together to make her legs grow weak.

His face was inscrutable as he came to a halt mere inches before her. A highly charged silence rose between them. Claire forgot for a moment that she was standing on the creek bank, forgot that she was dripping wet and half-naked and too far from the house for anyone to hear her call for help.

Rand's gaze darkened while it raked hungrily over her. The knee-length chemise she wore was almost transparent. If the boy had become a man, so had the girl become a woman. Her breasts were full and rose-tipped, her waist slender. A pair of well-rounded hips tapered down to silken thighs and long, shapely legs.

His eyes traveled back up to her face. She was even more beautiful than he had remembered. A damn sight more.

TEXAS WEDDING

Catherine Creel

FAWCETT GOLD MEDAL • NEW YORK

A Fawcett Gold Medal Book
Published by Ballantine Books
Copyright © 1995 by Catherine Creel

ISBN 0-449-14787-8

Manufactured in the United States of America

First Edition: July 1995

10 9 8 7 6 5 4 3 2 1

With love to my little son, Cameron. You may have to climb a few more mountains than the rest of us. But I'll be with you every step of the way.

Chapter 1

Texas, 1876

The good people of Parmalee would never let Miss Claire forget the wedding.

Six years had gone by. Six long years. And still there was no escaping the despised handle of "kissless bride."

It didn't matter quite so much anymore, of course. In days past, she had dreaded going into town. Her stomach used to knot up with both anger and humiliation whenever someone asked if she had heard anything from "that no-account young buck" she had married. Those cruel, pointed reminders of her shame had always been enough to bring on a flood of self-pitying tears.

But things were different now. *She* was different. Time and trouble had a way of toughening a person's skin.

At least that's what she kept telling herself.

The painful memories were buried deep in her mind on this particular April morning as she guided the horse and buckboard to a halt in front of Parmalee's lone general store. Her fine jewel green eyes were alight with determination as she tossed a quick glance overhead at the endless blue of the North Texas sky.

The day promised to be a typically bright one. The sun's rays were hindered by only a few whisper-thin clouds, while the air, smelling of horses and wood smoke and overboiled coffee, was already warm. There was scarcely a hint of the wind that more often than not came whipping around every corner to stir up fiendish, gritty columns of dirt. If the town's unpaved streets weren't being cursed for their choking dust in dry weather, they were being damned for the rivers of thick black mud they became whenever it rained.

Although it wasn't yet nine o'clock, the rough-hewn boardwalks lining either side of the main thoroughfare were already sounding a brisk clarion call of activity. Farmers had hitched up their teams and headed into town at first light to buy tools and provisions, ranchers to buy feed, and women to gather at the general store for near equal amounts of shopping and gossip.

The courthouse square was crowded with wagons and horses; the two-story, red brick courthouse stood like a beacon amid the hustle-bustle of the county seat. Brightly painted storefronts, a new hotel, and the start of yet another church (a Methodist one this time) gave further evidence of its prosperity. In every corner, life had taken hold. Only the saloons were quiet and still for the moment, their windows securely shuttered after a hard night of what some called entertainment.

Claire allowed her gaze to make a broad, encompassing sweep of the town that had been named in honor of her late father. She felt the usual contradictory mixture of pride, affection, and bitter resentment. No doubt about it, she mused with an inward sigh, Samuel Parmalee would have taken joy in the prairie metropolis the little frontier town had become ... but he'd have raged something awful at its scorn and mockery of his beloved only child.

Frowning, she gave one final tug on the reins. Her eyes narrowed ever so slightly when they moved to the group of bonneted and calicoed ladies assembled just within the mercantile's open doorway. She would have to run the gauntlet. The prospect caused her to mutter an oath of annoyance under her breath.

"You go on over to the livery stable and tell Mr. Cooper I'll be needing that new mare after all," she instructed the man seated beside her in the buckboard. She set the brake, secured the reins, and climbed down without waiting for her companion's help.

"Yes, ma'am," he replied dutifully enough, though a brief shadow of reluctance crossed his face. He was still young, no more than thirty, his body sturdy and his getup the trademark denim trousers and striped cotton work shirt of a cowboy. His short, curly hair was black as night, and his brown eyes held a wisdom far beyond his years. But the color of his skin was the only thing most people noticed—and the thing that continued to set him apart no matter how much he wished otherwise.

"Oh, and Micah?" Claire called out before he had done more than turn away.

"Ma'am?" Broad-brimmed hat in hand, he peered back at her in expectation. His boyishly attractive features gleamed dark and smooth in the morning sunlight.

"Don't let Graham Cooper waste your time with any of those crowbaits he keeps trotting out. He's been trying to pawn them off on some poor soul since the beginning of time, and I have very little doubt he'll try the same today."

"I'll keep an eye out, Miss Claire," promised Micah. His mouth curved into a brief, lopsided grin, and his eyes twinkled across at her before he took himself off to do battle with the town's most notorious purveyor of horseflesh.

Claire couldn't help smiling as she watched him stride away. The smile faded, however, when she turned back to her own task at hand. Impatiently tucking a wayward strand of hair into place again, she found herself hesitating to go forth.

She wasn't the least bit afraid of facing the group of women. Fear, and embarrassment for that matter, had long since vanished. She simply would have preferred to avoid the inevitable confrontation awaiting her. But there could be no avoidance, and she knew it. She knew it all too well.

Another sigh, this one audible, escaped her lips. Resolutely squaring her shoulders, she gathered up her long skirts and sailed through the doorway. All eyes flew to her, just as she had expected they would, while a sudden and heavily charged silence filled the cluttered, aromatic interior of the store.

"Mornin', Miss Claire," the proprietor offered from his position behind the counter. He was a tall man, rail-thin, with a full head of coppery hair and an amiable disposition. His greeting to Claire held its customary warmth. "Fine day, ain't it?"

"Yes it is, Mr. Hunnicutt," she replied, smiling briefly at him. She directed a curt nod toward the short, buxom woman at his side. Martha Hunnicutt, as sour as her husband was sunny, did nothing more than scowl in return.

"What a pleasant surprise," one of the assembled gossipers remarked, insincerely. Brunet, fine-boned, and unmarried, Harriet Thompson might have been considered attractive if not for her perpetual air of disdain. It was said that she set great store by the fact that she was descended from a wealthy, connected family back East. It was also said that she was as proud as a peacock. "I must say, Claire, I didn't think we'd be seeing you in town again so soon."

"Didn't you?" parried Claire. She swept blithely past the five women, unmindful of the fact that their collective gazes raked over her with ill-disguised envy. She had no idea how young and lovely she looked, even in her plain blue gingham work dress, nor of the way the sun lit fire in her unswept mass of honey-blond hair when she stepped through the soft, dust-dancing rays streaming in through the front window.

"You haven't brought that Bishop woman with you today, have you?" a second, much older member of the group queried sharply. Lydia Cassidy had been among the first settlers, and had never been particularly shy about speaking her mind. Today was no exception. "You mark my words, Claire Parmalee, she'll do you harm yet!"

"Whatever made you go and hire someone like that?" Jane Willis saw fit to demand. Not much older than Claire, Jane wasn't a particularly unkind person. But she tended to follow Lydia's lead. She exchanged a superior, knowing look with the others as she drew herself stiffly erect. "Truth be told, I'd be downright ashamed to have that kind of woman in *my* house."

"She ought to be run out of town," muttered Lydia.

"She ought to be run out of Texas!" said Jane.

"Yes, and that half-breed child of hers as well!" Harriet saw fit to add.

Claire moved across to the far end of the counter, pretending a sudden interest in the barrel of slightly green apples George Hunnicutt had just that morning rolled into place. Her blood was boiling, but she mentally counted to ten and schooled her features to impassivity. She wasn't about to give these harpies the satisfaction of knowing how much their mean, spiteful words angered her. God grant her strength, though, it was all she could do to bite her tongue. . . .

Taking their cue from her silence, the women proceeded to launch a full-scale attack, while George watched in helpless, masculine bemusement.

"It's bad enough you've got a former slave workin' for you," sniffed the gray-haired Lydia, her pale blue eyes fairly snapping. "Lord knows, I'm as full of Christian kindness as the next person, but he doesn't belong here. And neither does Sadie Bishop." Pulling her crocheted shawl more closely across her ample bosom, she lifted her double chin to a self-righteous angle and charged for what was easily the hundredth time, "You had no call to take on a fallen woman when there are plenty of decent folks who'd be glad of the work!"

"Your poor father is probably turning over in his grave," Violet McLaughlin expounded quietly. A pretty young woman of strong moral character, but no measurable share of common sense, she was usually much too

busy minding everyone else's business to look to her
own. She lowered her voice even further, as if she were
afraid Samuel Parmalee himself would suddenly materi-
alize before them. "Why, it absolutely chills my spine
to think—"

"You can be sure *he'd* never have allowed their kind
to step foot on Glorieta," the blond, sharp-featured
Anne Denney finally chimed in. The mother of six
grown sons, she had been acquainted with Claire's father for a number of years. "Sam wasn't one to suffer
fools gladly. And that's what you're being, Claire. A
stubborn little fool who's too caught up in her own defiance to see the right of things!"

"Haven't you given a mind at all to what the whole
town's saying?" Martha challenged severely. Her comment earned her a swift—albeit gentle—elbowing from
her husband, but she shot him a quelling glare and went
on. "You mark my words, your reputation's going to
suffer!"

"*What* reputation?" Harriet sneered. There was a general shaking of heads at that—half in pity, half in judgment.

Claire stiffened, her lips compressing into a tight,
thin line. She picked up an apple, then put it down
again and stepped across to the shelves, where row
upon row of tins and jars and boxes were stacked in
well-ordered disarray. She was still determined to do
her shopping and be on her way without surrendering to
the temptation to give back every bit as good as she was
getting. But it was growing more difficult with each
passing minute.

"Just so you know, we're aimin' to take this up with

the new preacher," announced Lydia. She pointed a plump, accusatory finger at Claire. "I expect he'll be readin' you from the pulpit any day now."

"I swear, Claire Parmalee," Martha felt duty-bound to threaten, "if you dare to try bringing that—that *Jezebel* to church, you'll find yourself cast out for good. Yes, and your whole bunch of sorry, ragtag misfits right along with you!"

"We'll see they get what's comin' to them!"

"Tarring and feathering might be just the thing—"

"Or riding a rail!"

For Claire, that was the last straw. By heaven, she told herself while her temper flared to an almost dangerous level, it wasn't humanly possible to endure any more. Rounding on her tormentors with her emerald eyes splendidly ablaze, she marched forward to confront them.

"Sadie Bishop is worth more than the whole lot of you put together," she declared in a tone of furious calm, stopping mere inches away from where they stood gathered together like so many chickens. "She has every right to go anywhere she pleases. So does Micah. *And* Sully."

A faint smile of irony touched her lips as she met the women's wide, startled gazes. They were unaccustomed to hearing her offer any kind of response at all to their taunts; she hadn't done so in a long, long time.

"You can say whatever you please about me," she said, then warned, "but never again make the mistake of turning those vipers' tongues of yours against the others. They don't deserve your condemnation. And I'll be hanged if I'll let you hurt them!"

"Claire!" Violet said sharply, visibly shocked at the profanity.

"I know, Violet," she drawled, with more than a hint of sarcasm. "I'm going straight to hell. In a hand basket." Briskly turning her back on them again, she withdrew a piece of paper from her skirt pocket and handed it to George. "I've made a list of everything I need, Mr. Hunnicutt. If you would be so kind as to fill my order, I'll return later to collect it."

"It'll be my pleasure to do it for you, Miss Claire," he assured her earnestly.

"You'll be paying cash, of course?" demanded Martha, her attitude more belligerent than ever.

"I've never yet asked for credit," Claire answered, with remarkable equanimity. She found herself battling a sudden, powerful urge to strike the woman. Violence had never been an integral part of her nature ... but there was always a first time for everything, she mused, her gaze sparkling with ironic humor again as she turned and swept toward the doorway. Anne Denney's voice followed her outside.

"Just remember, Claire Parmalee—you're certain to reap whatever it is you sow. I hope the good Lord shows you mercy. No one else will."

Only the wicked need mercy, Claire retorted silently. She stepped into the welcoming sunshine once more and took a deep breath. More rankled by the unpleasant encounter than she'd ever care to admit, she responded to a passerby's greeting with nothing more than a wan, preoccupied little smile. Her gaze traveled northward to the livery stable. Wondering about Micah's progress—or lack of it—with the rascally Graham Cooper, she headed off to join in the fray. She was certainly in the mood for a fight.

With an ease borne of many years' practice, she dodged an assortment of wagons, horses, and ever-curious glances as she made her way across the main street. She approached the entrance to the stable just in time to overhear Micah's response to the other man's latest attempt to rid himself of some of his less valuable inventory.

"I don't think Miss Claire had it in mind to buy a swaybacked cayuse on its last legs." Micah's tone was respectful enough, but Claire's ears detected an underlying note of sarcasm. A faint smile tugged at her lips. On sudden impulse, she crept closer to the doorway and paused to listen some more.

"Well now, boy . . . Venus here might not be a regular gut twister," Graham conceded begrudgingly, his bloodshot eyes narrowing as they shifted back to the horse beside him. He was an unattractive man, potbellied and ill-kempt and given to drink even on Sunday. He had long since earned the designation of "town character"—even more so than Old Man Arbuckle, whose one true claim to infamy was a propensity for shooting at anyone fool enough to ride past his house.

"But she's reliable," Graham went on to insist to a solemn-faced Micah as they stood together inside the smelly, hay-strewn coolness of the stable. He spat a stream of liquified tobacco onto the ground and frowned. "Damn reliable. Hell, Miss Claire don't want no animal with lightnin' in its belly!"

"You don't know her too well if you can say that," Micah countered smoothly. He reached up and settled his hat lower on his head. "We've wasted enough time, Mr. Cooper. Let's get down to business."

"I got nothin' else to show you," the older man insisted, his craggy, unshaven features reddening. It was clear that he was irritated by Micah's unwillingness to be taken in.

"Are you sure about that?"

"You callin' me a liar, boy?"

"I'm not a 'boy,' Mr. Cooper," Micah pointed out in a low voice edged with steel. His eyes glinted coldly, but he kept a tight rein on his temper. "And I'm not calling you anything at all."

"You're mighty uppity for a colored man, ain't you?" complained Graham. A sudden, ugly notion took root in what little brain he had. "Could be you're one of them fancy, gol-durned carpetbaggers come down here to cheat us out of what's ours. We already had enough of your kind, boy!"

Claire rolled her eyes heavenward. *Shut your mouth, you old fool,* she thought, alarmed by the hazardous turn of the negotiations. She called an abrupt halt to her eavesdropping now. Hastening inside, she skillfully positioned herself between the two men.

"Good morning, Mr. Cooper," she said, with deceptive nonchalance, then turned to Micah. "Have you made a decision yet?"

"No, ma'am." The only outward sign of his struggle was a tautness about his mouth. But Claire read the lingering anger in his eyes. "Mr. Cooper and I haven't gotten that far."

"Well then, maybe I can lend a hand." She folded her

arms beneath her breasts and told Graham, "I need a good strong mare. A sorrel, if you've got one."

"I can give you a right fair price for Venus," he offered, slicing Micah a glare that was both hostile and defensive.

"Venus hasn't improved with age," Claire remarked dryly. She gathered up her skirts and turned to leave. "Thank you for your trouble, Mr. Cooper. But if that's the best you can do, I'll simply have to take my business elsewhere. I've heard about a new livery stable over in the next county—"

"Now, now, Miss Claire. There ain't no call for that!" Graham exclaimed. He spoke in such a rush that he swallowed some of his chewing tobacco. Coughing loudly, he hurried to clear his throat. "I—I do recollect now . . . I've got another mare out back. A right fine one, come to think of it. A pretty little roan. I was savin' her for Miz Thompson, but seein' as how you're in need . . ." His words trailed away as he began leading Venus toward the corral behind the stable.

Claire looked at Micah. She was relieved to see the glimmer of sardonic amusement in his gaze. There was no need for words between them as they turned and followed after Graham.

Less than half an hour later, they were on their way home, with the supplies from the mercantile loaded in the buckboard and the new roan mare trotting at the end of a halter tied behind. A gentle breeze had begun to stir the air, and the blazing gold of the sun cast fewer and fewer shadows on its way to straight-up noon. A lone hawk circled lazily overhead. The sound of gunshots—a common enough occurrence in these parts—echoed in the distance somewhere.

Claire gave a light flick of the reins and shifted her hips a bit on the wooden seat. All about her, the country-side stretched out in broad sweeps of rich black earth. It was mantled in the green of springtime, and treeless ex-cept for the oaks and cottonwoods clustered along the numerous springs, creeks, and occasional rivers. When she and her father had first come to the prairie, the grass had been so tall in some places that a child could be-come lost in it. Back then, vast herds of wild longhorn cattle had roamed across the plains, and the threat of an Indian attack had been a constant worry. The memory of those early days was a bittersweet one.

Heaving a sigh, she turned her thoughts elsewhere. Her eyes gleamed in triumph at the realization that she had just bought Harriet Thompson's horse right out from under her. There was a certain poetic justice to it, she mused with an inward smile. Though Harriet prob-ably wouldn't see it that way.

She stole a quick glance at the man beside her. He was still something of an enigma, in spite of the fact that he had worked for her for more than a year. She knew that he had been born a slave in Georgia, and that he had escaped to fight for the North during the war. He claimed to have wrangled for some outfits down in South Texas; she had never bothered to investigate his story. From the very first moment he had ridden onto Glorieta and asked her for a job, she had sensed that he was trustworthy. His past didn't really matter.

Graham Cooper's foolish, hateful words suddenly

burned in her mind again. She frowned and broke what had been a companionable silence.

"Micah?"

"Yes, ma'am?"

"I hope you're not going to let what Mr. Cooper said—"

"He didn't say anything I haven't heard before, Miss Claire," Micah assured her. He dropped his gaze to the hat in his hands before adding quietly, "And nothing I won't hear again."

"You've got an awful lot of patience, haven't you?" she marveled aloud.

"No, ma'am. I've just got enough sense not to stick my hand in a hornet's nest."

"At least you didn't let him sell you Venus." There was a teasing light in her green eyes now.

"I may be nothing but an 'uppity darky' to some folks, Miss Claire," he allowed, raising the hat to his head again, "but the color of my skin doesn't affect my eyesight." His mouth suddenly curved into a grin. Claire gave a soft laugh and flicked the reins again.

It wasn't much longer before they reached the boundaries of Glorieta. Situated in the midst of the rolling plains, only a few miles from town, the ranch had borrowed the name of a small family church back in Samuel Parmalee's native South Carolina. Samuel had never completely forgotten his homeland—nor the betrayal that had combined with the South's heartbreaking defeat to send him searching for a fresh start elsewhere. He had found it here, in the rugged, sparsely populated frontier known as Texas.

He had done everything in his power to make a good

life for his daughter. Fate may have dealt him a series of cruel blows, but he hadn't become embittered. Only toughened. And even though he had been a strict father, he had also been a loving and attentive one, trying his best to make up for the lack of a mother. Of course, Samuel had always given everything his all. Glorieta was certainly proof of that.

Claire's heart swelled with pride as her gaze traveled across countryside that was still wild, still open and free. This was *her* land. Thank God, she had been able to keep the ranch going after her father's death nearly two years ago. Glorieta was one of the most successful ranches in all the county now, a prairie kingdom ruled with a fair hand. There were times when it seemed like a world all in itself, she reflected, times when she wished there would never be a need to leave the sanctuary it provided.

She drove the buckboard toward the half dozen buildings that had come into view just ahead. The main house was a whitewashed, two-storied clapboard, sheltered by tall oaks and boasting of decorative gingerbread trim. It bore little resemblance to the simple log cabin it had once been. Two large red barns—one for stock, one for hay—rose across the yard, while the long, low-roofed bunkhouse, stone springhouse, and corral fenced with split rails lay nearby. A small wooden "convenience" still sat nestled among the greenery behind the house, serving as a reminder of the days, not so long ago, before Samuel had finally yielded to the inevitability of progress and added an indoor bathroom just off the kitchen.

Guiding the horse to a halt before the main house,

Claire set the brake and climbed down. Micah wasted little time in starting to unload the supplies from the buckboard.

"I'll see to the horses once I've gotten these inside," he said, hoisting a sack of flour.

"Sadie and I can do that. You go ahead and take the wagon around to the barn. And if you happen to see Sully, would you please tell him I'd like a word with him?"

"Yes, ma'am."

She helped him transfer the other sacks and boxes to the front porch, then called to Sadie while he led the horses away. The housekeeper was quick to answer the summons.

"I didn't realize you were back yet!" Sadie Bishop declared breathlessly, wiping her hands on her clean white apron as she materialized in the doorway. Only a few years older than Claire, she was tall for a woman and possessed a trim, shapely figure, which she did her best to hide beneath loosely gathered dresses. Her long black hair was twisted up into a severe chignon. She rarely smiled. And her blue-green eyes held a sadness that Claire could only guess at.

"Wolf usually trumpets my arrival," noted Claire, her mouth curving briefly upward. She lifted a box in her arms and allowed her gaze to sweep across the deserted front yard. A mild frown of bemusement creased her brow. "I wonder where that silly mongrel is."

"More than likely, he's gone off with Harmony," Sadie offered, her tone apologetic. Opening the screen door, she stepped forward and bent to scoop up one of the sacks. "I hope you don't mind that she keeps him—"

"I don't mind in the least. To tell the truth, I'm glad he has someone else to badger for a change. He does tend to get underfoot. Sully keeps threatening to put him out of his misery." She carried the box inside, with Sadie following close behind. They headed through the entrance foyer, down a wide, rose-papered hallway, and on toward the sunlit kitchen at the back of the house.

"Mr. Greene wouldn't really do such a thing, would he?" Sadie asked worriedly, having failed to detect the amusement in Claire's tone.

"Of course not!" Claire hastened to deny. She crossed the kitchen's bare wooden floor, which offered up the pleasant aroma of lemon and beeswax, and lowered the box to the sturdy worktable near the sink. A sudden gust of wind sent the lace curtains at the window flapping as she turned to give the other woman a kind, quizzical look. "Come now, Sadie. Surely you've learned by now that his bark is far worse than his bite. He *is* a gruff man, downright ornery at times, but he has a heart of gold."

"Harmony took to him right enough."

"Well then, I'd call that proof of his true worth, wouldn't you?" Smiling again, she dusted off her hands and was about to set off for the porch again when Sadie unexpectedly detained her.

"Claire?"

"Yes?" She paused in the doorway and tossed a casual glance back over her shoulder.

"Did—did anyone in town ask about me?"

The shadow of pain crossing her friend's face was unmistakable. Claire felt her own heart twisting with compassion.

"No," she lied, though she told herself it wasn't really a falsehood. "Were you expecting someone to?"

"Yes," answered Sadie, then shook her head and dropped her gaze to the overstuffed cloth sack she had just set atop the table. "I mean, no. It's just that people have a hard time forgetting what lies behind."

"A good memory isn't always an asset, is it?" Claire remarked, half to herself. The pangs of sympathy she had felt on Sadie's behalf a few moments ago were nothing compared to the sharp pain that burned through her now as a sudden—completely unbidden—image swam before her eyes.

It was a man's face. *His face.*

"Maybe someday . . ." Sadie murmured, without any real hope or conviction.

"My father used to caution me against living for 'somedays,' " Claire recalled. She forced a smile to her lips and added, "He was fond of giving advice, but not always capable of following it himself."

"That's the way of it with most folks, I guess." The other woman sighed. She managed a weak, fleeting smile of her own before a faraway look came into her eyes. A man's face rose in her mind, too. Only the memory of it had become blurred a bit now, either by pain or the simple passage of time. The nagging sense of shame she felt, however, was all too vivid. Shame for having worked in a saloon . . . shame for having allowed herself to be valued so cheaply. "Sometimes I think I was wrong to come here." Her voice was barely audible.

"Nonsense."

"But I could cause trouble for you."

"You let me worry about that."

Claire started to say more, but thought better of it and returned outside to the porch. She refused to think about where her traitorous mind had just led her. There was nothing to be gained from dwelling on the past. Nothing at all.

"That filly you brought home ain't even saddle broke yet." A familiar masculine voice interrupted her reverie.

She looked up to observe Sully approaching the house. Sullivan Greene was a crusty old Irishman hired by her father not long after their arrival in Texas. Born in Dublin, yet reared on the harsh American frontier, he seemed to know more about cattle and horses than anyone else who cared to stand up for comparison. He was more family than employee after all this time. And every inch a benevolent dictator, Claire mused wryly.

"I know." She moved forward to curl an arm about one of the porch columns. "But Micah and I thought she looked worthwhile."

"Worthwhile?" His craggy, weather-beaten features, darkened to the color of leather by too many years spent beneath the Texas sun, screwed up into an eloquent gesture of disgust. "Hell, girl. Ain't you learned nothin' yet about horses?"

"Apparently not," she countered, her eyes sparkling

with warm, indulgent humor. "That's why I keep *you* around."

He offered no response to that, but climbed the steps and stood squinting at her with his thumbs hooked negligently in the curve of his front pockets. Although not very tall, he was strong and wiry, and he could still hold his own with men half his age. Of course, no one knew exactly what his age might be. He had never talked much about himself. But it was generally acknowledged that, if he so wanted, he could argue a gopher into climbing a tree.

"Have any trouble in town?" he asked Claire in his usual gruff, no-nonsense tone.

"None to speak of." Averting her gaze from the gray steadiness of his, she dropped her arm back to her side and pivoted about to lift the last of the sacks.

"That so?"

"It was nothing, really," she insisted, only to find herself confiding in the next instant, "Graham Cooper showed his bone-deep ignorance again. And some of the 'ladies' of the town decided to voice their displeasure with my new housekeeper."

"Damned she-rattlers," muttered Sully. "I could set 'em straight right enough."

"Yes, and I'm sure their ears would be burning for years afterward." Her mouth twitched at the thought. "But you're something of a pariah yourself, Sullivan Greene, and I doubt if anything outside of a well-aimed bolt of lightning could persuade them to listen. Besides," she concluded, her voice full of weary resignation now, "there's nothing to be gained by trying to reason with them. People tend to believe what they want to believe."

"If your pa was still alive, he'd give 'em hell."

"He would indeed." Her eyes clouded with a remembrance that was at once fond and rueful. She glanced at Sully and saw that his did the same. "Will the men be heading into town tonight?" she asked, purposely changing the subject.

"It's Saturday, ain't it?" He leaned against the opposite post and squinted at her again. "That what you wanted to talk to me about?"

"It was. I certainly have no desire to see them coming home all busted up again tomorrow morning," she declared sternly.

"Boys will be boys." He flashed her one of his rare grins, his teeth yellow and tobacco-stained amid the peppery stubble of his chin.

"That's what I'm afraid of." She did her best to conceal her own amusement and said, "Why don't you go along with them this time? You can leave Micah in charge while—"

"You lookin' to replace me?" he demanded, abruptly straightening.

"I might be, you old reprobate, if you don't stop interrupting me!" she shot back in mock exasperation. Her eyes sparkled across at him. "You know as well as I do that it would take ten men to replace you. I was merely suggesting that you accompany the hands into town so that you could keep them out of trouble. That new saloon is wreaking havoc. And anyway, it might do you good to take a night off and let down your guard for a change. You haven't stepped foot off Glorieta in ages."

"No need to. I'm past my prime, in case you ain't noticed." He heaved a loud, disgruntled sigh and headed back down the front steps at a brisk pace. "If you're so all-fired set on me playin' nursemaid, I'll do it. I won't like it none, but I'll do it."

"I knew I could count on you!" Claire called after him, her voice brimming with laughter. He was, without a doubt, the most prickly, bullheaded man she had ever known, she mused indulgently. Outside of her father, of course. It had been impossible to sway Samuel Parmalee whenever he had set his mind on something. What had happened six years ago had certainly proven that—

"Don't!" she commanded herself in a furious whisper. It was the second time that day she had thought of *him*. Great balls of fire! she lamented silently. Why, after all this time, should she start thinking of him again? It was over and done with. *Over and done with.*

Dismayed at the way her throat constricted, she finally turned and carried the sack inside.

The day wore on, just like any other. By the time afternoon faded into twilight, the ranch was practically deserted.

Sully, proving true to his word, had ridden off with the ranch hands for a traditional Saturday night in town. Micah had been only too happy to remain behind. He had made the mistake of joining the others once before; it had taken a considerable degree of argument on Claire's part to keep him from being locked up in jail for a week afterward. As he himself had readily admitted, strong spirits made him less willing to overlook slights and insults. And heaven knew, there were always plenty of those.

"You sure you don't need me for anything else tonight, Claire?" asked Sadie. She stood in the kitchen doorway, clasping the apron she had just drawn off. The supper dishes had been done, and the house, still holding the faint aroma of roasted chicken and potatoes, was quiet except for the sound of a child's laughter drifting down from the floor above.

"No, thank you," Claire replied, smiling as she poured herself another cup of coffee and allowed her eyes to stray toward the ceiling. "You can go on up now. And you might want to caution Harmony against letting Wolf sleep in her bed."

" 'You lie down with dogs, you get up with fleas.' " Sadie provided the old saying. The corners of her own mouth turned crookedly upward for a moment. "I heard that often enough myself. I guess there's more truth to it than most folks know." She sobered again before murmuring, "Good night."

"Good night, Sadie."

She watched the other woman go, then set the cup beside the stove and shifted her gaze to the window. It would be dark soon. Another night at Glorieta . . . another night spent sitting alone in the parlor with her books or out on the front porch with her thoughts.

A sudden, strange restlessness seized her.

Frowning, she left the coffee untouched and wandered to the back door. She opened it, leaned against the frame, and stared out across the rugged beauty of the plains. A coyote's distant, plaintive howl rose in the gathering darkness. Overhead, the North Star burned strong and steady, waiting to be joined by a million twinkling bursts of light.

Claire closed her eyes and breathed deeply of the sage-scented air. It was then that the idea of a visit to the pond entered her head. Her eyes flew open, her face brightening at the prospect. She told herself that it had been far too long since she had indulged in a nighttime swim. There was nothing like it to take a person's mind off their troubles, real or imagined. And besides, she rationalized, it made perfect sense to take advantage of the hands' absence.

She wavered for a moment, wondering whether or not to take Wolf with her, but decided against it. He was probably curled up at the foot of Harmony's bed by now. The little girl had formed a powerful attachment to him, and vice versa. He was becoming increasingly useless as a cow dog, but she couldn't be sorry for it.

Pausing only to catch up her rifle, she hurried off across the backyard, toward the creek, which lay a short distance behind the house. The light of the rising moon illuminated her way as she tread carefully over rocks and dodged low-lying branches. The possibility of snakes didn't frighten her, but she kept a watchful eye out just the same.

The "pond" was in actuality just a wider portion of the creek. Situated within the protective shelter of the trees, it was no more than chest-high at its deepest point, yet plenty big enough for a relaxing swim. As a child, Claire had often stolen away to splash and play with gleeful abandon. And even though she visited the spot with less frequency now, she never failed to experience a pleasurable, guilty sense of freedom while in its welcoming depths.

Propping her rifle against a tree, she hurried to strip off her clothing. She unfastened the buttons on the front of her dress and stepped out of it, then flung it across a limb. Her single petticoat came next, followed by her drawers. Taking a seat on the ground, she removed her boots and tugged off her stockings. She was clad only in her white cotton chemise as she stood and waded into the pond.

A delicious shiver ran the length of her spine when she bent her knees and plunged forward. The water was cool, but not uncomfortably so, and she smiled at the sensation of the mud squeezing between her toes when her feet touched bottom. She ducked underneath the surface, swimming to the opposite side before she splashed upward to suck in a deep breath. Her long hair escaped the pins to come streaming down about her face and shoulders, but she merely swept the wet mass of curls away from her face and dived beneath the pond's surface again.

She lost all track of time as she swam and floated blissfully along in the glistening coolness of the water. The night deepened, with the moon casting its soft, silvery radiance upon the prairie landscape. The leaves rustled gently in the wind, and the faint lowing of cattle filled the air. To Claire, everything seemed peaceful. Peaceful and orderly . . . yet incredibly lonely. What in heaven's name was the matter with her?

The spell abruptly broken, she rose from the water at last. Her hands lifted to smooth the hair away from her face once more as she climbed up to the creek bank to retrieve her clothes.

Suddenly, and without warning, a man's voice reached out to her in the darkness.

"It's been a long time, Mrs. Logan."

Chapter 2

A sharp gasp of startlement broke from Claire's lip. She froze. Her whole body tensed with alarm as her eyes flew wide.

It took only the fraction of a moment for the sense of danger to bring her to life again. She reached instinctively for the rifle, only to feel her heart sink in dismay when she discovered it gone.

"Who's there?" she called out in a loud, tremulous voice. Panic gripped her at the realization that she was alone and defenseless, but she refused to show any fear. She held her breath and straightened while her eyes made a hasty search of the area.

She gasped again when she spied the tall outline of a man beneath the trees only a few feet away. He stepped slowly from the shadows.

"Don't you remember me, Claire?" he challenged in a low tone.

His words threw her into confusion. She couldn't make out his face just yet, but there was something oddly familiar about his voice. It was warm and deep timbred, its splendid resonance washing over her in the darkness.

"Who are you? And what are you doing here?" she demanded, uncertain whether to be relieved or even more on guard. She was poised for action, ready to take flight if need be. *"Who are you?"*

He said nothing in response, but instead moved closer. The leaves and twigs crunched softly beneath his boots. He walked with an easy masculine grace, like a man accustomed to life outdoors.

Claire's mouth fell open in shocked amazement as he finally emerged into the moonlight. Her pulse took a wild leap. She blinked, unable to believe the evidence of her own eyes. It couldn't be, she told herself numbly. Dear God, it couldn't be!

But he was here.

He had changed. Gone was the boy. In his place was a man, matured by life and all its harsh realities. He was still handsome, even more so now, his features rugged and tanned above the collar of his pale blue shirt. His body was lean and hard, powerfully muscled. His dark brown hair, streaked gold by the sun, was cut short in the military style, and he wore a revolver holstered low on one hip. His eyes were as incredibly blue and fathomless as ever. They seemed to cut right through her.

"Rand," she whispered, still too thunderstruck to move. *This can't be happening,* she told herself. Her heart fluttered. Pain and pleasure joined together to make her legs grow weak.

His face was inscrutable as he came to a halt—mere inches before her. A highly charged silence rose between them. Claire forgot for a moment that she was standing on the creek bank, forgot that she was dripping wet and half-naked and too far from the house for anyone to hear her call for help.

Rand's gaze darkened while it raked hungrily over her. The knee-length chemise she wore was almost transparent. It clung to her body, revealing every sweet curve. If the boy had become a man, so had the girl become a woman. Her breasts were full and rose-tipped, her waist slender. A pair of well-rounded hips tapered down into silken thighs and long, shapely legs.

His eyes traveled back up to her face. She was even more beautiful than he had remembered. A damn sight more.

"It's good to see you again, Claire," he decreed softly. Although he made no move to touch her, she felt branded by him nonetheless.

The initial shock finally wore off. In its place came an intense, whirling flood tide of emotion. She gave a strangled cry and snatched her dress from the tree limb, then draped the gathered folds of fabric across the front of her body. She was acutely conscious of her vulnerable position now. And painfully aware of the fact that Rand Logan had her at such a disadvantage.

"How—how long have you been here?" she stammered. Her cheeks crimsoned at the smile that suddenly played about his lips.

"Awhile," he drawled, his eyes aglow with an unholy amusement—and something else she dared not put a name to.

"Why did you come?" Taking refuge in anger, she lifted her chin to a proud, defiant angle that belied the utter chaos inside her.

"I was passing through."

"Passing through?" Her eyes flashed green fire, and she gave him a look that would have scorched lesser men. "All of a sudden, after all this time, you just happened to be *passing through*?"

"I was sorry to hear about your father," he told her, his features sobering. "He was a good man."

"How did you—?"

"I've had my sources," he said enigmatically. He took a step closer, resisting the urge to smooth a stray curl from her forehead. His gaze burned down into hers. She could have sworn a shadow of remorse crossed his face before he queried, "You've been well?"

"You have no right to ask me that. No right at all!" She shook her head, still incredulous that he should appear out of the blue like this. Never in her wildest dreams— No, that wasn't true, she thought dazedly. She *had* dreamed of his return. She had imagined him coming back a broken man, begging for forgiveness and confessing that his life had been absolute misery ever since he had deserted her.

But he didn't look like a broken man. And he sure as hell wasn't begging for anything.

"Claire—"

"I don't know what brought you here," she ground out, "and I don't care. But I want you to leave. *Now*."

"You don't mean that."

"Don't I?"

"Aren't you even the least bit curious to know why I didn't come back before now?" he demanded, his own emotions in more of an uproar than he'd ever care to admit.

"Why should I be?" Claire shot back. "You ran out

on me six years ago, Rand Logan, and as far as I'm concerned you can keep on running!"

Hot, bitter tears suddenly blinded her. She spun about and fled along the grassy bank. Rand caught up with her in two long strides, his hand closing about her arm. She cried out and struggled to pull free, but he held fast.

"Let go of me!" she raged, lifting one hand to strike at him. He seized her wrist and started to pull her close, only to unexpectedly release her in the next instant. Staggering backward, she clasped the dress to her breasts, then shivered as a rush of cool night air swept across the exposed dampness of her flesh.

"I didn't intend for it to be like this, Claire," Rand told her quietly.

"How did you think it would be?" she choked out.

Furiously dashing at her tears, she took a ragged breath and lifted her stormy countenance to the grim, damnably appealing planes of his. He stood a full head taller, and there was no denying the masculine superiority of his strength. It occurred to her that he could easily do her harm if he took it in mind to do so; he appeared entirely capable of getting whatever it was he wanted. But strangely enough, she wasn't afraid of him. Fear was about the only thing she *didn't* feel at the moment.

"Did you expect me to be overcome with joy and gratitude?" she asked, with biting sarcasm. "To welcome you home like the prodigal son or—or to act like these past six years never happened?"

"No." His mouth curved into another faint smile, this one entirely humorless. "No, I didn't." His eyes smol-

dered like molten steel. She felt her head spinning
wildly.

"You never should have come, Rand," she declared
in a voice raw with hurt and fury. "You should have let
the past stay buried."

"You can't bury something that isn't dead, Claire."

His reply struck fear in her heart. It wasn't just the
words themselves. It was the way he said them.

She felt a sharp, knifelike pain deep inside. Her fiery
emerald gaze flew back up to meet the piercing, cobalt
blue steadiness of his. He was like some mysterious and
hard-edged stranger; yet at the same time, he was still
the Rand Logan she had once been prepared to give
herself to, body and soul.

Another involuntary shiver danced down her spine.
Desperate to put an end to the torturous encounter, she
turned and ran again. This time, he let her go.

She could feel his eyes burning into her back, but she
did not slow her frantic pace as she raced, barefoot,
across the ground. It wasn't until she had reached the
house again that she realized she had left the rest of her
clothing, and her rifle, beside the pond. But she would
not go back for them.

Hurrying up the stairs to her darkened room, she
closed the door and stumbled across to the iron bedstead. She flung herself facedown upon the quilt, her
body wracked with sobs that would no longer be denied. The tears streamed freely onto her pillow. She
cried as she hadn't cried since the death of her father.
She lay there until the terrible storm of weeping had
passed, until she could think more clearly about what
had happened.

Dear God, why? she lamented, rolling onto her side and wiping at her face with the skirt of the gingham dress. Why had he come back?

She sat up now, swung her legs over the edge of the soft feather mattress, and dragged herself from the bed. Making her way unsteadily across to the open window, she raised a trembling hand to tangle within the folds of the muslin curtain. She caught her lower lip between her teeth and stared outward at the quiet, moonlit yard below. Rand's face swam before her eyes once more.

It was still difficult to believe he was actually here. She had thought she would never see him again. She had believed herself safe. But he had come back. He had stolen her peace of mind, just as he had stolen her heart six years ago.

The memory of that fateful night, and the events leading up to it, came back to haunt her. She saw it all again with vivid, agonizing clarity. . . .

She was only seventeen then. Only seventeen when Rand Logan came looking for work at Glorieta.

Twenty-one, hot-tempered, and rakishly handsome, he was just the sort of dangerous man every father feared—and every daughter found irresistible. His history was both tragic and fascinating, especially to a girl whose whole world up till then had revolved around horses and ranch work.

She had never met anyone like him before. Orphaned by an Indian attack while still a child, he had been on his own for most of his life. Confederate soldier (at the tender age of fourteen), ranch hand, cattle driver, even deputy sheriff—he had held a variety of jobs, always managing to stay footloose. It went without saying that he had left a trail of broken hearts behind him, but that wasn't at all surprising. "Still cuttin' the wolf loose," Sully once remarked of him.

Samuel hired the good-looking young stranger against his better judgment. He had been able to tell right away that Rand was something of a firebrand. Yet he believed, mistakenly as it turned out, that nothing amiss would happen so long as he kept a tight rein on things. He warned Rand to stay away from his daughter, just as he had warned all the other hands.

The warning did little good.

To *her*, Rand Logan seemed like he had stepped from the pages of a book. A dashing, almost heroic figure come to life, ready to make a stand against evil and protect all that was good. That was a contradiction in itself, of course, for he was full of devilish charm and supremely confident of his own abilities.

A powerful attraction blazed to life between them at the very beginning. Within a matter of days, she tumbled head over heels in love with him. He made her no promises, but he also made no secret of the fact that he desired her. She dreamed of a future with him. Believing that his feelings were as strong as her own, she longed for the day when he would ask her to be his wife. She was a complete innocent, untested by love and all its accompanying tribulations. It never occurred to her that Rand might want anything other than a permanent relationship.

One warm, starlit summer night, the two of them were locked in a passionate embrace inside the barn when her father caught them. The scene that followed was frightening. She cried out and guiltily snatched the edges of her unfastened bodice together. Rand tried to make a run for it, only to find a rifle aimed directly at his heart. An enraged, vengeful Samuel considered killing the younger man there and then. But he managed to quell his more bloodthirsty inclinations and instead decreed that his daughter's "spoiler" would do the honorable thing and marry her at once.

It was Rand's turn to grow furious at that point. He tried, without success, to convince Samuel that they had done nothing more than share a few kisses. When he appealed to her to confirm the truth, to assure her father that she was still a virgin, she said nothing.

Her silence owed its origins to Samuel's fearsome, overpowering wrath, and to her own foolish belief in the power of love. Once Rand's temper cooled, she told herself, he would realize that their marriage, no matter how it came about, had been ordained by Providence after all. And anyway, she rationalized, hadn't he said that being with her was the closest thing to heaven on earth?

A preacher was fetched that same night. The wedding took place downstairs, in the parlor of the house, just after ten o'clock. There were no fancy trimmings, no white satin wedding dress or well-wishers or even guests—except for a grim-faced Sully. And as fate would have it, there was no honeymoon to follow.

The ceremony had scarcely ended when Rand bolted. He disappeared into the night, riding hell-bent for leather away from Glorieta and his new wife. He ran away without saying good-bye. And without claiming his husbandly rights.

She was left heartbroken and alone on her wedding night. An abandoned bride whose scandalous, hastily arranged marriage made her the talk of the town. Shotgun weddings were rare in Parmalee.

For a long time afterward, she prayed that he would return. She refused to surrender to despair, for she couldn't believe it possible that she could love someone so much and not be loved in return.

But he did not come back.

She was trapped in a cruel sort of limbo, neither wife nor widow, still loving him, yet forced to accept the truth of his betrayal. He never even bothered to write. She had no idea where he had gone, if he was alive or dead, or if he ever thought about her. Time crawled onward. Weeks turned into months, and months into years. She vowed to forget him . . .

Forget him. She had tried to do that. God knew, she had certainly tried. The grief she'd suffered had been just short of unendurable. Eventually she had learned to put aside her heartache and get on with her life, to dull her pain with long hours of work. But nothing had ever been quite the same again. Sully said that some of the fire had gone out of her the day "that randy, cocksure young son of a bitch took off." And her father . . . well, in his way, he had suffered right along with her.

"Damn you, Rand Logan," she whispered hoarsely, her fingers clenching within the curtains until her knuckles turned white. "Damn you straight to hell."

The man who had inspired such extreme, newfound rancor in her was at that same moment headed back to town. His hat was pulled low on his head, and he kept an easy grip on the reins as the horse beneath him cantered across the night-cloaked plains. He was lost in his own thoughts, his mind filled with memories more recent—and far less painful—than Claire's.

If not for that report the adjutant general had given him, he might never have known the truth. "Miss Claire Parmalee, owner of the Glorieta Ranch"—the words had leapt off the page at him. He had been taken aback by them at first, but his surprise had quickly given way to a deep, exhilarating pleasure. A swift investigation on his part had provided him with the news of Samuel Parmalee's death, and with a number of other details that were overshadowed by the discovery that there had been no annulment. For the first time in years, he had dared to hope.

She was still his wife.

His eyes gleamed with warm satisfaction at the thought. Fate, or merely some strange coincidence, perhaps, had led him back to her. Whatever it was didn't matter. He had been granted a second chance. And by damn, he was going to take full advantage of it.

He shifted in the saddle, his gaze darkening when he recalled their fiery—unexpectedly intimate—meeting. He had been drawn to the pond by the sounds of her splashing; standing quiet and still beneath the trees, he had watched her for a long time. The voice of reason deep inside his brain had warned him to leave, to wait until she had finished and returned to the house before making his presence at the ranch known, but he hadn't been able to tear his eyes away.

The sight of her emerging from the water, all wet and

soft and lovely in the pale moonlight, had set a fire to raging in his blood. More than anything, he had wanted to sweep her into his arms and kiss her until she begged for mercy. Only by virtue of an iron self-will had he been able to refrain from doing just that. Or from *trying* to, he amended silently, remembering the way she had struggled.

His mouth curved into a brief smile of irony. She was even more of a hellcat than before. A golden-haired spitfire capable of holding her own with any man. But he was the man born to tame her.

The light of determination in those magnificent, piercing blue eyes of his would have filled Claire with trepidation. She might well have been tempted to greet him with a loaded gun if she'd had any notion of what he was planning.

Life was still full of surprises. At long last, Rand Logan had come back to claim his bride.

Chapter 3

Her rifle was on the front porch when she stepped outside after breakfast the following morning. She discovered it propped up against the old slat-back rocker in the far corner, its long metal barrel glinting in the sunlight that crept from around the side of the house.

She paled at the sight of the gun. The realization that her "husband" had been so close to where she lay, tossing and turning restlessly in her bed the whole night long, prompted her to close her eyes and give an inward groan of dismay. So, she told herself ruefully, it hadn't been just a nightmare after all.

Rand Logan had come back.

The thought was every bit as nerve-rattling in the cold light of day. She shivered and folded her arms tightly beneath her breasts. Try as she would, she couldn't forget the strange, inscrutable expression on Rand's face the night before. The touch of his hand upon her arm was another memory she'd just as soon cast out. And the way his smoldering blue gaze had traveled over every square inch of her with such bold possessiveness . . .

"Why now?" she wondered aloud once more. Her

low, uneven tone was scarcely audible to her own ears. She was thankful for that in the next moment.

"You're up mighty damn late."

Her eyes flew wide at the sound of Sully's voice. *Like a rusty gate hinge,* her father had once described it. Guilty color sprang to her cheeks as she whirled hastily about. She saw the old wrangler surveying her from his vantage point in the yard at the opposite end of the house. The porch had been built well above the ground; Sully reached only waist-high to its surface.

"I see you made it home all right," observed Claire, anxious to steer the conversation elsewhere. She uncrossed her arms and wandered toward him.

"Did you think I wouldn't?" he countered somewhat testily. His eyes brimmed with wry amusement as he stepped up to the porch and braced a hand against its whitewashed edge. "Most of the boys look like they've been pulled backward through a knothole. Good thing it's Sunday."

Sunday, Claire echoed silently. She had forgotten what day it was.

"You headin' into town?" he asked, though he was already pretty sure of the answer.

"I suppose so," she responded, with a heavy sigh. She'd have to hurry if she wanted to make it to church on time.

"Then you'll be hearin' about the train robbery."

"Train robbery?" Her eyes grew round with surprise. "What train robbery?"

"Happened yesterday, on the four-thirty out of Dallas," Sully told her gravely. "A gang of six, maybe seven. They'd killed a steer and dragged the carcass onto the tracks. More than five hundred dollars in gold went missin'.''

"Was anyone hurt?" she queried in alarm. "Did they catch the men who did it?"

"One of the guards got his head broke, but it's said he'll live. And no, the thievin' bastards got clean away." He tugged the front brim of his dusty, sweat-stained felt hat lower and turned to set off toward the barn. "I'll hitch up the wagon."

Claire nodded mutely in his wake. She forgot all about her rifle and returned inside to the kitchen. The room still held the lingering aromas of coffee and bacon. Sadie and Harmony were seated together at the table. The little girl, a six-year-old beauty with long raven hair and eyes so deep a brown as to be called black, was chattering happily to the scruffy-looking giant of a dog at her feet, while her mother peeled potatoes for the traditional Sunday dinner. As soon as Sadie caught sight of Claire, she silenced the child with a quick, well-understood shake of the head and rose from her chair.

"Are you planning on going to church today, Claire?" she asked, wiping her hands on her apron.

"I am. Why don't you and Harmony come with me?"

"Oh, no. We—we couldn't do that." A dull flush rose to her face; she swiftly averted her gaze.

"Why not?" demanded Claire. "You seldom leave the ranch. A trip into town would do the both of you a world of good." Recalling that she had said much the same thing to Sully yesterday, she managed a brief yet warmly lit smile for Harmony and knelt beside Wolf. Her hand moved to the top of his furry brown head as she raised her eyes to Sadie again and pointed out kindly, "You'll gain nothing by keeping yourself hidden away out here. The best thing for you to do is show them you're not afraid of being seen."

"They don't want us there," argued Sadie, looking pained. "Especially not in church."

"And what better place is there for you to be?"

"*I* was in church once," Harmony interjected at that point. She stole a hasty glance at her mother before elaborating. "I was only a baby. Mama said the preacher put some water on my head."

"Well then," Claire replied, keeping her expression appropriately solemn, "I think a second visit is long overdue, wouldn't you agree?"

"Can we take Wolf?"

"Harmony, don't be silly," came her mother's gentle admonishment.

"We'll let Sully look after him until we get back," Claire reassured the little girl. She climbed to her feet and crossed back to the doorway. "I'm afraid we haven't much time to get ready. The service begins at eleven."

Anticipating further protests from Sadie, she hurried upstairs to her room. She exchanged her faded gingham work dress for a "Sunday best" ensemble made of printed Scottish cambric. Its plain fitted bodice and bustle skirt were still fashionable, and the square, lace-trimmed neckline made it all the more becoming. She had never developed the sort of obsession with clothing that so many other women of her acquaintance exhibited—there had been little enough opportunity for dressing up while running a ranch—but she *had* been taught to take pride in her appearance. An inner voice demanded archly if she might be hoping to impress Rand Logan. There was, after all, a distinct possibility that she would have to face him again very soon.

She muttered a highly unladylike oath. Coiling up her long hair, she jabbed the pins into place, then went back downstairs to the parlor. Sadie and Harmony joined her there a short time later. Although Sadie had chosen to wear a loose-fitting wrapper of gray calico, its dowdiness could not fully conceal her beauty. Harmony looked quite pretty in the new red calico dress her mother had made her. She was so excited about the journey ahead that she virtually bounded out of the house and down the front steps. Preoccupied though she was, Claire couldn't help laughing softly at the girl's childish enthusiasm.

The morning sunlight was warm on their backs as they drove away in the buckboard. Sadie kept Harmony occupied with a discussion about the vast array of insects that returned each spring to transform the countryside into a buzzing, teeming sea of miniature legs and wings. Claire, guiding the horse with a steady and practiced grip on the reins, found her thoughts drawn irrevocably to Rand once more.

Her reasons for going to church were more than social or theological. Since she had no idea when *he* would show up again, it seemed best to get away from Glorieta for a while. Her actions were cowardly, perhaps, she conceded with an inward sigh, but advisable just the same. The prospect of yet another confrontation with him filled her with dread. Heaven help her, she was as nervous as a long-tailed cat under a rocking chair. But she was nevertheless determined for life to go on as usual. The man had turned her world upside down once before. She would not let it happen again.

She wondered if anyone else knew he was back. The thought of certain people's reactions, of their hateful gossip and their knowing smirks and their predictions about what was likely to happen now that her worthless, long-lost husband had finally returned, made her offer up another silent curse. It was probably too much to hope that he would stay away from Parmalee altogether, or that if he did go there, he would use an assumed name. He had changed a great deal; maybe, God willing, no one would recognize him.

She tugged on the reins to slow the horse's pace as they reached the outskirts of town. Pulling up in front of the quaint, steeple-topped frame church just as the last bell sounded, she swung Harmony down and hastened around the buckboard. Sadie alighted as well, but held back when Claire started inside.

"Claire, I—"

"Oh, Sadie. You can't lose courage now." She placed a bolstering hand on the other woman's arm and said quietly, "Don't you think I understand how you must feel? Winning their acceptance won't be easy. But nothing worth having ever is."

"You might have fallen from grace, but you didn't fall as far as I did," Sadie remarked, with a sad irony, keeping her voice low as her eyes moved to where Harmony had wandered away to play beneath a tree. "I'll never win their acceptance. And I'm not sure I even want to."

"I can't blame you for that. They *are* unforgivably cruel and judgmental at times. But that's precisely why

I refuse to let them beat me down. This is my home as much as it is theirs. And by thunder, I have no intention of wearing sackcloth and ashes for the rest of my life simply because they're too goshawful mule-headed to try and understand." She paused for a moment, her beautiful green eyes narrowing before she challenged, "Now, Sadie Bishop—are we going to church or not?"

Sadie did not immediately answer. She appeared to be weighing Claire's encouragement against her own apprehensions. Finally her features relaxed into a soft, capitulating smile. She called to Harmony, and the three of them headed toward the church steps again.

Claire's eyes strayed about, instinctively searching for Rand before she disappeared inside, but there was no sign of him. She breathed a sigh, although she couldn't have said whether it was one of relief or chagrin. All of a sudden, she remembered how she had once dreamed of entering that same church in a fancy white wedding dress while Rand waited, tall and handsome, beside the altar. For the merest fraction of an instant, she clutched at the dream again. If only— *No.* It was impossible to turn back the clock. Why did she feel such a desperate yearning to do so?

Remembering Lydia's threat about the new preacher reading her from the pulpit, she lifted her head to a proudly defiant angle and led the way down the narrow aisle to a half-empty pew near the very front of the church. A loud, collective gasp of shocked amazement rose from the congregation. Had she really brought *that woman* into the sanctity of the Lord's house? they all seemed to be thinking.

The new preacher, blithely disregarding the murmur

of the crowd, continued with his greeting and announcements. Attractive and fair-haired, he had emigrated from Austria at the age of eighteen. He was now in his mid-thirties, a benevolent figure clad in the customary black robes of a clergyman. He cast a welcoming smile in the latecomers' direction as they took their seats. His gaze sparked with interest as it lingered on Sadie for a moment, and he found it necessary to stop and clear his throat before resuming.

The service lasted for the better part of an hour. It was not entirely successful in taking Claire's mind off her troubles, for she still found herself plagued by frequent and disturbing thoughts of Rand. She almost wished she *would* be read from the pulpit; at least she'd be able to vent some of the hurt and anger churning inside her.

Fortunately no one dared to storm from the church during the sermon or the hymn singing that followed. But there was a swift exodus immediately afterward, with the women gathering outside beneath the trees to fume in righteous indignation about Sadie Bishop's presence there, and the men forming their own groups to talk about the rising price of cattle, the downward spiral of politics in Texas, and the county's most recent train robbery. It was the second one in as many months; only a short time before that, a total of three stagecoaches had been relieved of their strongboxes by a gang of masked, astonishingly well-prepared gunmen.

Not even such momentous news as that, however, could deflect attention of the worst kind away from Claire and her two companions. The last to emerge from the church, they were surprised to find the preacher waiting for them on the front steps.

"Thank you for coming, ladies," he offered earnestly. His smile was meant for the entire trio, but his blue-green eyes kept drifting back to Sadie. "I do not believe I have yet had the pleasure of making your acquaintance. I am Reverend Thomas Mueller." He was quite tall, his voice mellow and flavored with the evidence of his Tyrolean heritage. Sadie colored faintly and looked away, while Harmony made a game of scampering up and down the steps.

"I'm Claire Parmalee." Claire dutifully performed the introductions. "This is Sadie Bishop. And *that* is Harmony." She smiled toward the child.

"Miss Parmalee. Miss Bishop." He nodded politely at each of them in turn.

"It's *Mrs.*," Sadie corrected him, her gaze falling self-consciously beneath his again.

"Oh, I see." Although he was long accustomed to masking his emotions, he could not fully prevent a shadow of disappointment from crossing his face. "And did your husband not accompany you today, Mrs. Bishop?"

"No, he—he passed away two years ago."

"I am sorry. Please accept my condolences, belated though they are." He finally transferred his gaze to Claire. "I seem to recall being told that it was your father who founded the town, Miss Parmalee."

"I'm sure you were told a great deal more than that, Reverend Mueller," she remarked in a wry tone. She was pleasantly surprised to glimpse an answering light of amusement in his eyes.

"I make it a point never to listen too closely to idle gossip, especially when I am assuming the leadership of a new church."

He glanced at Sadie again, and his expression grew pensive. He had heard about her, too, of course. And now that he thought about it, there *had* been some mention of a half-breed child. Yet his sources had neglected to tell him that the notorious Sadie Bishop was a widow. She was not at all what he had expected. It was difficult to believe the shy, delicate-looking woman before him had once been caught up in the immorality of the saloons. She looked more like an earthbound angel than a fallen one.

"We have a dog named Wolf!" Harmony sang out from the bottom step. "But he isn't really a wolf."

"That is a most peculiar coincidence, Miss Bishop. You see, when I was only a boy, I had a dog named Wolfgang." A low chuckle escaped his lips. "He was the meanest four-legged beast in all of Austria."

"*Our* dog isn't mean," the little girl declared, with all the compelling gravity of a six-year-old.

"We should be going now," announced Claire. She was aware of the fact that dozens of pairs of eyes were fairly burning at the sight of their conversation. It gave her a certain perverse satisfaction. "Good-bye, Reverend," she said, then told him in all sincerity, "I hope you're planning to stay on for a while."

"Good-bye, Miss Parmalee. And I do, indeed, have every intention of remaining." To Sadie, he suggested, "Perhaps I will see you in town this week, Mrs. Bishop."

"I don't think so, Reverend. I—we don't leave the ranch very often."

"Then would you grant me the honor of calling on you in the near future?" He hastened to clarify in the next moment, "And on Miss Parmalee and your little daughter as well, of course."

"I . . ." Her voice trailed away as she looked to Claire for help.

"You're welcome anytime, Reverend," said Claire. "To tell the truth, we don't get many visitors at Glorieta."

She swept down the steps and across to where she had left the horse and buckboard waiting in the coolness of the shade. Sadie retrieved Harmony, and then quickly joined her up on the uncushioned wooden seat. She was in the process of releasing the brake when Lydia Cassidy's loud, grating voice rose from the midst of the assembled womenfolk.

"Shame on you, Claire Parmalee! Shame on you for bringin' them here!"

"God will not be mocked!" someone else proclaimed. It sounded suspiciously like Harriet Thompson.

"Ladies, please!" a horrified Reverend Mueller appealed. He sprang down the steps and across the grounds in an attempt to put a stop to the persecution. Some of the onlookers also tried to intervene, for they were able to view Sadie with at least a small measure of the compassion and forgiveness they had been exhorted to display in that very day's sermon. But they were far less vocal, and too far outnumbered, by those determined to rid the town of a known sinner.

"Harlot!"

"Jezebel!"

"We'll not be lettin' you poison *our* town with your wickedness!" one of the men now joined in. Warming to his Christian duty—and conveniently forgetting about his own frequent visits to the saloons—he scowled darkly and sneered, "Get on back over to Dallas where you belong!"

"Mama?" Harmony asked, visibly perplexed by what was happening. She peered up at her mother, then twisted back around to stare in childish wonderment at the angry, vengeful crowd. "Why are they yelling at us?"

"Please, Claire. *Let's go!*" Sadie entreated in an anguished tone. Her face looked pale and stricken, and her hand was trembling as she slid an arm protectively about Harmony's shoulders.

"The devil take them all!" Claire ground out. Resisting the urge to counter the vicious, unwarranted attack with a few well-chosen words of her own, she clenched her teeth and abruptly snapped the reins together above the horse's head. The buckboard lurched forward.

" 'For it is disgraceful even to speak of the things which are done by them in secret'!" Lydia offered up the scripture in malevolent triumph. She was blind to her own hypocrisy. Reverend Mueller, however, did not hesitate to try and make her aware of it.

The wagon wheels bounced and rolled across the dusty road as Claire struggled to regain control of her temper. She waited until they were well away from town before offering up a heartfelt apology.

"Sadie, I'm sorry," she declared, her emerald gaze full of contrition. "It's all my fault. I knew there might be a scene. But I thought if they turned against anyone at the church it would be *me*, not you. I was a fool! I never should have—"

"It wasn't your fault, Claire," the brunet disputed, with a weary resignation. She pulled her daughter closer and battled the tears glistening in her eyes. "I'd just as soon not talk about it anymore."

Claire nodded in mute agreement. She certainly couldn't blame Sadie for looking so miserable. It was strange—after all the difficult times the woman had endured, a person might have expected her to be cynical and tough as nails. But she wasn't like that at all. She was sensitive and good-hearted, a hard worker and a loving mother. Sadie Bishop was no Jezebel.

Dear God, she thought while casting a fiery, bewildered glance up toward the heavens, why was there so little kindness for those who needed it most?

The rest of the journey homeward passed in silence. Even Harmony seemed to understand the melancholy that fell over both women. Once back at the ranch, Sadie disappeared inside the house with her daughter to prepare dinner. Claire toyed with the idea of offering to help, but decided against it and instead hurried upstairs to change into a plain brown skirt and white cotton blouse—both of which had seen better days. Her appearance no longer mattered. Once again, she would use work to forget everything else. To forget Sadie's troubles . . . and her own.

She had believed the day couldn't possibly get any worse. She was wrong.

It was much later, long after the hands had roused

themselves enough to spend a few leisure hours washing their clothes or writing letters or simply killing time,
when a lone horseman was spotted bearing down on
Glorieta. Sully was the first to catch sight of him.

"Rider's comin'," he noted, squinting against the
blaze of the afternoon sun. He and Claire stood together
at the corral. They were both leaning their arms on the
topmost rail as they watched Micah lead the new mare
around at the end of a halter. The animal tugged wildly
at the unfamiliar restraint now and then, snorting and
kicking up her heels. But Micah had a way with horses.
There was little doubt that he would win this latest battle between man and beast.

Claire tensed at Sully's announcement. Her eyes narrowed and shot toward the horizon. *Rand.* She could tell
it was him, even from that distance. No other man sat
quite so tall and easy in the saddle. No other man filled
her with such dread.

Her stomach knotted painfully. She had known he
would return sooner or later. The prospect had kept her
on pins and needles the whole day long. Now that the
moment had finally arrived, she found herself fighting
the impulse to turn tail and run.

"You expectin' someone?" questioned Sully. He had
not failed to notice the way all the color suddenly
drained from her face.

"No. That is . . . I might be," she said nervously.
With an inward groan, she moved away from the corral
and crossed the yard to stand beneath the trees. Sully
was close behind her.

Rand slowed his mount to a walk as he approached
the house. Reining to a halt in front of Claire and Sully,

he swung agilely down from the saddle and tugged the hat from his head. The rich darkness of his hair gleamed in the sunlight. The double-breasted cotton shirt he wore beneath a deerskin vest was a near perfect match for his eyes. His denim trousers molded the lean hardness of his lower body. His boots were plain and sturdy rather than the fancy, stitched-leather kind favored by so many young cowboys anxious to impress. The Colt .45 revolver was once again holstered low on his hip.

To Claire, he looked even more dangerous than he had the night before.

His steady, penetrating gaze caught and held the angry defiance of hers. She lifted her chin and opened her mouth to speak, only to be cut off by Sully.

"State your name and business, mister," he directed brusquely. His fingers tightened about the rifle he was ready to use.

"Your memory's worse than ever, old man," drawled Rand, a sardonic half smile playing about his lips.

His remark earned him a narrow glower from Sully. Seconds later, recognition finally lit in the ranch foreman's eyes.

"Logan," he muttered. His features twisted into an expression of furious contempt. Without warning, he raised his rifle and aimed it at Rand.

"Sully, don't!" Claire cried breathlessly. She rounded on him in alarm. "Put down that gun!" Behind her, Rand made no move toward his own weapon.

"I swore if I ever laid eyes on you again, I'd blow you straightaways to hell," Sully told him, his gaze still holding murder.

"Don't be a fool!" snapped Claire in exasperation. She thrust aside the barrel of the gun and spun back around to face Rand. "I told you last night I didn't want to see you again."

"I'm here in an official capacity."

"What 'official capacity'?" she scoffed, her tone edged with acid disbelief.

She watched as he unhurriedly withdrew something from the pocket of his vest and held it up for examination. Her eyes grew enormous within the stormy, delicate oval of her face when she saw that it was a five-point silver star. The badge of a lawman.

"I'm with the Rangers now, Claire," he informed her, slipping the badge back into his vest pocket. "The local authorities asked for our help. I've been assigned to investigate the robberies." He didn't add that he had volunteered for the duty. Or that nothing short of death could have prevented him from coming once he had learned she was still Mrs. Logan.

"You're a Texas Ranger?" she echoed, visibly stunned by the news. Sully's response was more to the point.

"The hell you say!" he rasped out. "An outfit like the Rangers wouldn't let no worthless, yellow-livered bastard like you join up! Now get off this ranch, or I'll blow you full of holes!" he threatened, his hands whipping the rifle up once more.

"For heaven's sake, Sully! Stop behaving like such a burr-pricked jackass!" Claire commanded, her voice rising along with her temper. She tried to take the gun from him, but he held fast.

"Take aim again, Sullivan Greene, and you'd better

be willing to make it count," Rand warned the older man. His tone was deceptively low and even-tempered, but the glint in his eyes was hard.

"Just *go*!" Claire ground out before Sully could respond. She flung Rand a venomous glare. "Get back on your horse and—"

"Not until we've had a talk."

"We have nothing to talk about."

"In private," he decreed firmly, ignoring her protests.

"When hell freezes over!" she shot back.

"Are you having some trouble, Miss Claire?" asked Micah, his features somber and his gaze vigilant as he strode forward to take a protective stance beside her. Although he carried no gun, he gave every appearance of a man who knew how to handle himself just fine without it.

"Nothin' *I* can't see to," Sully growled. It was obvious that he'd like nothing better than to test Rand's warning.

"There's no trouble, Micah," Claire denied. Her words were in direct contrast to her emotions. But she managed to regain her outward composure, lifting her head proudly to say, "Mr. Logan was just leaving."

"I've got some questions to ask you," Rand stated, with maddening equanimity. "And I'm not leaving without answers."

"What possible—?" she started to object.

"In private," he reiterated.

She furiously clamped her mouth shut, her green eyes hurling invisible daggers at his head. The realization that it was his job that had brought him to Glorieta— not a desire to see her again—hurt her far more deeply than she would ever admit. *He hadn't come back for her after all.*

"Miss Claire?"

Drawn from her inordinately upsetting reverie by Micah's prompting, she heaved a sigh and gave him a faint, tight-lipped smile.

"It's all right, Micah. Please see to Mr. Logan's horse."

"What the hell good do you think it'll do to ask *us* about the robberies?" Sully argued. "You're wastin' your time here." His eyes became mere slits, his words heavy with suspicion when he submitted, "Could be the real reason you've come back is to stir up trouble with Claire again. Could be you think you've got a chance of takin' up right where you left off six years ago. Ranger or no Ranger, I say you take that damn 'official capacity' of yours and clear out!"

"I have an investigation to conduct," Rand countered in a quiet tone laced with steel. His own eyes narrowed imperceptibly. "And unless you want to find yourself under arrest, I suggest you think twice before interfering."

"Save your threats!" Claire flung at him. She drew herself rigidly erect. "I'll answer your questions, and so will everyone else here at Glorieta. You'll have our complete cooperation." Her long skirts swirled up about the tops of her boots as she abruptly turned and started toward the house. "Now let's get on with it. The sooner we're done, the sooner I'll see the last of you."

Rand watched her go, his eyes warming with appreciation while he noted the angry sway of her hips. He handed the reins of his horse to Micah, who took them with a curt nod. Sully, meanwhile, could not resist issuing one last warning to him as he attempted to walk past. "You lay a hand on her, and I'll kill you."

"I'm glad to know you've been looking after her," he replied. It was difficult to tell if he was serious or not. The older man subjected him to a dour, scrutinizing look, then finally stepped aside. Rand allowed the merest hint of a smile to touch his lips before he followed after Claire.

Without a backward glance, she continued up the steps and inside to the parlor. It was a pretty, comfortable room, bathed in the soft gold of the afternoon sunlight. In the center was a floral-upholstered sofa and two dark leather wing chairs. Lace curtains fluttered softly at the open windows. Along the far wall stood wide, towering oak shelves lined with the dozens of books Samuel Parmalee had brought with him all the way from South Carolina. A painting of Claire's late mother, a beautiful yet frail-looking young woman whose hair and eyes lacked the vibrance of Claire's, hung in the traditional place of honor above the stone fireplace.

Six years earlier, this same room had been witness to stolen kisses and whispered endearments between the rancher's daughter and the new hired hand. That memory was not lost upon Claire, whose heart felt incredibly heavy as she swept across to stand in front of the fireplace. A sudden lump rose in her throat when she turned her head and saw Rand's tall, muscular frame filling the doorway.

"Are you really a Ranger?" she demanded, eyeing him dubiously. "Or was that only—?"

"It's true," he reaffirmed. "I joined up right after I came back to Texas, more than a year ago."

"A year ago?" The news provoked another sharp twinge of resentment.

"I was in California until then, serving as a federal marshal." He sauntered forward now, his hat still in his hand. His boots connected almost soundlessly with the polished wooden floor as he advanced upon her. "Before that, I spent some time in the U.S. Cavalry. Arizona Territory."

"What ... makes you think any of that matters to me?" she parried, mentally cursing the unsteadiness of her voice. It *did* matter, of course. It mattered too much. "I thought you were here to 'interrogate' me about the robberies. Well then, let's stick to that!"

"If that's the way you want it."

"It is." She crossed her arms against her chest before impulsively taunting, "You don't appear to be fulfilling your duties very well."

"Don't I?" His mouth twitched, and his blue eyes glowed warmly when they met the flashing green of hers.

"No, you don't. For instance, where the devil were you when the train was robbed yesterday? I thought you were supposed to prevent crimes—not gallivant all over the countryside while they're happening."

"I'll keep that in mind." Tossing his hat onto the sofa, he stopped directly in front of her. His expression grew solemn, and all traces of amusement vanished from his gaze before he directed, "Tell me what you know."

"I know only what I've been told. The stage was held up three times this year, the train twice."

She tightened her arms beneath her breasts, acutely conscious of his proximity as he stood towering above her. She could literally feel the heat emanating from his virile, hard-muscled body. Her breath caught in her throat, and she found herself remembering what it had been like to rest within the strong circle of his arms while his lips moved upon hers. He was the first man she had ever kissed ...

"Maybe you can think of someone desperate enough, someone who's fallen on hard times and might suddenly take it in mind to turn against the law."

"No." Coloring faintly, she shook her head and looked away. "There's not a soul around here who hasn't experienced a fair share of hard times."

"You managed to keep the ranch going." His deep-timbred voice was brimming with secret pride. "You did a good job of it, Claire."

"What other choice did I have?" Her eyes blazed anew as they flew back up to his. "In case your memory's as bad as your timing, my father didn't raise me to surrender without a fight."

"I remember a lot more than you think I do."

He yearned to pull her close, to devour the sweetness of her lips and crush her body to his. Like her, he could recall every detail of those passionate, youthful embraces they had once shared. But he forced himself to hold back. He had waited six years already; he could wait awhile longer.

"Are there any newcomers who could be involved?" he asked, returning with no small amount of difficulty to the subject at hand. "Ranch hands, wranglers looking for work, or even someone starting up a new spread in the county?" He studied her face closely. Her reaction was not what he had hoped it would be.

"No, I—" She broke off, hastily averting her gaze again while another dull, telltale flush crept up to her cheeks. For a moment, her mind was filled with the vision of an attractive young man with sandy-colored hair and an easy laugh. He had been in the area for less than a year. . . . She immediately chided herself for the absurd, completely unfounded suspicion and asserted with a good deal more conviction, "No. I can't think of anyone who would ever stoop so low. God knows, my neighbors are far from saintly, but none of them are criminals."

"All right," he said quietly. He wondered how much of what he'd read in that report back at headquarters in San Antonio was true. *Rumored to be friendly with the primary suspect.* His gaze darkened at the thought. Just how friendly was she?

"Is that all?" demanded Claire, uncrossing her arms and giving him a cold, dismissive look. She congratulated herself on having retained her dignity throughout the ordeal. Not so long ago, she wouldn't have been capable of facing him like this without falling to pieces.

"Not quite."

"I have nothing else to tell you. You've asked your questions, now—"

"I'll be moving into the bunkhouse tonight."

"What?"

"You'll have to keep quiet about who I am," he cautioned. "I'll have a word with Sully and Micah as well."

"But, this ... You—you can't possibly stay here at Glorieta!" she stammered, her head spinning and her eyes wide with shocked disbelief.

"Why not?"

"You know good and well why not!"

"I've already been to town," he continued, oblivious to her protests. "No one recognized me. I'm using the name Jake Parker. You can tell everyone I'm the new hand."

"Have you gone completely loco?" She took a deep, highly erratic breath and insisted, "You can't do this! You have no right—"

"I have the authority." His tone was low and commanding, and the look in his eyes set off a warning bell deep within her brain.

"Your 'authority' be damned," she stormed rashly. "I will not have you here, Rand Logan! Go ahead and arrest me if it suits you, but I won't agree to this—this beef-witted little scheme of yours."

"I never would have taken you for a coward, Claire." The ghost of a smile played about his lips.

"I'm not a coward! I'm not afraid of you ... I'm not afraid of anything!" *So much for dignity,* she thought with an inward groan. Folding her arms across her chest again, she battled her rising temper. "Do you really think you can come waltzing in here after six years, without a single word in all that time, and—?"

"I wrote to you," he revealed unexpectedly. His eyes burned down into hers as he inched closer. "A few months after I left."

"Am I expected to believe that?" she retorted, taking an instinctive step backward.

"Believe what you will."

She could have sworn she detected an undercurrent of pain in his voice. But that couldn't be so, she told herself. *He* hadn't been the one left behind.

"You can't do this, Rand," she maintained, shaking her head in a firm, calm denial. "You can't stay here. We both know why."

"Do we?" He closed the gap between them again. His steely gaze captured and held the luminous depths of hers when he challenged softly, "Is it the past you're running from, Claire—or the present?"

"I don't know what you mean." She was forced to tilt her head back in order to face him squarely.

"Yes, you do." He frowned and appeared to be struggling with his own instincts before he said, "Maybe it's time we set the record straight."

"Set the record straight?" She swallowed hard and sought desperately to avoid the inevitable. "There's no need—"

"I wanted to come back," he confided in spite of her obvious reluctance to hear him out. "But circumstances prevented my return. The cavalry takes a pretty dim view of desertion." His mouth curved into a faint smile of irony before he sobered again. "The letter I sent was returned, unopened."

"Save your lies for someone addlebrained enough to believe them," she flung at him, surprising the both of them with her vehemence. "I'm not the same girl you left behind. I learned my lesson—the hard way!"

"So did I." His frown deepened, his eyes clouding

with regret when he admitted, "I was a hotheaded young fool back then. But getting married with a shotgun jammed into my back was something I'd never counted on."

"And you think I wanted that?"

"I didn't know what to think. Everything happened too fast."

"This has gone far enough," she murmured tremulously. Tearing her gaze from his, she started for the doorway. A sharp gasp broke from her lips when Rand moved to block her path.

"When you played that trick on me, I swore I'd make you pay," he told her. A shadow of remembrance crossed the rugged perfection of his features. "I was furious with you and your father, but most of all with you. I believed you'd gone and set me up, that you had it all planned for him to catch us. I blamed you for everything that happened. And I tried to forget you. I tried for a long time."

"Did you?" She willed away the tears that threatened to gather in her eyes. Her voice was admirably— deceptively—level when she pointed out, "What difference does it make now? Nothing's changed. You left. I carried on. It's too late to—"

"Damn it, Claire. I put it all in the letter. About how I'd joined up in anger and then couldn't get leave. About how sorry I was for running off."

"If this is an apology, it is most definitely *not* accepted!" She would have pushed past him, but his hand shot out to seize her wrist in an iron grip.

"I didn't expect you to understand," he said, his fingers branding her flesh even through the fabric of her sleeve. "Not yet."

"Not ever!"

"Fine." With startling abruptness, he released her wrist and gave her a look that was at once hard and yet, oddly, dangerously stirring. "Either way, I'm back. Get used to the idea." He signaled an end to the conflict by turning on his booted heel and heading back across the room.

"Find yourself a more willing victim, Rand Logan!" she cried, left fuming in his wake. She watched as he caught up the tan felt Stetson on his way to the door. "You're not the only one who swore revenge. As God is my witness, if you ever step foot on Glorieta again, I'll shoot you myself!"

"Careful, Mrs. Logan," he warned in a lazy drawl. He paused, his gaze smoldering across into hers one last time while he raised the hat to his head. "You don't want to be a widow before you're a wife."

A strange, powerful tremor shook her, and she was dismayed to feel her face flaming. It took several long seconds before she recovered her voice.

"I'm not *Mrs. Logan!*" she hotly refuted. But it was too late. He was already gone.

Chapter 4

Darkness had fallen hours ago, and there was still no sign of Rand.

Claire pulled her scarlet crocheted shawl more closely about her shoulders as she strolled beneath the canopy of trees in the front yard. The shawl was a family heirloom, handed down from mother to daughter for the past three generations. The color had been considered quite shocking at the time it had been made—red was customarily reserved for the sort of ladies desirous of flaunting their charms—but her great-grandmother Fitzgerald had proclaimed it "uplifting." With that small gesture, and with many more significant ones as well, she had established a legacy of spirit and defiance. It was a legacy Claire was only too willing to uphold.

She released a long, uneasy sigh and tossed a quick look skyward. The night was calm and deep and quiet . . . the kind of night meant to be shared, she mused idly. Another frown creased the smoothness of her brow.

"Harmony and I will be heading on up to bed now if it's all right with you, Claire," Sadie called gently to her from the porch.

"Wouldn't the two of you care to go for a walk with me?" she asked on sudden impulse, then smiled and drew closer to the soft golden lamplight radiating outward from the house's windows. "The weather's certainly fine enough for it. We should take advantage of it while we can. As unpredictable as this time of year can be, we might just find ourselves in for a real gully-washer come tomorrow."

"True enough. But we've already stayed up too late," the other woman said, declining. Although she managed a brief smile, there was a discernible catch in her voice when she added, "Thanks all the same. It's . . . well, it's been a long day."

"Good night then," said Claire. She experienced another sharp pang of guilt when she watched Sadie turn and open the door again. "Tell Harmony I intend to make good on my promise to take her swimming tomorrow."

"She'll be too excited to sleep if I tell her now. I'll wait until morning." She disappeared back inside, closing the door behind her.

Left alone again, Claire wandered farther from the house. Her eyes strayed toward the bunkhouse. The hands, eight of them in all if Sully and Micah were included in the count, were more than likely asleep by now. They tumbled out of bed at first light each morning, startled awake by the rude, ear-splitting clang of an iron triangle struck by the cook, a gap-toothed giant of a man they called Red. There was still plenty of work to be done about the ranch, in spite of the fact that roundup had taken place several weeks earlier. The line camps had to be manned, the cattle and horses tended, the buildings and windmills kept in good repair, and the ranch protected against the ever-present threat of rustlers. Glorieta had lost more than twenty head in the past year alone.

Her eyes darkened at the thought. There had been talk of fencing the range, of planting posts in the ground and stringing mile upon mile of barbed wire between them to mark the boundaries of the land. It was difficult to imagine such a thing happening. Texas was open-range country and always had been. Trying to tame it too much would surely bring on disaster.

She neared the small stone springhouse behind the barns. Her gaze softened with the memories the sight of it invoked. It had been among her favorite hiding places when she was young, a haven from the world in general and from her father's volatile temper in particular. Sully was the only one who had known about it, and he had never divulged her secret.

He wouldn't divulge Rand's, either, she told herself. Sully liked the plan no more than she did, and had certainly let her know it, but he had given his word. Micah, on the other hand, had kept his opinions to himself, merely accepting the situation as it was and offering to help in any way he could. *Help.* She needed help all right . . . help in figuring out how to get rid of the only man alive who had ever gotten under her skin.

She hastened her steps a bit as she approached the springhouse now. Driven by a sudden impulse to try and escape her troubles the way she had done in those many years past, she opened the splintered wooden door and slipped inside. It was quite dark, for there were no windows. She was greeted by the faint yet highly distinctive aroma of cabbages and onions. Her arms reached for the oil lamp hanging beside the door. She lifted it down and raised the smoke-darkened globe. Striking a match, she held it to the wick, then slid the glass back down into place and returned the lamp to the peg above.

She took a seat on the ground, unmindful of the fact that her skirts would bear stains from the damp earth when she rose again. Her eyes drifted downward to the stream that flowed through the building. Gurgling softly on its way to join with the waters of the nearby creek, it served to keep the springhouse several degrees cooler than the outside. There were only a few jars and baskets of food stacked along the wall at present, but come summer, the room would be filled with vegetables from the garden, fresh fruit purchased in town (or sent over from the Widow Taylor's much-envied orchards), and anything else needing protection from the heat. She could well remember the joy of losing herself among the mountains of sweet-smelling peaches and figs and plums. On more than one occasion, she had eaten so much that she had barely touched her supper.

Drawing her knees up to her chin, she wrapped her arms about her legs and looked back to the door. She was beginning to wonder if Rand had changed his mind about the whole thing. Maybe he had come to his senses, she mused as she closed her eyes and dropped her face to rest atop her knees. Maybe he had realized the futility of dredging up the past.

"Why couldn't you have stayed away forever?" she whispered against her skirts.

As if on cue, the door swung open.

Claire jerked her head up. Her eyes flew wide in startlement while a gasp caught in her throat. *Speaking of the devil,* she thought with bitter irony.

Rand's gaze captured the green fire of hers. Without waiting for an invitation to enter, he tugged off his hat and ducked inside. He straightened to his full height once more and directed a nod up toward the lamp.

"I saw the light." Closing the door softly behind him, he turned back to her with a strange half smile playing about his lips.

"Why in heaven's name must you keep sneaking up on me?" Claire demanded indignantly. She scrambled to her feet at last and smoothed her skirts down into place. Two bright spots of angry color rode high on her cheeks, while her breasts rose and fell rapidly beneath the snowy white cotton of her blouse and chemise. "I was hoping you had changed your mind."

"About what?" His face looked rakishly handsome in the lamp's glow.

"About staying here. I still don't see why you think it's necessary." Yanking her shawl about her shoulders again, she tried desperately to ignore the frenzied racing of her pulse.

"I can learn more this way," he explained. Like a moth to flame, he was unable to resist moving closer to where she stood beside the stream. He had been able to think of nothing but her the whole day long. And even though he was determined to summon as much patience as it took to win her back, he found himself burning like hell to touch her.

"Well, I intend to have a word with the sheriff," she declared, alarmingly conscious of the fact that they were alone once more. The springhouse was so very small. And Rand had closed the door. *Why had he done that?* "I'm sure the two of you can put your heads together and—"

"He doesn't know I'm here yet."

"But you said the local authorities had asked for your help," she pointed out, her brows knitting together into a frown of bewilderment as he stopped to loom ominously over her. He was so close they were nearly touching . . . so close she could almost feel his heart beating against hers. His eyes seared down into hers, and she swallowed hard before stammering, "Why, he—he has to know!"

"He will." Again, that enigmatic smile tugged at the corners of his mouth. "When the time's right."

"You can't do this, Rand," she argued once more, striving to keep her voice steady and her expression cool. "It isn't going to work."

She stared up at him in the lamplit darkness, feeling inexplicably light-headed and cursing the fact that he was still the most handsome, downright *masculine* man she had ever known. Her every instinct told her to flee, to get out of here before she made an absolute fool of herself, but she refused to obey. She was still resolved not to look like a coward. And there was something else, something she couldn't quite put a name to, that prompted her to stay.

"Maybe you really are what you claim to be," she continued, "and maybe you really do have the governor's backing when it comes to staying wherever you please, but I'll be hanged if I'll let you run roughshod over me or anyone else here at Glorieta. You can threaten all you like, but—"

"Why didn't you ever get the marriage annulled, Claire?" he suddenly demanded, his tone low and challenging.

"*What?*" she gasped in stunned disbelief. "What does that have to do with—?"

"Was it because you hoped I'd come back?" He cut her off again. His gaze darkened with barely suppressed emotion as it raked over her upturned countenance.

She caught her breath and retreated a step, so disturbed by the turn of the conversation—and the look in Rand's eyes—that she didn't notice her shawl slipping downward to trail in the water.

"No!" She shook her head in a furious denial. Her color deepened while her own eyes shot emerald sparks. "No, by heaven, that wasn't it at all. My father wouldn't allow it. He said it would only make things worse, that it would—it would bring further dishonor upon the family name."

"Samuel's been dead for two years."

"That didn't make any difference," she cried, her voice rising along with her temper. "I wouldn't expect *you* to understand, Rand Logan. If you'd possessed even a fraction of his sense of honor and decency, you wouldn't have been able to abandon me the way you did."

"Honor and decency," echoed Rand, his mouth curving into a slow, faint smile of ironic humor as he closed the distance between them again. He tossed his hat atop the stack of jars beside the wall. It was a simple enough gesture, yet one that held a foreboding significance. "Is that what made you lie to him that night in the barn?"

Claire felt as though she had been struck. Hurt and anger blazed through her—six years' worth of it. Her temper flared out of control. Acting solely on impulse, and without pausing to consider the wisdom of her actions, she ground out an oath and raised her hand to slap him.

Rand, however, was too quick for her. His hand shot up to seize her wrist, his fingers tightening with near bruising force. A loud, shocked gasp escaped her lips when he suddenly yanked her up hard against him.

"There was always fire between us, Claire," he recalled, his voice husky and his deep blue eyes smoldering down into the wide, stormy green depths of hers. "Yes, by damn, there was always that!"

Before she could do anything more than give a strangled cry of alarm, he encircled her with his strong arms and brought his warm lips crashing down upon the parted softness of hers.

Claire struggled furiously in his grasp, but to no avail. He gathered her even closer, imprisoning her supple, well-rounded curves against his virile hardness. His mouth ravished hers, showing no mercy and demanding a response she was determined to withhold.

She might as well have tried to lasso the moon. She was only flesh and blood. As he was so effectively reminding her . . .

His lips moved hungrily, masterfully, upon hers, and she moaned low in her throat when the velvety heat of his tongue thrust inside her mouth. With trembling fingers, she pushed feebly at his broad chest, then suffered another sharp intake of breath as one of his hands swept downward to close upon the firm, shapely curve of her buttocks.

Her head spun wildly. Her legs threatened to buckle beneath her. All her resistance melting away, she could not prevent her arms from stealing up toward his neck. Time stood still as passion intensified and the kiss deepened.

Claire moaned again and gave herself up to the madness, her mouth welcoming the sweet, conquering invasion of Rand's. She hadn't been kissed since . . . since the night of her wedding. The night he had shattered her dreams. No other man had been allowed to get this close since then. No other man had dared to try.

The memories of those long-ago embraces suddenly flooded her mind once more. Painful and vivid, they were what called her back to reality.

Tearing her lips away from Rand's, she renewed her struggles with a vengeance and choked out a declaration of furious, heartfelt defiance.

"No! No, damn you! I—I won't let you make a fool of me again!"

"Claire, don't—"

"Let go of me!" Her eyes flashed murderously as she glared up at him. "I hate you for what you did to me, Rand Logan," she uttered between clenched teeth. "I'll hate you till my dying day!"

"Will you?" he parried with deceptive nonchalance. Desire still raged hotly through him, but he forced himself to deny it. He could understand her sense of betrayal. He could understand her pain. And more than anything, he regretted having been the cause of it.

His steely gaze was filled with a dangerous light as he reluctantly drew his arms away. He watched while she stumbled backward in her haste, snatched up her shawl, and flew across to the doorway. Resisting the urge to go after her, he retrieved his hat and settled it low on his head.

"Go ahead and hate me," he told her softly. "Hate me all you want to. But know that this isn't the end of it." He was satisfied when she stopped dead in her tracks and spun about to face him again.

"Any fool knows that lightning never strikes twice in the same place." Her voice was quavering with emotion—in truth, not all of it unpleasant.

"It doesn't have to." He moved toward her with slow, measured steps. The look on his face was more unnerving than ever. "It struck the first time I set eyes on you. And the fire's still burning."

Claire was dismayed to feel her heart pounding thunderously within her breast. She opened her mouth to offer up another vehement denial, but the words wouldn't come. Flinging him one last highly eloquent glare, she turned and wrenched open the door. Her feet raced back across the quiet moonlit ground to the safety of the main house.

Rand stared after her for several long moments. Then, extinguishing the lamp on his way out, he strode from the springhouse. He would find a place to bed down in his new quarters. But he wasn't optimistic about getting any sleep.

* * *

Though chagrined at her own lack of courage, Claire avoided "Jake Parker" the following day. And the day after that.

It wasn't so difficult to do. Rand played his role of new ranch hand to perfection. He kept his distance from her—a fact that both surprised and—strangely enough—annoyed her. As Sully grudgingly admitted, he was as capable about the place as ever. He performed his duties without complaint, whether it was riding the range to check on the herd, or taking his turn at one of the line camps, or even cleaning out the barn. It turned out that he was every bit as good with the horses as Micah. Although Sully continued to grumble about him to Claire, the other hands seemed to accept him easily enough. But then, none of them had been at Glorieta six years ago.

For Claire, his presence there was a constant thorn in her side, a burning reminder of everything she had tried so hard to forget. She could almost manage to make it through the daylight hours without thinking of him too much. Yet, every time she happened to catch sight of him, her hard-won peace of mind would be vanquished by a mixture of guilt, anger, and confusion. She stayed close to the house most of the time, helping Sadie with the spring cleaning, setting the account books in order, and working in the garden. Twice, she sought escape on horseback. But it was no use. As long as *he* was here, her emotions would remain in utter chaos.

The nights were the worst. Lying in the darkness of her room, she would stare up at the ceiling and listen to the crickets chirping softly below her window. Her thoughts were inevitably drawn to Rand. She would remember the feel of his arms about her, the strong warmth of his lips upon hers. The memory of the fiery, passionate kiss they had shared out in the springhouse provoked such bedlam within her that she found it next to impossible to sleep.

She despised herself for the weakness of that moment. She despised him for taking advantage of that weakness. It would never happen again, she vowed, no matter how damnably pleasurable it had been. He would be gone soon. He would ride away just as he had done six years ago. And her life would return to normal. *Why did that prospect give her so little comfort?*

On the third evening following Rand's arrival, she received another unexpected visitor. She was seated beside Harmony on the steps of the front porch, helping the little girl brush the latest tangle of grass burrs from Wolf's thick coat, when her ears caught the sound of hoofbeats. She shifted her gaze toward the horizon, only to frown when she realized the identity of the lone horseman. Thoughts of Rand sprang to mind once more, but she determinedly pushed them aside.

"Looks like Tate Jenner," observed Sadie, securing the bowl of snap beans in her lap as she got up from the rocking chair. She stole a quick glance at Claire. "Will you be wanting him to stay to supper?"

"No," Claire murmured, heaving a sigh as she, too, stood and shook out the skirts of her red gingham dress. People didn't usually come calling so late. The sun had already begun to set, turning the sky into a blaze of color. The hands were finishing up their work for the day; both Sully and Micah stopped what they were doing to keep a vigilant eye on the approaching rider.

Wolf leapt belatedly to his feet and started barking. Scrambling up beside him, Harmony demanded in a stern voice that he stop creating such a ruckus. She tangled a hand in the fur on the back of his neck to keep him from bounding down the steps. Sadie quickly ushered her daughter and the growling dog inside, leaving Claire to greet the slender, fair-haired young man who was by that time reining to a halt beneath the trees.

Tate Jenner swung down from the saddle, tugged off his hat, and led his horse closer to the porch. Still on the sunny side of thirty, he and his three brothers had taken over the old Hanson spread only a few months ago. It was rumored that they had purchased it with money won at the gaming tables down in San Antonio, but Claire wasn't at all inclined to listen to gossip. Tate was a frequent visitor to Glorieta. She considered him a friend, even if he *did* sometimes make her uncomfortable with his attentions. His pale blue eyes were brimming with ill-disguised admiration as he smiled up at her now.

"Evenin', Claire." He was attractive, in a decidedly Anglo-Saxon way, and only a few inches taller than her.

"Hello, Tate," she said, finding it easy enough to return his smile. "What brings you here this time of day?"

"I hadn't been by in a while. Thought I'd see how you were gettin' on."

"We're doing just fine, thank you." She hesitated for a moment, her eyes straying with a will of their own toward the bunkhouse before she offered politely, "Would you care to stay awhile? I'll fetch us some lemonade."

"I was hopin' for an invitation," Tate confessed, his mouth curving into an unrepentant grin. He looped the reins of his mount about the hitching post, then climbed the steps and waited, hat in hand, while Claire disappeared inside the house. She emerged a few moments later with two glasses of lemonade, gave one to him, and led the way over to the wooden porch swing. Taking a seat, she was not at all surprised when he chose to sit beside her.

"The place looks good as ever," he noted, his gaze traveling leisurely about the grounds as he took a drink and rested his hat atop his knee. "Come this time next year, Claire Parmalee, I'll be givin' you all the competition you can stand."

"I believe we're more than equal to the challenge, Mr. Jenner." She raised the glass to her lips. Her eyes moved back to the bunkhouse. She wondered if Rand was inside, if he was perhaps watching them at that very moment . . .

"I heard about what happened in town the other day."

"What?" Coloring guiltily, she looked at Tate and flashed him an apologetic smile. "I'm sorry. What did you say?"

"I said I heard about that little set-to at the church." He frowned, his eyes glinting harshly. "Damn it, Claire! Why don't you let me teach all those Holy Rollers a lesson? Between me and my brothers, we could—"

"No, it would only make things worse." She heaved a sigh, then managed a faint smile of irony before adding, "And besides, I wouldn't want to chance your getting hurt. Heaven knows, I've got few enough friends as it is."

"I could be a lot more than that if you'd let me."

"Tate, please. I—" she entreated, rising to her feet in

sudden alarm. She had always suspected that he would demand more from her someday. She had dreaded the prospect. But, of all times, why did it have to be now?

"Hear me out, Claire." He lowered the glass to the porch and drew himself up before her. His gaze bored down into hers. "I know all about what happened six years ago. I know all about that yellow-bellied son of a bitch who was fool enough to run off and leave you. But none of that matters to me. Not one damn bit of it."

"You don't understand," she said unevenly, shaking her head as she moved past him to the steps. "I'm still a married woman, Tate."

"In name only," he was quick to amend behind her.

Her face flamed, and she breathed an inward curse. Her fiery gaze shot back to the bunkhouse again. Mentally consigning Rand Logan to the devil, and trying to ignore the ache deep inside her, she tightened her fingers about the glass she still held. Some of the lemonade had spilled onto her dress, but she was too preoccupied at the moment to notice.

"All right," she conceded in a low, bitter tone. "In name only. But that doesn't change the fact that I'm legally bound to someone else. And it doesn't change—"

"I can take care of that."

"What do you mean?" She spun about to face him. Her eyes widened with apprehension.

"Let's just say I've got friends in high places," he quipped evasively, a crooked smile tugging at the corners of his mouth. His features grew solemn again in the next instant when he promised, "If that husband of yours is still alive, I'll find him."

"No!" she cried, startling them both with her vehe-

mence. She could feel her color deepening as she firmly shook her head and declared with an attempt at more composure, "No, Tate. I don't want him found. I don't want things stirred up all over again. Let it rest. Please, just let it rest."

"Maybe you don't want to be free," he suggested, his eyes narrowing in sudden suspicion. He swiftly covered the distance between them and subjected her to a hard scrutiny. "Maybe you like havin' a long-lost husband. It sure as hell makes it *convenient*, doesn't it?"

"I don't know what you're talking about."

"With one man's name hangin' over you, you don't ever have to make up your mind about takin' on another. I think you're damn well quakin' in your boots at the thought of lettin' me close. I think you're afraid what happened before will happen again."

"That isn't true," she denied hotly, her own gaze reproachful.

"Then why not give me a chance to show I'm different from him?" he persisted. His hands lifted to close gently, almost reverently, about her arms as he vowed, "I'd treat you good, Claire. I'd never hurt you. And sure as I'm standin' here, I'd never let anyone else hurt you, either."

His expression was so earnest and his eyes so full of tender devotion that Claire felt a lump rise in her throat. She could not find the heart to stop him when he slowly bent his head and pressed his lips to hers. The kiss was sweet and warm, evoking little more than a small twinge of pleasure within her. It was almost like being kissed by a brother, she mused absently.

There had certainly been nothing brotherly about

Rand's kiss. The memory came back to hit her full force again. She gave an inward groan and drew her lips away from Tate's.

"I'm sorry, Tate," she told him, with a brief, unsteady smile of regret as he frowned quizzically down at her. "Even if I were free, I still couldn't marry you."

"Why not?"

"Because I—I don't love you." She cursed the fact that it was necessary to hurt him.

"Give it time," he insisted, his tone flippant, yet underscored by pain.

"No. Time won't change anything." She moved past him to the swing. "I hope you'll try and understand. I value your friendship very much."

"If that's the way you want it." He crossed to her side, caught up the hat he had tossed onto the swing, and raised it to his head. He paused to capture her gaze again, and the look in his eyes made her throat constrict in renewed alarm. "I'm not licked yet, Claire," he proclaimed quietly. "Not by a long shot."

"Please, Tate," she tried to appeal, shaking her head for emphasis, "don't—"

"Come next Sunday, I'll be here to take you and Sadie to church. Who knows?" he added, with another wry grin. "The preachin' and fightin' might do me some good."

She opened her mouth to protest, only to inhale upon a gasp of astonishment when he suddenly leaned closer and brushed her cheek with his lips.

"Am I interrupting something?"

Claire stiffened at the sound of that familiar, deep-timbred voice. Her face crimsoning, she pulled guiltily away from Tate. Her gaze kindled with fire when it lit upon Rand. He was standing at the end of the porch, his hat in his hand and a faint, humorless smile playing about his lips. His eyes burned across into hers.

"What in heaven's name do you think you're doing?" she demanded. She battled the urge to hurl the glass of lemonade at his handsome head.

"Sorry, ma'am," he drawled, without an ounce of contrition. "Micah asked me to tell you the new mare'll be saddle-broke tomorrow."

"I don't know who you are, mister, but it looks to me like you could use a lesson in manners," snapped Tate. He was visibly annoyed at the intrusion. "Didn't anybody ever teach you to respect another man's privacy?"

"The name's Parker. Jake Parker. And I've learned a lot of things you haven't even heard of yet."

Claire suffered another sharp intake of breath. Her eyes were round as saucers as they flew to Tate. She was dismayed to observe a dull, angry flush rising to his face. Setting the glass down at last, she hastened to intervene.

"Thank you, *Mr. Parker.*" Her words were heavy with meaning when she directed, "You can go on about your business now."

"I need to have a word with you first," he announced, standing his ground. His gaze, disturbingly unfathomable, locked with the other man's in silent combat. Finally, after several long seconds, Tate looked back to Claire.

"I'll be back on Sunday," he reiterated. Before she could argue, he strode down the steps. He unlooped the reins from the hitching post and mounted his horse.

Eyeing Rand narrowly one last time, he reined about and set his heels to the animal's flanks.

He had scarcely cleared the trees in the front yard when Claire whirled to confront Rand.

"You were spying on me," she accused. Her tone was low and seething, her eyes gloriously ablaze. She was so angry that it would have required very little encouragement on Rand's part to send her flying across the porch at him. "How dare you! How dare you—"

"Who was he?"

"Tate Jenner—not that it's any of your business," she flung at him, folding her arms resentfully beneath her breasts. "The man happens to be a neighbor of mine. *And* a friend."

"A close one, from the looks of it." The name was familiar to him, of course, but he gave no indication of it.

"Very!" She was surprised at the urge to taunt him. She was further surprised at the near savage gleam that suddenly appeared in his eyes.

"You're still a married woman, remember?" His chiseled features growing dangerously taut, he moved toward the front steps.

"Why should that make any difference to me?" With a reckless disregard for both his anger and her own secret, rapidly increasing trepidation, she raised her head to a lofty angle as she watched him drawing closer. "I'm quite sure it hasn't made any difference to *you* these past six years." He had probably known a lot of women in all that time. . . . Dear God, why did the thought make her feel so wretched?

"It would have," Rand said grimly, noting the sudden

shadow that crossed her face. "If I had known." He climbed the steps now, raked the hat from his head, and stood towering above her while white-hot jealousy blazed through him. The memory of the kiss that bastard Jenner had given her (*suspected* bastard, an inner voice amended mockingly) was enough in itself to make his blood boil.

"What are you talking about?" demanded Claire, frowning up at him in complete bafflement.

"When my letter to you came back unopened," he explained in a quiet, controlled tone meant for her ears alone, "I wrote to Reverend Blackstock."

"Reverend Blackstock? But he left town a few months after—"

"—your father talked him into performing the wedding," he finished for her. "Yes, I know."

"Why on earth would you write to *him*?"

"Because I was fool enough to think he might plead my case. And because I wanted to find out how you were getting on." He paused for a moment, his blue eyes clouding with bitter remembrance. "The good parson answered my letter all right. He told me you had gotten the marriage annulled. He told me you were planning to marry someone else."

"Why, I—I don't believe you," she stammered, her head spinning at the incredible news. "John Blackstock would never do such a thing. A man of the cloth would never lie like that."

"Wouldn't he?" countered Rand. He raised a hand to brace against the porch column, his eyes glinting dully. "I didn't learn the truth until last week."

"What possible reason could he have had . . . ?" she

wondered aloud, her voice trailing away as her thoughts tumbled backward over the years. She had known the kindly, bespectacled preacher since she was a child. He had been a particular favorite of her father's, in spite of the fact that Samuel Parmalee rarely set foot inside a church. It was difficult to imagine him perpetrating such an unethical little scheme.

"No doubt, he believed he was doing what was best for you," Rand speculated. "Maybe he thought you'd stand a better chance of starting over if I was out of the picture for good. It could be he even received a bit of 'persuasion' from your father. Either way, I'm sure he wanted to spare you further pain. And I guess lying to me was a small price to pay for that."

Claire felt another sharp pain slice through her heart. Still reeling at the news, she slowly turned and wandered back toward the swing. Rand followed, his gaze warming with both tenderness and desire as it traveled possessively over her.

"That's the only reason I stayed away," he declared softly, though his voice sounded raw. "I wanted to come back. I wanted to more than anything. But I couldn't bear the thought of seeing you as another man's wife."

"Do you really think I'm going to swallow this latest cock-and-bull story of yours?" she furiously choked out. She rounded on him again, balling her hands into fists and planting them on her hips. Her eyes flashed up into his. "Even if you *were* telling me the truth, it wouldn't make any difference. It wouldn't change the fact that you ran away." Her arms fell back to her sides, and she momentarily dropped her gaze while battling the accursed tears that always seemed ready to fall since he had returned. "I was so very young and naive then. You told me you cared for me. You led me to believe your intentions were honorable. And then you broke my heart!"

"I know," he readily admitted. "And you're right—I can't change the past. But you're still my wife."

"Not for long!"

"What the hell is that supposed to mean?"

"Only that I'm finally going to file for that annulment, Rand Logan. I'm going to see to it that you'll never again be able to make any claims on me. This time, when you ride out of my life, you can stay gone for—" She broke off with a gasp when he took a menacing step toward her.

"There will be no annulment." His eyes, piercing in their intensity, seared relentlessly down into hers. "You're mine, Claire. I'll be damned if I'll let you go."

Although he did not touch her, she was certain an invisible current passed between them. Her heart leapt into her throat. She could feel the barely suppressed violence in him, could feel his heat and strength and undeniable virility. The words he spoke were frightening . . . and yet strangely thrilling at the same time.

"I'm not yours," she denied in a harsh whisper, backing away until her legs came up against the edge of the swing. "I never was."

"Liar," he murmured. Her eyes flew wide, and she opened her mouth to launch a verbal barrage at him, but he gave her no time. His arm suddenly clamped about her waist while his mouth swooped down upon hers. For the second time that day—and for only the third time in six long years—she found herself being kissed.

The comparison between the most recent two was un-avoidable. Whereas Tate's kiss had been mildly divert-ing, Rand's was fiercely captivating. His mouth was quite thorough in its bold, passionate conquest of hers, his arm sweeping her so close that she found it difficult to breathe. She struggled as best she could. But her head swam and her whole body trembled. She was acutely conscious of her breasts pressing against the hard and powerful warmth of his chest.

It ended as abruptly as it had begun.

Her eyelids fluttered open when she felt him reluctantly—yet firmly—drawing away from her. She stared up at him in dazed bemusement, her face becom-ingly flushed and her green eyes still soft with passion's glow.

"Just like old times, Mrs. Logan," drawled Rand. Lifting the hat to his head, he tugged the front brim low. A single muscle twitched in the rugged, clean-shaven smoothness of his cheek; it was the only outward evi-dence of the battle raging within him. His eyes filled with a devilish light when he added, "Only better."

"Why, you— *Go to hell!*" Claire sputtered wrath-fully. She might have said a good deal more at that point, but he turned and left her alone with her thoughts. And with her equally turbulent emotions.

Watching him stride back toward the corral, she sank heavily down upon the swing. The entire world had gone topsy-turvy. Tate Jenner had proposed marriage to her. And Rand Logan had vowed never to set her free.

She raised a hand to her lips. They still tingled from the warm, intoxicating pressure of his.

If Sully had seen what had happened, she thought as

a deep frown creased her brow, he'd have come barreling across the yard with his finger already on the trigger. That possibility apparently hadn't troubled Rand. No, by heaven, he hadn't seemed to let that bother him at all.

"Mama wants to know if Mr. Jenner might be staying for supper after all."

The sound of Harmony's voice made her start guiltily. She sprang to her feet and whirled toward the doorway, anxiously wondering if the child who stood surveying her with wide and innocent eyes had witnessed her tempestuous encounter with Rand.

"No," she answered, managing to sound halfway tranquil. "Mr. Jenner has already gone home."

"Mama said Mr. Jenner likes you," the little girl impulsively confided. She pushed the screen door open and allowed it to bang shut again. The look on her face was completely guileless.

"Did she?" murmured Claire. She couldn't prevent her eyes from straying toward the corral. Rand was easy enough to spot. He stood tall and self-assured as he talked with Micah. Looking at him, she was reminded of the day—an eternity ago—when he had first come striding so confidently across the front yard to ask her father for a job.

"Yes. But I don't think he likes you as much as Mr. Parker does."

Claire tensed. She felt the telltale color staining her cheeks. Gently clearing her throat, she shifted her gaze back to the child.

"What makes you think that?" She held her breath while waiting for the answer.

"I don't know," Harmony replied, then gave a shrug of childish unconcern. She offered nothing further on the subject before singing out, "I've got to help Mama!"

Claire was left totally perplexed in the six-year-old's wake. Sinking back down onto the swing, she rolled her eyes heavenward and released a long, uneven sigh. The situation was growing more impossible with each passing day.

You're mine, Claire. Those words, along with all the others he had spoken, continued to echo within her mind . . . just as his kiss still burned upon her lips.

Chapter 5

"Says he's got to ride into town today."

"I don't give a tinker's damn what he says!"

"It seems like I told him that," recalled Sully, squinting against the brightness of the late afternoon sun as he looked back to where Rand had just led his horse from the barn. "Only I wasn't so pure-dee elegant about it."

Claire muttered an oath underneath her breath. Angrily gathering up her skirts, she swept down from the porch and across the yard. Her eyes were bridling with extreme irritation when she took up a rigid, querulous stance before Rand.

She noticed the way his thick hair shone with a mixture of gold and brown in the sunlight, the way he smelled of soap and leather. As usual, she felt thoroughly unsettled by his nearness. She couldn't help but remember what had happened between them the previous day. It only added fuel to the fire.

"What do you think you're doing?" she demanded.

"Saddling my horse." His mouth twitched, but he didn't stop. With no apparent effort, he lifted the saddle to the sleek, gently fidgeting sorrel's back and bent to tighten the cinch.

Claire's gaze was drawn to the lean hardness of his hips. She was perturbed to feel a strange warmth spreading outward from the vicinity of her abdomen. Blushing at the wicked turn of her thoughts, she folded her arms against her chest and lifted her head to a haughty angle.

"You're not going anywhere!"

"I thought I was." He pulled the stirrup back down into place and moved to adjust the bit in the animal's mouth.

"The hands only get Sundays off," she informed him. Then she cast a quick look about the grounds and cautiously lowered her voice to add, "It was *your* idea to pretend you're one of them, remember?"

"I remember." Catching up the hat he had left hanging from a nearby fence post, he finally turned to face her. "I'll make up for it on Sunday."

"I forbid you to go."

"Forbid?" His eyes twinkled down into hers. She felt her heart fluttering when his mouth curved into a slow, disarmingly crooked smile. "Well now, 'Boss,' I guess you'll have to think about firing me."

"I never hired you in the first place," she retorted acidly.

"I've been here several days now, Claire." His tone was one of quiet authority now, his expression growing serious. "I've learned all I can by staying put. It's time I headed into town again."

"Are you going to have a word with Sheriff Howell?"

"Maybe." His evasiveness was maddening as ever.

"What makes you so sure you can learn anything in town?"

"I plan to keep my ears open." He lifted the hat to his head now and gathered up the reins. "I should be back before morning."

"Morning?" she echoed, her eyes widening in surprise. She wondered what could possibly keep him in Parmalee that long. The saloons, most likely, it occurred to her. The thought provoked more than a twinge of displeasure. "If you must go," she decreed on sudden impulse, "you'll have to take Micah with you."

"I work better alone," he stated, frowning.

"It will arouse less suspicion that way," she argued firmly. "We can say the two of you are going to settle some accounts for me at the livery stable, the mercantile, and such. Micah and I usually do that together, but it probably won't look too out of the ordinary to make an exception just this once. I can assure you, he is completely trustworthy."

"It isn't a question of—"

"For heaven's sake," she interrupted in exasperation, "do you want to make this believable or not?"

"I didn't know my job mattered so much to you," he challenged mockingly. He took a step closer and pushed the front brim of his hat upward a bit. The light in his eyes deepened to a warm glow. "Or maybe it's my personal safety you're worried about."

"Don't be silly. It's Glorieta I'm thinking of. How will it look if I allow the new hand to take a night off while the others have to bide their time until Saturday?" She peered stormily up at him for a moment, endeavoring (with her usual lack of success) to ignore the effect his proximity had on her. "Well," she prodded, "what's it to be? Are you going to take Micah with you—or are you going to get your things together and clear out?"

"Ultimatums have never set too well with me." He gave her a hard, penetrating look. "You of all people should know that." He tugged his hat lower on his head once more and reluctantly conceded, "But it could be that having Micah along might just serve a purpose."

Claire's gaze sparkled with triumph. Her victory, however, was short-lived.

"While I'm gone," he directed, suddenly thrusting the reins into her hands, "you can be thinking about what I said yesterday." He did not wait for her reaction before sauntering away to find Micah.

"What?" she gasped. Her eyes grew very round, then narrowed and blazed at the broad, retreating target of his back. "It so happens that I intend to forget every blasted word of it!" She thought she heard a low chuckle drifting back to her on the wind, but she couldn't be certain.

A short time later, Rand and Micah were on their way to Parmalee. It was one of the few opportunities they'd had to speak privately.

"I know who you are," Micah suddenly announced when they slowed their mounts to a walk a short distance from town. They had chosen to stick close to the road, and had thus far encountered few other travelers on their way across the vast, gently rolling prairie. The sun hung low in the sky by now. A thick tumble of gray-white clouds had gathered on the horizon, offering up the promise of a nighttime storm. "I know you're the one."

"The one what?" asked Rand, a faint smile of wry amusement playing about his lips.

"The one who married Miss Claire and then lit out."

"That was a long time ago." He frowned, his blue eyes suffused with a dull, guarded light as he tightened his grip on the reins and shifted in the saddle.

"Not long enough," Micah commented gravely. He shot Rand a look that was at once critical and pensive. "Miss Claire took me on when no one else would. Took on Mrs. Bishop and the little girl, too. She's a fine woman, good-hearted as they come."

"I know that."

"There's something else you ought to know. If you ever hurt her, I'll kill you." He offered the threat simply, without any discernible trace of rancor. Rand took no offense at it.

"You're pretty fond of her, aren't you?" he asked, the corners of his mouth turning briefly upward again.

"I am," Micah was only too willing to admit. His dark eyes softened with reminiscence. "Like I said, she was just about my last hope. I was a buffalo soldier, stationed at Fort Davis. When I was mustered out, I had no place to go, no family and not much to show for all those years in the cavalry. Miss Claire didn't mind about my color. Said we're all the same under our skin. She gave me a new start." He looked to Rand again, concluding, "I reckon you've got some decency in you if you're in the Rangers, Mr. Logan. Maybe you've come back a changed man. Either way, I'll not be letting you hurt her."

"I guess I should thank you for the warning." His gaze was steady and honest as it met the other man's squarely. "But there's no need for it. I want only what's best for her. You have my word on that."

"Just so we understand each other."

"We do." He gave Micah a curt nod before urging his mount into a canter once more. His eyes gleamed with a touch of humor while he mused that Claire sure as hell inspired loyalty in those who worked for her. She was worthy of it. And he'd never stop being grateful for the second chance fate had offered him.

Afternoon was deepening into the first hint of twilight when, back at the ranch, Claire walked from the stock barn and tugged off her worn, fringed leather gloves. Bits of hay still clung to her skirts, and several wayward strands of honey-gold hair had escaped the pins to tumble across her damp forehead. She had spent the past hour currying horses and cleaning stalls. The work, physical and mercifully engrossing, had helped to take her mind off other matters—"other matters," of course, centering around the tall, blue-eyed Texas Ranger who had bedeviled her waking hours and haunted her dreams for the past several days. Any respite from that particular curse was a real blessing.

Raising a hand to her throat, she unfastened the top two buttons of her high-necked, white cotton blouse and took a deep, cooling breath of air. Her nose suddenly caught the distinctive scent of rain. She tossed a swift glance northward. Sure enough, the approaching clouds had darkened to a more ominous shade of gray. There was little wind at the moment. Perhaps, she thought idly, the storm would pass by. But it was useless to try and second-guess Mother Nature. The weather, much the same as life itself, was always so damnably capricious.

Her gaze widened and sparked with curiosity when it fell upon the small, canvas-topped buggy rolling straight over the grassy plains toward the ranch. Incredibly, Glorieta was about to receive yet another visitor.

"Who in tarnation. . . ?" she murmured, frowning. She strolled across the yard, then stood waiting beneath the trees in front of the house while the buggy drew nearer. A flicker of recognition lit in her eyes just before its driver pulled the horse to a halt and raised a hand in greeting.

"Good afternoon, Miss Parmalee," said Reverend Mueller. "I hope you will not mind that I have come to call without an invitation." He climbed down from the buggy, his mouth curving into a smile as he swept the hat from his head.

"Not at all, Reverend," she assured him earnestly. "I told you, you're welcome anytime." She smiled in return and stepped forward to offer him her hand. He clasped it within the warm strength of his. When he released it again, his blue-green eyes instinctively searched about for Sadie.

"Is Mrs. Bishop home as well? And Harmony?"

"I think they're out back at the moment. Today was wash day," she explained, then gestured toward the house. "Please, come inside. I'll see if I can find them."

"I would not wish for you to trouble yourself."

"It's no trouble at all."

She led the way up the steps and inside the house to

the parlor. Leaving the parson to admire her mother's portrait, she hastened through the kitchen to the backyard. Just as she had expected, Sadie and Harmony were still there, gathering the last of the clean, sunfreshened sheets from the clothesline.

"Sadie?" Claire called to her.

"Yes?" Sadie turned and smiled. Dressed in a faded blue homespun dress and white apron, she looked even younger than her twenty-six years. Her cheeks were pink and glowing from her efforts, and her opal eyes held no trace of their usual sadness at the moment.

"We have a visitor," announced Claire, joining her. "Reverend Mueller has come to call."

"Reverend Mueller?" Sadie echoed in surprise. She caught her lower lip between her teeth and quickly looked away, her color deepening while her brows drew together into a disconcerted frown. With painful clarity, she recalled the scene in front of the church. What must the man think of her?

"Can I show him Wolf, Mama?" Harmony queried eagerly, all too willing to leave the remainder of her chores behind. She flew to her mother's side. The great, devoted mongrel was hot on her heels.

"If Miss Claire doesn't mind," murmured Sadie.

"Of course not," said Claire. Her eyes twinkled conspiratorially down at the little girl. "I'm sure Reverend Mueller will appreciate Wolf's many talents." She smiled as Harmony disappeared inside with the dog. "Are you coming?" she asked Sadie, her features sobering. She hadn't failed to notice the housekeeper's sudden discomfort; she was fairly certain of its origin.

"Yes." She nodded and began untying the strings of her apron. "I'm coming." Pausing long enough to wash up and tidy her hair, she took the other woman by the arm.

Thomas Mueller—completely oblivious to the possible damage to his black serge suit—was down on one knee in the parlor, playfully ruffling Wolf's fur, when he glanced up to observe Claire and Sadie watching him from the doorway. He immediately drew his tall, slender frame upright and came forward to meet them with a smile of genuine delight on his face.

"It is a pleasure to see you again, Mrs. Bishop," he told Sadie, his gaze so warm and steady that she felt her pulse quicken.

"Thank you, Reverend." More than a little embarrassed to have been caught in her oldest work clothes, she instinctively lifted a hand to tuck a wayward tendril of hair back into place.

"Would you care for some lemonade, Reverend Mueller?" Claire offered. "Or perhaps some coffee?"

"Lemonade would be very nice, thank you."

"I'll get it," declared Sadie. She was surprised to feel Claire's hand close gently about her arm.

"No. You stay and entertain our guest. I'll do the fetching for a change." Smiling at Harmony, she coaxed, "Come along. You can help me squeeze the lemons."

The little girl needed no further encouragement. Naturally, Wolf followed along after her, his massive tail wagging with such enthusiasm that it thumped resoundingly against the doorframe.

"Your daughter is quite lovely," Thomas remarked to Sadie once they were alone. Gallantly waiting until she had perched on the edge of the sofa, he chose to sit in the wing chair opposite. His voice sounded mellow and pleasant to Sadie's ears. "Such beautiful hair and eyes."

"Thank you," she replied, meeting his blue-green gaze tentatively. "She looks quite a lot like her father."

"Does she indeed?"

"He was half-Indian. Cherokee." She was startled to hear that particular bit of information falling from her tongue. It wasn't the sort of thing she usually confided to people. And yet, she realized, there was something about this man that caused her to feel at once nervous and wonderfully secure. It made no sense at all.

"You could not have been married very long," the parson opined, with another soft smile. "You are still a young woman."

"I was eighteen when we met." Her gaze fell beneath the admiring kindness of his, and she folded her hands tightly in her lap before confessing in a low, uneven tone, "I was working at a saloon over in Dallas. Daniel was one of the regular customers." She looked back at him, fearing she would encounter the usual condemnation. But, oddly enough, there was none. "That's why those women didn't want me at the church. Because of what I used to be."

"They were very wrong to treat you so cruelly." His features tightened with anger at the memory.

"It's all right," insisted Sadie, though he could read the pain in her eyes when she raised them to his once more. "I can't really blame them."

"You are much too forgiving." He gave a soft chuckle at the expression of astonishment on her face.

"That, of course, was not what you expected to hear from someone who preaches forgiveness each Sunday."

"No, it wasn't." Her eyes fell toward her lap again, only to fly back up at his next remark.

"I am sure your husband was a good man, Mrs. Bishop."

"Yes, he—he was." She felt only a dull ache now whenever she thought of Daniel. Their marriage might not have been made in heaven, but her life with him had, for the most part, been a happy one.

"And how long have you worked for Miss Parmalee?"

"Only a few months." Her opal gaze momentarily clouded with remembrance. Again, she found herself revealing things she had made a habit of trying to forget. "There was very little money when Daniel died. I went back to the saloon for a while, just until I'd saved enough to get out of town. We headed up to Denton. A cousin of mine helped me find a job in one of the hotels there. That's how I met Claire." Dismayed by the alarming tendency to pour out her life's story to a man she had only met once before, she sought to change the subject. "What about you, Reverend? How did you end up in Parmalee?"

"I have an old friend to thank for that," he told her, his eyes lighting with amusement now. "He was to have taken the church here, but he decided at the last moment that he could not endure life among the 'barbarians.' I, however, was eager to come. The frontier had long held an appeal for me, you see."

"And is Texas what you'd expected it to be?"

"It is. And much more."

There was something in the words he spoke that caused her heart to stir in a way it hadn't done in a long, long time. Nonplussed by the sensation, she was relieved when Claire and Harmony returned from the kitchen a few moments later.

The visit, pleasant and filled mostly with talk of the weather and other local interests, lasted only a short time longer. After the parson had taken his leave of Sadie and Harmony, Claire accompanied him back outside.

"Thank you for dropping by, Reverend," she offered in all sincerity. She liked him. And from what she had just observed, she wasn't the only one. "I hope you'll come again soon."

"I would enjoy that very much, Miss Parmalee." He donned his hat, climbed up into the buggy, and took hold of the reins. "I look forward to seeing you and your two charming companions at church on Sunday."

"Does this mean you're not planning to read me from the pulpit?" Her eyes sparkled teasingly across into his. She was pleased by the droll, appreciative smile that tugged at his lips.

"I can assure you, it was never my intention to do so."

"Well then, I can think of a few ladies who will be disappointed." Folding her arms across her chest, she stepped away from the buggy. The distant rumble of thunder reached her ears. Frowning, she looked up at the darkening sky. "You'd better get started. With any luck, you'll be able to make it home before the storm breaks." The storm . . . *Micah and Rand.* She turned back to the parson and impulsively queried, "You didn't happen to come across two of my ranch hands on your way out, did you?"

"As a matter of fact," he recalled, "I did meet two horsemen on the road, though I am sorry to say I did not stop to introduce myself to them."

"It doesn't matter," she murmured, giving him another brief smile. "Good-bye, Reverend."

"Good-bye, Miss Parmalee."

She stood and watched as he drove away. Thunder echoed forebodingly across the land in his wake.

"My bones are tellin' me we're in for a bad one this time."

She turned to find Sully approaching her from the barn. His craggy features wore a deeper scowl than usual, and there was a worried look about his eyes.

"What exactly do you mean by 'bad'?" Claire questioned dryly, one hand lifting to smooth the wayward strands of hair from her temple.

"The air's too damn hot and still." He tugged off his hat and brought it slapping downward against his leg. A small shower of dust fell to the ground. "Feels like trouble. Look at the way those clouds're startin' to boil up," he noted, slicing a quick, narrow glance toward the horizon. "I've seen it plenty of times before. Rain for certain, maybe hail or worse. I'll tell the boys to pull in for the day. You and Miz Bishop and the little girl had best be shuttin' up the house."

"All right." His prediction filled her with more uneasiness than she was willing to admit. A sudden vision of Rand's face rose in her mind. *I should be back before morning . . .*

Mentally shaking herself, she pivoted about and hurried inside the house. Sadie and Harmony wasted no time in bringing in the rest of the laundry, while she went from room to room latching the shutters, closing the windows, and stockpiling pots and pans in case the roof decided to leak—as it did all too frequently. She, too, could remember a number of "devil-beating" storms at Glorieta, and she wasn't about to be caught off-guard.

Outside, Sully and the hands set about their own preparations. The horses, increasingly skittish as the storm neared, were sheltered in the barn with plenty of oats and water to see them through what could turn out to be a difficult night. Red and one of the younger men volunteered to stay and keep watch over the frightened animals. In the other barn, the bales of hay had to be covered with canvas tarpaulins to prevent a disastrous soaking, and the bunkhouse secured against the possibility of winds that had been known to rip huge trees out of the ground, tear roofs from buildings, and even stab pieces of wood clean through windowpanes without shattering the glass.

"No matter what happens, stay inside," Sully said, returning to the house to caution Claire. The warning was unnecessary, of course, but she nodded in agreement as they stood together on the front porch. Overhead, the encroaching mass of clouds had begun turning the sky to black well before the usual hour of darkness. "If you hear what sounds like a train barrelin' through sudden-like, you and the others take cover, understand?" *Tornado* was a word to be avoided—it was sort of like tempting fate to say it aloud. But Claire understood exactly what he meant.

"What about you?" she demanded anxiously, her hand grasping at his arm when he turned to go. "Where will you—?"

"Hell, you got no reason to worry about me," he grumbled, then allowed his lips to curl into a rare grin. "I'm too damn mean to die." He pulled his hat low on his head and headed off to issue last-minute instructions to the men in the barn, leaving her to frown heavenward with growing apprehension.

Finally there was nothing to do but wait.

The wind was the first indication that the storm would not simply pass by. Whipping fiendishly across the ranch, it tore at the shutters and howled through the cracks in the walls. Soon thereafter, lightning flashed and crackled, setting fire to the sky and revealing the ominous swirl of the moisture-choked clouds. Loud, earthshaking thunder rumbled frighteningly in its wake.

And then the heavens opened up. Initially the cold droplets of water smashed against the roof like so many bullets, but within seconds the rain came down in heavy sheets. It pummeled the waiting earth with relentless, near blinding force, streaming along the ground in a crisscross of newborn rivers and filling the air with a dreadful roar.

Claire sat in the lamplit warmth of the kitchen, her hand curling absently about a cup of coffee while she listened to the storm raging outside. A tired yet wide-eyed Harmony sat cradled on her mother's lap across the table, while Wolf lay sprawled underneath. The smell of the rain—somewhat oppressive under the circumstances—had crept into the room, but so far the roof was holding its own against the deluge.

"I'd hate to be caught out on a night like this," murmured Sadie, her arms tightening instinctively about her daughter as her eyes strayed toward the ceiling again. "At least it isn't hailing yet."

"Maybe we'll still be spared the worst of it," Claire remarked on a note of hopefulness. Her thoughts, however, were not so much on the storm itself, for Rand's face continued to swim before her eyes with disturbing frequency. For some inexplicable reason, she was plagued by a sharp, nagging uneasiness about him.

Fool, she chided herself in disgust. He and Micah were no doubt enjoying themselves immensely ... Rand, most of all. He was probably sitting in one of the town's wickedest saloons at this very moment, his eyes brimming with too much whiskey and his knee occupied by a pretty, willing girl with more bosom than brains. His "activities" would all be for the pursuit of information, of course. And the storm would hold no real significance for him.

Frowning, she drew in a slightly ragged breath and raised the cup to her lips. At least she could trust Micah to keep a clear head. But Rand? She couldn't even begin to predict what he would do.

"When will the rain stop, Mama?" Harmony asked, squirming restlessly on Sadie's lap now.

"I don't know. The storm might last the rest of the night."

"Then how will Micah and Mr. Parker get home?"

Claire choked on the coffee she had just swallowed. Coughing, she lowered the cup to the table. Her hand moved to her throat, while her glistening eyes fastened closely upon the little girl.

"How did you know Micah and Mr. Parker were gone?" she managed to ask.

"I saw them on their horses," Harmony replied simply. She looked up at her mother before adding, "Micah said they were going to town. He said I can go with him sometime."

"Did he?" Sadie smiled indulgently and glided an affectionate hand down over the child's arm. "Well, we'll see."

"Reverend Mueller said we can come back to church."

"Oh, Harmony. I—I'm not sure that would be such a good idea."

"Why not?" Without waiting for her mother's reply, she turned her dark, intelligent gaze upon Claire and announced, "Mr. Parker said I could call him Jake."

"That was very nice of him," remarked Claire, her own gaze falling.

"*You* don't call him that."

"Harmony," Sadie admonished gently.

"She called him Rand, Mama," Harmony persisted, twisting about to assert in a stubborn, defensive tone, "I heard her! Why does she call him that when his name is—?"

"Harmony, that's enough!"

"Don't scold her, Sadie," Claire intervened, a dull flush staining her cheeks. "She's only telling the truth." Rising from the table, she wandered across to the window and stared distractedly outward at the rain-lashed blackness. Her voice was fraught with simmering emotion when she promised, "I'll explain it all to you sometime. Only . . . not now. Not tonight."

"You don't owe me any explanations," Sadie insisted firmly. Easing Harmony from her lap, she stood and cast another anxious glance toward the ceiling. "We'd best be getting upstairs to check on the roof again, else we're liable to find ourselves sleeping in damp beds tonight."

"God willing, it will let up soon." Claire sighed. Forcing her thoughts back to the present dilemma, she hastened from the kitchen and up the stairs.

It was approaching midnight when Claire slipped quietly out of her bedroom. The flame of the candle she was holding flickered in the darkness and cast subtle shadows on the rose-papered walls as she crept toward the stairs. Anxious to avoid waking either Sadie or Harmony, she gathered up the long, clinging folds of her nightclothes and tiptoed down the carpeted steps. She headed into the kitchen, where she lit the lamp, stoked the fire in the cast-iron stove, and set another pot of coffee on to boil. Then, tugging the belt of her blue muslin dressing gown more securely about her waist, she padded barefoot across to the window and peered outward.

A sudden shiver ran the length of her spine. She folded her arms against her chest and drew closer to the stove's warmth. Her thick golden locks were tumbling riotously down about her face and shoulders, for she had neglected to tame them into the single braid she usually favored each night. But she had been too preoccupied with other matters to bother about her hair.

The beds had been spared a soaking, thank goodness, but the roof in two of the second-story rooms had sprung leaks. Wolf, for some reason known only to him, had decided to make off with several of the pots they had placed on the floor to catch the intruding drops of water. Downstairs, one of the shutters latched in place at the parlor window had finally surrendered to the wind's ferocity. And rain had gathered under every door and window, making it necessary to keep a constant supply of towels on hand.

But, within the past hour, the merciless downpour had given way to a steady, almost restful drumming upon the roof. The thunder and lightning had moved along to lay siege farther southward, and the winds had tapered off considerably. There could be no way of knowing the full extent of the damage done until morning. And there was always the possibility that another squall line could blow through. The air still held a strange charge, a tension and heaviness that Claire knew had as much to do with the storm inside her as it did with the one that had so recently battered the house.

Heaving a sigh, she wandered to the table and sank down in one of the chairs. She was tired, near exhaustion really, yet sleep had once again eluded her. No sooner had her head hit the pillow than Rand's parting words had filled her mind: *You can be thinking about what I said yesterday.*

"Damnation," she muttered, crossing her arms atop the table and wearily dropping her head upon them. Why couldn't she forget about that? And why did she find it so difficult to stop thinking about what he might or might not be doing in town?

She could well imagine women throwing themselves at him. Yes, and she could well imagine *him* catching them. As sure as the day was long, he hadn't lived the life of a monk these past six years. But . . . he was still her husband. Just as he himself had taken such obvious pleasure in reminding her, they were still legally bound to each other. And even though she didn't want him, no other woman had a right to him. Not yet, anyway. Not until she had found a way to dissolve their marriage. Not until he rode away from Glorieta and never, *ever* darkened her door again.

As if on cue, the wind suddenly regained its previous wrathful strength. It began whipping the rain about, sending leaves and branches pelting against the outer walls of the house. Claire raised her head and looked to the window. Lightning streaked through the storm-tossed darkness once more. Thunder rumbled and swelled, roaring across the prairie with such clangorous intensity that the ground shook.

And then, the back door crashed open.

Claire leapt to her feet, her eyes flying wide in startlement. She caught her breath and stood as if transfixed while she watched Rand step inside and close the door against the wind's fury.

"Wha—what are *you* doing here?" she sputtered, her pulse still racing from his unexpected and highly melodramatic entrance. Water streamed from his hat and yellow canvas slicker. His boots were covered with mud. And raindrops sparkled softly on the tanned, rugged perfection of his features.

"I told you I'd be back before morning." He tossed her a brief, enigmatic smile and peeled off the slicker. Hanging it on the hook beside the door, he removed his hat as well and ran a negligent hand through the wet, glistening thickness of his hair.

"Yes, but I never thought— For heaven's sake, are you out of your mind?" She cast a swift, anxious glance up toward the room where Sadie and Harmony lay sleeping. Lowering her voice to a whisper, she demanded in furious disbelief, "Whatever possessed you to go gallivanting about during a thunderstorm? And where is Micah? Did he—?"

"He's out in the bunkhouse," Rand assured her. Crossing unhurriedly to the stove, he poured himself a cup of coffee. "We headed back after the storm cleared through Parmalee."

"Why didn't you just wait until daylight?"

"Because I was worried about you." He turned to face her again. His expression was serious, and his gaze held none of the mockery she had expected to find.

"You were worried. . . ." repeated Claire. Her voice trailed away as she felt warm color flooding her face.

"I've been back in Texas awhile now, remember?" he remarked, another faint smile playing about his lips. "I know how a night like this can go from bad to worse." He frowned and raised the steaming cup toward his lips before adding, "And from the sound of it, the worst might still be coming."

Claire swallowed a sudden lump in her throat. She couldn't help but notice the way his eyes, more incredibly blue and penetrating than ever, traveled over her with bold intimacy. It seemed that he could see right through the clinging layers of fabric. The blush in her cheeks deepened to crimson, and she snatched the upper edges of her dressing gown more closely together. Desperately wishing she weren't standing before him in nothing but her nightclothes, she lifted her chin to a haughty angle that belied her current dishabille.

"You might at least have bothered to knock."

"I saw the light on." He offered no apology for the intrusion. And he looked anything but sorry for it.

"It seems like I've heard *that* before," she retorted sarcastically, referring, of course, to the time he had disturbed her out in the springhouse. Then, as now, his proximity set her every nerve on edge. "Now that you've let me know you're back," she told him in a simmering undertone, "you can finish your coffee and get out."

"Don't you want to know if I learned anything in town tonight?" he asked, with infuriating calm. Setting the cup beside the sink, he slowly closed the distance between them.

Claire caught the faint scent of whiskey hanging about him. It set her eyes to blazing.

"I've no doubt you enjoyed your 'investigation,' " she seethed indignantly. "And I'm sure the saloon was glad of the extra business."

"The best place to loosen a man's tongue—" he started to reiterate.

"The best place to loosen a woman's buttons," she flung at him, the storm raging outside all but forgotten now. Her outrage increased tenfold when she observed the light of unholy amusement glowing in his eyes.

"Jealous, Mrs. Logan?" he challenged softly.

"Not even if you were the last man on earth," she was quick to deny. "And stop calling me that."

"It's your name, isn't it?"

"It won't be for much longer." She folded her arms angrily beneath her breasts and leveled a curt toss of her head at the back door. Her long, shimmering tresses danced about her shoulders while she commanded, "Now get out!"

"I only had a couple of drinks, Claire," offered Rand, unscathed by the fire in her eyes. "It was necessary. Otherwise, I'd have looked as out of place as a steer in a chicken coop. And I did learn a thing or two that might prove useful. As for those buttons," he concluded in a low, dangerously compelling tone, "the only ones I'm interested in loosening are yours."

"Why, you—you *have* gone loco," she breathed. Once again, his words had struck a note of fear deep inside her. And provoked a dismaying weakness in her knees.

"Maybe." His expression was grim, his voice raw with a long-denied yearning. "But if I'm out of my mind, it's because of you. Six years of regret, of loneliness and rambling—and wanting something so bad you'd swear it burned a hole in your heart—can do a lot to a man. It can make him determined to take advantage of second chances." Reaching for her, his fingers curled about her upper arms.

"No!" She lifted her own hands to push at his chest. "There aren't any second chances. You can't change the past, you can't make things right simply by—"

"The past is part of us. But it's the future I care about. Yours and mine."

"We don't *have* a future. We never did. You killed any hope of that the night you ran away. If you had cared for me, if you had wanted me at all, you couldn't have left me behind like that. You couldn't have broken the promises you made."

"I wanted you. More than I'd ever wanted anyone. But I made you no promises," he said, disputing her. His gaze smoldered like molten steel as it bored down into hers. A sharp gasp broke from her lips when he suddenly yanked her close. "Damn it, Claire," he ground out, his handsome face thunderous now, "you lied to your father. You tricked me into marriage. Maybe I did lead you to believe I was ready for it. Maybe I deserved to be horsewhipped for taking advantage of your innocence that night in the barn, but no man likes to have something forced on him. Especially something as permanent as marriage. If you had only—"

"If I had only what?" she demanded bitterly, cursing the pain twisting at her heart. "Told him the truth? All right, I should have! It was wrong of me to let him believe the worst. Is that what you wanted to hear? I should have told him and spared myself the humiliation of these past six years. But I was young and in love—or *thought* I was—and you let me go on dreaming. You're every bit as much to blame for what happened as I am, Rand Logan. No, by heaven, you're *more* to blame!" she amended, glaring reproachfully up at him. "You were so cocksure, so confident of your ability to get whatever it was you wanted. And you haven't changed."

"Haven't I?" His mouth curved into only the suggestion of a smile.

"No." Frightened by the look in his eyes, as well as by her own light-headedness, she tossed a swift, fiery glance up toward the ceiling again and hissed, "Now take your hands off me. Sadie and Harmony are bound to hear—"

"Let them."

With an impatience that quite literally took her breath away, he gathered her close and bent his head to capture her mouth with the strong, sensuous warmth of his.

She fought him, struggling furiously within his embrace in spite of the sudden, alarming tendency to melt against him. He disregarded her moans of protest and tightened his arms about her. She gasped to feel her soft curves pressed to the virile hardness of his body. His lips moved demandingly upon hers, his tongue exploring the honeyed sweetness of her mouth while she tried, without success, to twist away.

The kiss was more hotly captivating than she would ever acknowledge, yet she forced herself to resist. Bending her knee, she brought it thrusting upward in a desperate attempt to break free. But he was too quick for her. In one lightning-swift motion, he swept her up in his arms, settled his hips on the edge of the table, and pulled her across his lap.

Another clap of thunder rang out, but Claire took no notice of it. The winds thrashed and swirled, while the rain slammed earthward with a newfound vengeance. It was all a perfect match for the chaos within her.

She squirmed with a fast-waning strength within his grasp, but he easily imprisoned her with one arm clamped across her knees and the other about her shoulders. The battle was already lost, and she knew it. She closed her eyes. The kiss deepened.

A delicious warmth spread throughout her body. Her head spun, and her arms crept upward to entwine about Rand's neck. Surrendering to the inevitable, she kissed him back with all the desire he had first awakened in her six years ago—with all the longing she had been denying since the night he had gone. It was almost as if time had stood still, as if she were seventeen again and the two of them were stealing forbidden, hungrily passionate moments together out in the barn. *Rand . . .*

He tugged the belt of her robe loose and swept the edges open, his hand gliding down to her buttocks. She felt branded by his touch through the delicate white cotton of her nightgown. Her hips moved restlessly atop the powerful hardness of his thighs, and she could not summon the will to protest when his hand next moved up to close upon her breast. His fingers caressed her with a tenderness and urgency that set her senses to reeling.

Suddenly his mouth left off its heart-stopping ravishment of hers. She drew in a long, highly uneven breath as his lips roamed feverishly across her face, then trailed a searing path downward to where her pulse beat so erratically at the base of her throat. With a swift and alarming dexterity, he unlooped the row of pearl buttons on the front of the nightgown's yoked bodice. He yanked the fabric aside, baring her breasts to his burning, fiercely possessive gaze.

Claire gasped to feel the rush of cold air upon her exposed flesh. Her eyelids fluttered open, and she managed a woefully feeble protest now, but to no avail. Gathering her further upward in his embrace, Rand bent his head and pressed his lips to the swelling, delectable fullness of her naked breasts.

Closing her eyes again, she moaned low in her throat. Her fingers lifted to entangle within the damp, sunkissed richness of his hair. She caught her lower lip between her teeth and instinctively arched her back while his mouth swooped down to capture one of the rosetipped peaks. His warm lips tantalized while his tongue flicked and swirled and teased.

At the same time, his hand returned to her hips. He swept the hemline of her nightgown upward; as usual, she wore no drawers beneath it. Another gasp escaped her lips, and her face flamed when his strong fingers spread appreciatively across the bare, firmly rounded curve of her bottom. He gave a low groan and captured her lips with his once more.

Though it seemed impossible, the kiss was even more wildly intoxicating than the first. Claire's mouth welcomed the conquering warmth of his. Caught up in the fury of the moment, she was nevertheless startled when his hand delved between her thighs. Her eyes flew wide once more. Not even six years ago had he dared to touch her *there*.

But he did so now. Lowering determinedly to the beckoning triangle of dark blond curls, his fingers parted the moist, silken flesh.

Claire felt wildfire streak through her. Inhaling sharply against Rand's mouth, she trembled and squirmed anew. The caress was wicked and shocking, and so pleasurable that she was certain she would faint. She clutched at his shoulders, her conscience battling with her passions. In that small part of her brain still capable of rational thought, she knew that she should put a stop to the madness. She knew that she would probably despise herself afterward. But heaven help her, she had never felt this way before. . . .

In spite of his own hot, achingly intense desire, Rand sensed her confusion. He raised his head and brought his lips close to her ear.

"I love you, Claire," he declared huskily.

Her reaction was not at all what he had expected—or hoped for.

To Claire, his words were a painful, taunting reminder of his betrayal. It never occurred to her that he might be speaking the truth. She knew better than to trust him. *Fool me once, shame on you. Fool me twice, shame on me.* The old proverb seemed all too appropriate for the situation. Six years ago, Rand Logan had said he loved her. Six years ago, he had run away and left her heart and her dreams shattered to bits.

"No!" she choked out. Scrambling from his lap so abruptly that he was taken off-guard, she backed away toward the sink and snatched the edges of her dressing gown across her breasts. Her eyes were blazing vengefully, her hair streaming about her face and shoulders in glorious disarray as she seethed, "No, damn you! I won't let you do it to me again. I let myself be deceived once before, but not this time. Never again!"

"Claire—"

"Get out! Get out, or so help me, I'll scream and bring everyone on the place running!"

Rand slowly drew his tall frame upright. His gaze, deep and penetrating, seared across into hers.

"I'll leave . . . for now," he said. Though his face was

inscrutable, his low, wonderfully resonant voice held a determination that knew no bounds. "But I meant what I said, Claire. What we had together all those years ago is still there. Try and deny it if you want to. But it won't go away. And neither will I."

"Get out!" Her voice rose perilously, and she felt hot tears stinging against her eyelids. She took another wary step toward the sink when he moved past her to the doorway. He donned his hat and slicker again, gave her one last, completely unnerving look, and disappeared into the turbulent darkness of the night.

As soon as the door closed after him, Claire made her way back across to the table and collapsed into the chair. She breathed a long, ragged sigh and stared, unseeing, toward the steady golden flame of the lamp, still burning beside the stove.

Dear God, she had almost let herself be well and truly seduced . . . and on her own kitchen table besides. She might have laughed at the utter absurdity of it all, if not for the fact that her heart ached so terribly.

She had nearly made the same disastrous mistake a second time. Her cheeks burned at the memory of Rand's kisses and caresses, and her own shameful response to them. How many other woman, she wondered bitterly, had found themselves charmed out of their inhibitions with such ease? He was a thoroughly appealing scoundrel, all right. A devil in the guise of an angel . . .

With the new storm still raging outside, she stood and raised her hands to fasten the buttons of her nightgown. Her eyes strayed to the back door. And before she finally returned upstairs to the empty comfort of her bed, she mused with a faint, humorless smile of irony that she'd better stop lighting lamps whenever she was alone.

Chapter 6

The deluge finally ended shortly before daybreak. It left the air smelling fresh and clean, the ground saturated and sparkling with an irregular patchwork of puddles, and the ranch hands facing the formidable, time-consuming chore of rectifying the mayhem it had wrought.

On Saturday morning, two days after the storm had first threatened Glorieta, Claire rose and dressed early. She planned to drive the buckboard into town to fetch the lumber and nails and other supplies needed to make repairs. And although it had required a great deal of persuasion on her part, she had convinced Sadie to accompany her.

Preceded by an ebullient and bright-eyed Harmony, the two women descended the steps of the front porch a little before eight o'clock. The buckboard was waiting, the horse already harnessed, and the reins looped in readiness beside the locked brake. But instead of the escort Claire had expected to find, she saw that it was Rand who stood in the shade of the wind-battered trees, his own horse saddled and pawing impatiently at the moist dirt.

"What are *you* doing here?" she asked, striving to keep her tone level. If not for the presence of the others, she would have behaved with far less civility.

"I'll be going with you," he announced calmly, then nodded at Sadie and Harmony. "Morning, ladies."

"Good morning, Mr. Parker," murmured Sadie. She stole a quick, dubious glance at Claire before gathering up her skirts and drifting around to the other side of the wagon.

"Can I ride on your horse, Jake?" Harmony entreated.

"Sure." He smiled down at the little girl and raised his hat to his head. "If it's all right with your ma."

"Where is Micah?" Claire broke in to demand. She was annoyed at the way her cheeks warmed beneath the disquieting steadiness of his gaze. Having scrupulously avoided any contact with him since that night in the kitchen, she now found herself recalling—with wicked clarity—everything that had passed between them. The mere sight of him was enough to send a renewed wave of shame and mortification crashing over her, but she lifted her head proudly and gave him a look that would have chilled a lesser man to the bone. "He was supposed to—"

"He offered to let me take his place."

"Then he'll have to take his offer back." She started toward the bunkhouse. Rand leisurely blocked her path.

"I've got some business of my own in town, Miss Parmalee," he decreed in a low tone edged with steel. His blue eyes seared commandingly down into the startled emerald depths of hers. Her face paled a bit, and she did her best to ignore the tremor that shot through her.

"Come on, Jake!" Harmony prompted. Her impatience earned her a sharp, reproving frown from her mother.

Claire was loath to give in. With a highly visible reluctance, she pivoted about and climbed up into the buckboard to take her place beside the other woman. Rand moved away to swing up into the saddle. He reached down, caught Harmony about the waist, and brought her up to the horse's back. She followed his instructions to put her arms around him and hold tight.

The newly washed earth was ablaze with sunlight as the foursome set off across the rolling plains. The wagon wheels cut into the muddy road, leaving ruts that would remain for days. There were other reminders of the storm everywhere—branches and leaves strewn haphazardly about, water glistening in the tiny, shallow canyons carved by the wind and rain, and more than one windmill towering nakedly against the vast Texas sky. Still, cattle grazed with their usual contentment, and seemed to have already forgotten about the storm's terrifying violence as they wandered freely across the range.

Reaching town, Claire guided the horse and buckboard to a stop in front of the general store. She had done the same last Saturday—the day Rand Logan had appeared out of the blue to turn her whole world upside down. It was difficult to believe all that had happened in only a week's time. It was even more difficult to believe she had changed from an admittedly prim, coolheaded woman who guarded her emotions to one who was so weak-spirited that she found pleasure in the kisses of a man who had already proven himself a rogue. Great balls of fire, she lamented in silent, ireful bemusement, when would the ordeal end?

The rains had transformed Parmalee's main street into a veritable sea of black mud, a quagmire difficult to maneuver either on foot or horseback. As a result, there were considerably fewer people in town that day. But the "regulars" would be there. Nothing short of death could keep them from town on a Saturday. It had been that way for as long as Claire could remember.

"I'll head on over to the lumberyard," Rand told her once he had reined to a halt as well. Reaching behind him with one arm, he caught Harmony about the waist and effortlessly swung her down. The child squealed with delight and beamed him an adoring grin, while he added, "Maybe they'll at least have what we need to get the roof patched up."

"Fine," snapped Claire. Refusing to look his way, she set the brake and started to secure the reins.

Rand dismounted, then helped Sadie down from the buckboard. He tied the reins of his horse to the hitching post, tugged the front brim of his hat lower, and surprised Claire by rounding the front of the wagon to approach her.

"I thought you were—" she said in puzzlement, rising from the seat.

"I am. After I walk you inside." His hands came up to seize her firmly about the waist.

"I am perfectly capable of—" she protested, but to no avail. He swung her down as though she weighed little more than Harmony. His fingers remained warm and strong upon her for several moments longer than was necessary. She flung him a virulent look before finally pulling away.

"I'd like to pay a visit to the telegraph office if you don't mind," Sadie announced quietly as she joined them on the mud-caked boardwalk.

"The telegraph office?" echoed Claire, turning to face her with a frown.

"Yes. I haven't written to my folks in a while. I thought I'd best be letting them know that Harmony and I are all right." A dull flush crept up to her face, and her eyes fell guiltily before she confided, "To tell the truth, they don't even know where we are. They—they wanted me to come home when Daniel died. But I couldn't go back."

"Take all the time you need," Claire insisted, giving her a brief yet compassionate smile. "Heaven knows, you certainly deserve it."

"Thank you, Claire." Her features relaxing in gratitude, she called to Harmony.

Left alone with Rand, Claire rounded on him again. Her voice was quite low and charged with anger when she said, "I'm sure you're proud of yourself for forcing me into this. But it was extremely careless of you. Don't you realize that if the two of us are seen together someone is bound to recognize you?"

"People believe what they want to believe," he replied, unconcerned. "Or what they're led to."

"Are you truly willing to risk being found out?" she whispered in disbelief.

"I'm used to taking risks. Remember?"

He took her arm and propelled her through the mercantile's open doorway, raking the hat from his head on his way in. Claire was relieved to find only George and Martha Hunnicutt inside. George smiled when he caught sight of her. Martha, on the other hand, favored her with a dissociable glare.

"Mornin' to you, Miss Claire," said the amiable, copper-haired George as he climbed down from where he had been stacking canned goods high on a shelf. He immediately moved to take his place behind the counter in front of Claire, who responded to his customary friendliness with a wan, preoccupied smile of her own.

"Good morning, Mr. Hunnicutt." Unhappily aware of Rand's presence at her side, she had no choice but to make the introductions. The Hunnicutts had been new to town six years ago; there was only a remote possibility they would even remember what Rand Logan looked like. "This is Jake Parker," she declared. "He recently signed on at Glorieta." To Rand, she explained with a deceptive cordiality, "Mr. and Mrs. Hunnicutt own the mercantile."

"Pleased to make your acquaintance," said the proprietor. He offered his hand to Rand, who accepted it in a firm grip.

"Thanks." He nodded politely to Martha. "Ma'am." She murmured a cold response before her hawkish gaze sliced back to Claire.

"Seems like I recall some folks named Parker over in the next county," George remarked idly. Then he asked Rand, "you wouldn't by any chance be kin to them, would you?"

"No. I'm from San Antone."

"Well then, I guess not." He smiled again, but the

smile faded into a slight frown of perplexity a moment later. His eyes narrowed a bit as they fastened on Rand's face. "You look mighty familiar to me, Mr. Parker. Ever been through Parmalee before?"

Claire tensed involuntarily. She held her breath and cast a surreptitious glance up at Rand. He didn't appear in the least nonplussed by the question.

"Not until a few days ago," he drawled. The ease with which he spoke the lie prompted Claire to muse resentfully that he was every bit as adept at bending the truth as he used to be.

"I don't suppose you're planning to attend the box social tonight, are you?" Martha suddenly demanded of Claire.

"Box social?" she repeated in bewilderment, her eyes widening.

"Over at the church?"

"I—I suppose I forgot." Now that she thought about it, she *had* heard something about it last Sunday. But other things had driven it from her mind.

"I just hope you don't plan on bringing that Bishop woman with you!"

"Now, Martha," George admonished gently. "You know what Reverend Mueller said."

"I don't give a fig what he said!" she retorted, with her usual prickliness. "I'll continue to hold my own opinions."

"I've brought a list of supplies with me again today, Mr. Hunnicutt," Claire interjected at that point, anxious to avoid a full-scale confrontation with Martha. She could feel Rand's eyes upon her. She stiffened and refused to allow her own gaze anywhere near him.

"I'll have everything ready for you in a little while, Miss Claire," George assured her. He looked pained by his wife's ill-bred behavior. In Claire's opinion—an opinion shared by a good many others in town—he had to be one of the least envied men in all of Texas.

Turning away, Claire swept back outside and untied the strings of her red calico bonnet. Yanking it off with an uncharacteristic disregard for her upswept, tightly pinned hair, she stood battling her temper when Rand emerged from the store. He was a convenient target for her wrath—particularly since he was the primary source of it.

"You have things to do, *Mr. Parker*," she reminded him, her green eyes brilliantly ablaze. "I suggest you stop wasting time and get to them."

"Yes, ma'am." He looked neither contrite nor subservient. With a faint, sardonic smile, he raised his hat to his head once more and stated, "I'll be back in about an hour."

"An hour? It can't possibly take that long to—"

"Is that the kind of wife you intend to be?" he challenged in a low, affectionately mocking tone. "The kind who demands an accounting of every damned minute?"

"I don't intend to be a wife at all," she said. Her fingers crushed the bonnet she held, while two bright spots of angry color rode high on the smoothness of her cheeks. If not for the fact that they were in such a decidedly public place, she might well have been tempted to strike him. "Not to you or anyone else!" she added in a furious whisper.

"Too late." His smile this time was devastating.

Stunned into speechlessness, she watched as he

headed across the street. His stride was confident and easy, in spite of the thick mud that grasped at his boots. Was there anything he didn't do well? she thought in a flash of resentment. Her traitorous mind conjured up yet another memory of his skillful and highly inflaming kisses. By heaven, she was acting like a schoolgirl. . . .

Blushing at her own foolishness, she whirled about and marched off down the boardwalk. Several passersby spoke to her, and she wondered if she was only imagining that they did so with more enthusiasm than usual. She was grateful for the fact that she encountered none of the "harpies." It had been a difficult week; she was in no mood for their nonsense.

She paid a visit to the saddlemaker's, where she ordered a new saddle for the cantankerous Sully. He would never own up to the fact that the old one was an absolute disgrace to his profession. And although she knew that he would protest the extravagance, she had little doubt that he would secretly be delighted with the gift.

After that, she directed her steps toward the telegraph office. She spied Sadie and Harmony standing in the morning sunlight nearby. Her mouth curved into a brief smile of satisfaction when she saw that they were talking with Reverend Mueller. Reluctant to disturb what appeared to be a promising conversation, she wandered back to where she had left the buckboard.

A loud, shrill whistle rent the stillness of the air, announcing the departure of the ten o'clock train bound for Dallas. Claire looked toward the small tin-roofed station at the end of the street, then found her eyes straying with a will of their own to the lumberyard next to it.

"I rode over yesterday to see how you'd fared durin' the storm."

Starting a bit, she turned to find Tate Jenner smiling at her. His pale blue eyes twinkled across into hers when he drew closer. Dressed in a striped chambray shirt, black cloth vest, and fitted denim trousers, he looked as attractive as ever. But the sight of him didn't make her heart skip a beat. Not like— *Don't,* she thought, groaning inwardly.

"You weren't there," Tate accused, with a mock frown of reproach as he stopped in front of her.

"Sully told me you'd been by," she replied. "I was out checking on the herd."

"How many head did you lose?"

"None, thank God. And you?"

"The same. We were lucky, too. Except we're missin' half of the stock barn. Will's down at the lumberyard right now, gettin' what we'll need to fix it up."

"The first year is always the hardest," Claire reassured him, though his words prompted her gaze to drift elsewhere again. She wondered how much longer Rand would be gone—and what his reaction would be if he saw her talking to Tate. Why the devil should she care what he thought? "I haven't seen those three brothers of yours in a long time," she noted, forcing her attention back to Tate. "Perhaps you'd care to bring them over for Sunday dinner tomorrow."

"They'll be thankful for the invite," he told her, with a mellow chuckle. "We've been eatin' too much of our own cookin'. Come summer, we hope to hire ourselves a real cook. Maybe a couple of hands, too."

"Then things *are* going well," she remarked, glad of his success.

"Well enough." He took a step closer, and the expression on his face grew even more appealing when he said, "I just heard there's to be a get-together over at the church tonight. Would you like to go with me?"

"Oh, Tate. I don't think I should. There's still so much to do because of the storm. And it wouldn't be fair to . . . well, to raise your hopes," she said.

"There's nothin' wrong with two friends enjoyin' each other's company."

"So you do understand about that?" she asked hopefully. "You're not—?"

"I'm not. But I *might* be if you don't say you'll go," he teased. "It's the least you can do after turnin' me down."

"I suppose it is." She smiled and shook her head at his backdoor methods of persuasion. "You certainly know how to get what you want, don't you?"

"I was beginnin' to think I'd lost my touch." He now tossed a negligent glance over his shoulder at the buckboard. "Are you headin' home?"

"Not yet. I'm waiting for Sadie and Harmony. They should be along soon."

"So it's just the three of you?"

"No." She averted her gaze now, her manner suddenly—and suspiciously—evasive. "One of the hands accompanied us."

"Micah?"

"No. Jake Parker."

"Parker," he repeated. His brow furrowed thought-fully for a moment, and then his eyes glinted with an unpleasant remembrance. "Isn't he the one who—?"

"He is." Hoping to avoid further talk of Rand, she asked lightly, "What time will you come by tonight?"

"Eight o'clock ought to be early enough."

"Early enough for what?"

They both turned to face the two men who were making their way across the muckish, practically deserted width of Main Street. Claire's eyes grew round with surprise at the sight of Rand walking alongside Will Jenner.

"Howdy, Miss Claire." Will greeted her with a gallant tip of his hat. He was the youngest of the four Jenners, not much more than a boy really, his hair a thatch of white-blond and his gray eyes always full of mischief. "Tate," he said, shifting his gaze eagerly to his brother, "this here's Jake Parker. He's the one bought me a couple of rounds over at the Empire the other night. I ran across him down by the station just now."

"Mr. Parker and I have already met," recalled Tate, his features tightening. Rand gave him a curt nod.

"What's eight o'clock early enough for?" Will probed once more, grinning while he looked to Claire and back again.

"Well, it . . ." murmured Claire. Coloring faintly, she allowed her eyes to fall to the bonnet she still held. It would be creased beyond repair by the time she got home.

"I'll be bringin' Claire back to town tonight," Tate was only too willing to announce. "To the box social at the church." He curled a hand possessively about her upper arm. A slow, triumphant smile spread across his face; it was clearly meant for Rand. "I'll be with the prettiest gal there."

"Not at all," Claire protested briskly. She raised her eyes to meet Rand's again. The fierce gleam in them made her lift her chin to a proud, defensive angle.

"I thought you'd already made plans for tonight, Miss Parmalee," he remarked, his features inscrutable at the moment.

"I changed my mind." It gave her a small measure of perverse satisfaction to throw his own words back at him.

"Maybe I'll come along," Will suggested, deliberately trying to get a rise out of his brother.

"Think again," advised Tate. He directed one last hard, challenging look at Rand before telling Claire, "See you tonight."

She nodded mutely. Her eyes followed the two brothers as they strode away to collect their own wagonload of supplies. When she finally, and reluctantly, turned back to Rand, she was not surprised by his disapproving frown. But she *was* more affected by it than she had counted on.

"You can't go with him," he decreed, his deep-timbred voice for her ears alone.

"I can and will."

"Jenner's trouble. More than you know."

"Thank you very much for the warning, Mr. Parker, but I didn't ask for it, and I certainly don't intend to—"

"You're playing with fire, Claire." His steely, penetrating gaze seemed to bore into her very soul.

"So are you," she retorted, almost forgetting to keep her own voice low. "And I hope you get burned. God forgive me, *I hope you get burned.*"

She pushed past him and fled inside the general store. But there was no respite to be found there. A highly expressive oath rose to her lips when she discovered Lydia Cassidy and Jane Willis deep in the throes of gossip with Martha. As she was all too painfully aware, news spread like wildfire in a small town like Parmalee.

"We hear you've gone and hired yourself a new man," Lydia remarked in place of a greeting. Her words were more of an accusation than a statement.

"Martha says he's quite attractive," Jane disclosed, with a little more charity.

"Does she?" parried Claire. Still furious with them for their churchyard attack upon Sadie, she swept purposefully across to the counter and asked George, "Is everything ready, Mr. Hunnicutt?"

"It sure is, Miss Claire. I was just fixin' to load it all up for you."

"Thank you. If you'll just—"

"I'll give you a hand there, Mr. Hunnicutt," Rand spoke behind her. His tall, splendidly hard-muscled frame filled the doorway. Taking off his hat, he favored the trio of women, who had been struck dumb at the sight of him, with a crooked half smile and a nod before sauntering forward to help George with the supplies.

Claire tossed a swift, exasperated glance heavenward. Her face colored warmly, and she was conscious of the fact that the other women's eyes followed every move Rand made as he and George carried the boxes outside.

"Is he the one?" Lydia demanded, obviously not caring if she was overheard.

"His name is Parker," Martha reiterated. "Jake Parker. And surely, Claire Parmalee, you should have known better than to hire a man who looks like that." Folding her arms across her more than ample bosom, she narrowed her eyes toward the doorway and pronounced, "It's plain to see he's cocky as all get-out. And too good-looking to be trusted."

"People will talk, that's for certain," Jane cautioned gravely.

"People always talk," muttered Claire. She pivoted about and started outside.

"It isn't decent," Lydia asserted, once again setting herself up as the town's arbiter of matters both social and moral. "A young woman livin' out there alone at that ranch with all those men. And now *this* one comin' along."

"Well . . . she's not exactly alone," Jane pointed out tentatively, then blanched at the waspish glare Lydia turned upon her.

"Sadie Bishop doesn't count." Looking back to Claire, she positively glowered while warning, "You let yourself be led into temptation once before, remember? Now, you'd best be markin' my words—this Jake Parker looks to be every bit as much a rounder as that husband of yours was."

Claire's eyes suddenly lit with amusement. It was all she could do to suppress a laugh at the irony of Lydia's words. If only the old brimstone knew how doubly appropriate the exhortation was.

"I'll keep that in mind," she promised dryly.

Sailing back outside, she was relieved to find Sadie and Harmony waiting for her. The three of them, along with Rand, were soon headed homeward. The wagon bed was loaded with foodstuffs, lumber, tin, and several bags of nails. By now, the morning was almost gone, and the wind had returned to whisper across the green-mantled prairie.

Harmony rode behind Rand on the horse again, her little arms wrapped about his waist. Her dark eyes were sparkling with a secret pleasure when she suddenly turned and gave Claire a broad smile.

"Mama and I are going to church tonight!" she announced in a voice loud enough to be heard above the creak and rattle of the buckboard.

"Are you?" Claire responded in surprise. Her gaze quickly traveled to the woman seated beside her.

"Reverend Mueller asked if he could take us to the box social they're having," explained Sadie, her own eyes softly aglow. "I said yes. I—I found it difficult not to." Her brows drew together into a worried frown when she appealed, "You don't think it was wrong of me to say we'd go, do you, Claire? After what happened last Sunday, I suppose it's foolish of me to hope—"

"No, Sadie. It isn't foolish. And it isn't wrong. The reverend assured me nothing like that will happen again. He strikes me as a man willing to back up his word. I think he may just have succeeded in putting the 'fear of God' in all those who dared to attack you." She certainly hoped so, anyway.

"Can we take Wolf with us, Mama?" asked Harmony.

"No. He'll have to stay with Claire."

"He'll have to stay with Sully." Claire corrected her, then admitted, "I'm going to the social, too."

"With Tate Jenner?"

"Yes."

She stole a look up at Rand. He sat tall and silent in the saddle, his face impassive beneath the brim of his hat. But when he turned his head to meet her gaze, she saw that his eyes held an intense—unmistakably dangerous—gleam.

She experienced a sharp twinge of guilt—and another of very real apprehension. Swallowing hard, she hastily looked away again and gave an impulsive flick of the reins.

Chapter 7

Reverend Mueller, with the promptness expected of a man in such a socially demanding line of work, guided his horse and buggy to a stop in front of the house at half past seven that evening. Sadie and Harmony were upstairs in the room they shared, making last-minute adjustments, when Claire opened the door to inform them that their escort was cooling his heels in the parlor.

"We're almost ready," Sadie proclaimed breathlessly. Her color was high, and her eyes were shining with more excitement than she had felt in a long time. Having cast aside her usual shapeless attire, she looked quite lovely in a fitted, two-piece dress of primrose muslin. She had even arranged her thick raven hair in a less severe style, leaving several tendrils to curl softly about her face.

"What's a box social, Claire?" Harmony queried, even though she had already posed the same question to her mother. Her own dark tresses had been plaited into a single braid and secured with a blue satin ribbon. She was wearing her new red calico dress, and like Sadie, looked very pretty indeed.

"Well, I suppose it's really just a picnic of sorts," replied Claire. Her lips curved into a smile of genuine affection as she moved forward to slip an arm about the little girl's shoulders. "Except that it's held to raise money for a good cause—tonight, of course, it's to put a roof on the new fellowship hall. The ladies bring boxes of food from home and the men bid on them, and the highest bidder wins the privilege of eating supper with the lady who cooked the food. Although, in my case," she amended, with a conspiratorial look, "your mother cooked the food. But we won't tell anyone."

"That's *all*?" said Harmony. Her disappointment was obvious.

"Well, sometimes there's dancing afterward. Of course, that depends on whether or not the parson believes dancing is a sin."

"Does Reverend Mueller believe it's a sin, Mama?"

"You can ask him yourself," Sadie told her. She started from the room now, but paused to ask Claire, "Are you sure you don't need any help with your dress before I leave? Mr. Jenner will be here soon and—"

"I'm sure. Now, go on. Your escort is waiting." She administered a gentle push to the other woman and led Harmony forward, commenting wryly, "Just because the man's a preacher doesn't mean he has the patience of a saint."

After she had watched them happily borne away in the comfort of Reverend Mueller's buggy, Claire returned upstairs to dress. She had enjoyed a warm, soothing bath earlier in the afternoon, and had washed her hair as well. Stripping down to her undergarments, she drew on a gown of corded, sky blue silk. It was by far the prettiest she owned, and she was glad now that she had surrendered to the temptation to purchase such an expensive fabric. The gown's simple lines suited her. The boned and fitted bodice, buttoning down the back, featured tiny puffed sleeves and a low rounded neckline that allowed an entirely proper—yet tantalizing—glimpse of the creamy swell of her breasts. The attached skirt was full and gathered, trimmed with three rows of flounces near the hem and caught up behind by a large self-fabric bow.

Perching on the edge of the bed, she donned embroidered white stockings and a pair of white kid slippers with front-cross lacings. Her mother's gold filigree locket, hanging from the center of a black velvet band about her neck, and a rose-colored lace fan completed the ensemble. Evening gloves were a nicety she had never learned to tolerate.

She stood and crossed to the mirror, twisting up her long golden tresses to pin them as she always did. But a sudden impulse compelled her to try something different. Her eyes searched for inspiration as they moved to the nearby dressing table. Spying a length of pink satin ribbon, she gathered her hair loosely and tied the ribbon about it. The style was much the same as the one she had worn six years ago ... when she had met Rand. She frowned darkly at her reflection and reached for the hairpins, only to stop when she heard Tate pulling up below.

A strange and sudden reluctance gripped her. Why, oh, why had she ever said she'd go? Everyone there would probably assume she was taking up with Tate

Jenner. She might well find herself branded as even more of a pariah. There was no sidestepping the fact that she was still a married woman, even if it was in name only. And what about her "husband"? She knew he would be furious if she went.

Rand. Her eyes kindled with the fire of defiance. He had no right to tell her what to do. No right at all.

Whirling about, she caught up her crimson shawl and hastened downstairs to greet Tate. He was waiting for her on the front porch, his hat in his hand and mouth turned up into an engaging smile.

"Just like I said—you'll be the prettiest one there," he pronounced. His eyes gleamed with warm, wholly masculine appreciation while they traveled slowly over her.

"Flattery will get you nowhere, Tate Jenner." Her saucy retort was an effort to mask the growing uneasiness she felt.

After pausing to collect the box of food Sadie had left waiting for her on the swing, she allowed Tate to take her arm in a familiar grip as they moved down the steps and across to his buckboard. He handed her up, then took his place beside her and unlooped the reins. She placed the box beneath the seat, her gaze straying instinctively toward the bunkhouse. Once again seized by the powerful urge to call the whole thing off, she told herself it was too late. She couldn't back out now. She couldn't do that to Tate.

Pulling her shawl more closely about her, she drew in a deep, ragged breath while the buckboard rolled away into the gathering darkness. With a sunset that was vibrant and multihued, and a sky unmarred by even a hint of clouds, the coming night promised to be a beautiful one.

The ride to town was easy and pleasant. They talked about their ranches, about the possibility of barbed wire coming to the local range, and about the still-unsolved robberies that had plagued the area in recent months. Claire tensed when the latter subject was introduced. The robberies, after all, were what had brought Rand back to Glorieta. Strangely enough, she had forgotten about that.

"Doesn't look like Sheriff Howell's much of a lawman," Tate opined, with a chuckle. He flicked the reins lightly together once more and turned his head to smile at her. "Then again, he might be a particular friend of yours."

"No, not really. He's only been in Parmalee for a couple of years." Casting a glance up at the twilight-cloaked heavens, she inhaled deeply of the fresh night air. Her ears caught the faint, mingling sounds of crickets and coyotes and—the region's lifeblood—cattle.

"A couple of years? That's more than a year longer than me."

"Yes," she conceded, her green eyes sparkling as they lowered to his face again, "but you were much easier to get to know. Still, I suppose the man is trying his best." His best might get even better if he knew a Texas Ranger had been assigned to the investigation, she added silently. Rand was apparently set on keeping his true identity a secret for a while longer. Then again, there had always been an air of mystery about him. She wondered if it was possible to ever get to know the real Rand Logan. . . . *Heaven help her, she had to get him out of her mind, if only for tonight.*

"I say they ought to string up the thievin' cowards who did it." Tate's voice drew her from her reverie.

"Sully has offered to do the job himself."

"He'd have plenty of help." He snapped the reins above the horse's back again and disclosed idly, "I heard some talk about the Rangers bein' called in."

"Did you?" Feigning indifference, she adjusted the folds of silk across her lap.

"I don't recollect who exactly, but someone told me the sheriff sent word down to San Antone. Maybe now we'll get results. The Rangers are a slam-bang outfit, all right. There was a time I thought about joinin' up myself."

"What made you decide against it?"

"I was the oldest and had to look after my brothers. Will wasn't more than half-grown back then."

"But," she pointed out, with a bemused frown, "the Rangers didn't start up again until two years ago." She recalled having read about the governor's decision, about how crimes such as cattle rustling and horse stealing had taken on such alarming proportions in some parts of the state that the people had clamored for relief. Parmalee, of course, had never suffered any real outbreak of lawlessness. Not until recently, anyway.

"True enough," admitted Tate, then smiled crookedly. "I guess I still thought of Will as a boy. He's changed a lot since we moved on. We all have."

"How old were you when your parents died?" she asked quietly. He had never talked about his past much.

She had always been curious to know more about him, but she hadn't wanted to pry. Her father used to say that a lot of men were running from something, but that no man could run forever. Was *this* man running from something—or someone?

"Fifteen. It was a fever that took them. Took my sisters, too."

"I'm sorry, Tate," she murmured, her eyes shining softly into his. "How terrible it must have been for you."

"It was a long time ago," he remarked, with a shrug. But a sudden shadow crossed his face. "We damn near starved to death before I could find work. I swore we'd never be in such a bad way again. Whatever happened, I was goin' to see to it that my brothers were taken care of."

"Well, it certainly looks as though all your hard work and determination have succeeded. You've done a good job, Tate," she declared in all sincerity, her heart twisting at the thought of his long, painful struggle. "I doubt if too many other young men in your situation would have shouldered the responsibility so well."

"I still say the Jenner ranch'll be bigger than Glorieta someday," he teased, the usual spark returning to his eyes now.

"Competition's good for the soul," she retorted in the same playful spirit.

Arriving at the church soon thereafter, Claire was mildly surprised to observe so many horses, wagons, and buggies waiting out front. She had thought the troubles caused by the storm might prevent some of the church members from attending. Evidently, however, it had only served to make them even more grateful for their blessings. And a day of sunshine had helped dry out the roads, so that anyone who wanted to venture into town would find the going a great deal easier than it had been that morning.

She carefully gathered up her full, ankle-length skirts and allowed Tate to help her down. A dull flush crept up to her face when his hands curled about her waist, and she frowned at the not so distant memory of another, far more unnerving—and possessive—pair of hands on her.

"Sounds like the party's in full swing already," Tate noted, looking toward the new fellowship hall beside the church. Its four walls were tall and sturdy, but the absence of a roof meant that it was open to the deep, starlit expanse of the sky; fortunately the storms had inflicted far less damage than had been feared. The lively strains of fiddle music drifted through the cool night air. "Maybe we'll get to find out if any of those Holy Rollers know how to kick up their heels." Grinning, he turned to retrieve the box of food from beneath the wagon seat.

"I just hope Sadie and Harmony weren't 'welcomed' the way they were last Sunday," said Claire, her eyes clouding with renewed worry at the thought. Surely, she told herself, no one would dare speak publicly against Sadie so long as the preacher himself was her escort. There had to be an end to the judgment and intolerance . . . and she had a feeling Thomas Mueller was just the man to perform such a miracle.

Accepting the arm Tate proffered, she held the fringed edges of her shawl together and walked along with him toward the hall. She took a deep, steadying breath when the two of them climbed the steps to stand framed in the doorway for a few moments.

The large, rectangular room was ablaze with the light of two dozen lanterns strung across the roofless space above. Laughter punctuated the conversations of the threescore men and women who, following the usual course of nature, had separated into small groups of their own sex to complain about the opposite one. A number of children darted through the crowd, their antics perilously close to upsetting the tables that had been set up along one wall and covered with bright checkered tablecloths. There, pitchers and punch bowls offered libation—spiritless, of course—while boxes and baskets of varying shapes and sizes waited to be auctioned to the highest bidder. Some were decorated with ribbons or flowers; others, like the ones Claire and Sadie had brought, were plain, yet contained a delicious and highly substantial meal of fried chicken, buttermilk biscuits, potato salad, baked beans, and homemade apple pie.

Searching for Sadie and Harmony, Claire's gaze made a quick—albeit unsuccessful—scan of the hall. She was pleased, however, to see that the center of the room had been left clear for dancing. Several benches lined the walls, and the bare wooden floor was still slightly damp from the rains. Up on a makeshift dais beside the tables, Floyd McLaughlin and Harold Denney were engaged in a friendly rivalry as they tried to outshine each other with their self-taught fiddling skills.

"I'd say we're attractin' a bit of attention, wouldn't you?" drawled Tate, his eyes twinkling down at Claire.

He was right, she noted with an inward frown. It seemed that every head in the room turned their way. She found herself the recipient of looks that conveyed startlement, curiosity, or blistering disapproval. But she would not be intimidated. Instinctively squaring her shoulders and lifting her chin, she forced a devil-may-care smile to her lips and asked Tate, "You don't mind, do you?"

"Nope."

"Good. Then we might as well attract some more."

Feeling particularly defiant that evening, she took the box from him and swept across the room to place it alongside the others. She tugged off her crimson shawl and draped it atop the box. Tate, who had followed close behind, was only too happy to oblige when she turned back to him with the suggestion that they take full advantage of the reel being played. His arm slipped about her waist, while his other hand entwined companionably with hers. Smiling down at her again, he swung her out onto the empty dance floor.

A shocked, breathless murmur rose from the crowd. Claire delighted in the sound of it. For far too long, she had behaved herself. She had played the role of an unfortunate, "tainted" woman to perfection all these years. Who cared if she created a ruckus, if a new scandal fell about her? Her innocence had been stolen from her—metaphorically speaking, anyway. There could be no going back. But she was still young, still very much alive. It was high time she acted like it . . . *and Rand Logan be damned.*

She threw herself into the dance with even more enthusiasm. In spite of the fact that she was out of practice, her efforts displayed an innate, enviable gracefulness. Her silken skirts twirled up about her trim ankles, providing the onlookers with a shameless glimpse of stocking. Tate showed himself to be a more than capable partner. His eyes glowed warmly down into hers as he swung her around and around.

Although they continued playing, Floyd and Harold exchanged a glance of uncertainty. They peered out into the crowd. Their wives, Violet and Anne, flashed them looks of stern, unmistakable censure. But, instead of obeying those silent commands, they suddenly cut the reel short and launched into a spirited, allegro rendition of "The Yellow Rose of Texas."

It was exactly the icebreaker the situation needed. No able-bodied, self-respecting Texan's feet could remain still whenever that tune filled the air. Within a matter of seconds, Claire and Tate were joined by three other couples. And then five more, and more, until the center of the room was astir with color and movement.

Another shock was in store for those who had turned a critical eye upon Claire and Tate—Reverend Mueller led Sadie Bishop into the midst of the dancers. No one had expected that. It was one thing to have the parson tolerate such questionable and worldly pursuits; it was quite another to see him join in. But he didn't appear in the least bit concerned about any possible damage to either his soul or his reputation. Pulling a reluctant, blushing Sadie close, he gave her no choice but to follow his lead as he waltzed with surprising agility.

Laughter and applause rang throughout the room

when the song ended a few minutes later. Flushed and breathless, Claire drew away from Tate and vigorously fanned herself with the lace fan looped about her wrist. She smiled at Sadie and Thomas, who came forward to greet them while the others broke away into their respective cliques once more.

"Good evening, Miss Parmalee," the reverend intoned politely. Claire noticed that he kept Sadie's hand tucked within the crook of his arm.

"Good evening." Her gaze shifted momentarily to Tate before she inquired, "Have you met Mr. Jenner yet?"

"I have indeed. It is good to see you here tonight, Mr. Jenner."

"Reverend," said Tate, shaking the other man's hand. "I didn't know preachers ever stopped walkin' on water long enough to kick up their heels."

"Ah, but I am only flesh and blood, the same as you." He smiled down at Sadie. "If you would please excuse me, I must begin the auction."

"Of course." Her eyes followed him as he headed across to the dais. Try as she would, she couldn't deny how wonderful it had felt to be in his arms.

"Where is Harmony?" Claire asked, interrupting the other woman's alarming reverie.

"The last I saw of her, she was playing on the front steps with some of the other children. I only hope she doesn't get into trouble."

"She's only a child. Surely no one—"

"Ladies and gentlemen, may I please have your attention?" Thomas appealed in his best ministerial voice. His words achieved the desired silence as the church members—along with several curious young cowboys who had drifted in from the street on their way to raise Saturday night hell at the saloons—looked to where he stood upon the dais. "I trust you are enjoying our time of fellowship. But now, we must get down to business. You are familiar, I believe, with the rules. Each of these lovely hampers you see before you will be auctioned off, and the highest bidder will enjoy both its contents and the companionship, however temporary, of the fair cook. The proceeds will put a roof above our heads. So, I encourage you to dig deeply into your pockets, my friends, and remember that what you spend is for the good of us all."

"No good'll come if you eat any of Annie Black's cookin'!" a towheaded youngster of nine cautioned from the back of the room. His remark elicited a number of chuckles, as well as a retaliatory pinch on the arm from his big sister Annie.

"We shall begin the bidding at twenty-five cents," announced Thomas, his own mouth twitching.

The first basket, a small one with a bright blue ribbon woven along the handle, was identified as the creation of one Julia Sue Willingham. The bidding for it was fast and furious; Julia Sue was a pretty, full-figured brunet of seventeen. In the end, it was awarded to one of the cowboys, who spent every penny of his drinking money for it. When he came forward to claim the meal and the shyly blushing girl, Julia Sue's father subjected him to a flinty-eyed scowl that left little doubt what would happen if he dared to take liberties.

The second item to be auctioned was a striped hatbox belonging to the aforementioned Annie Black. A single bid of twenty-five cents was offered and never sur-passed. It seemed that young Alan Black's warning had taken root.

The auction continued. Each time a container was de-clared sold, the fortunate winner—usually a husband, or at the very least an interested party—would collect his supper and his partner and find a place to sit. Some chose the hall, while others wandered outside to where additional benches had been placed randomly about the churchyard. The children in attendance weren't ne-glected, since extra hampers of food had been provided for them. Harmony was accepted into their midst with very little fanfare. Accustomed to the taunts and jeers of others, she simply turned a deaf ear to the few leveled at her and wisely aligned herself with a group of girls whose minds had not yet been poisoned.

Finally there were only two boxes remaining—Sadie's and Claire's. Thomas held the first one aloft, but hesitated to begin the bidding for it. He lowered it back to the table, his brow creasing into a slight frown as he found himself faced with a dilemma. Naturally it had been his intent to sell every lady's donation, yet now that the moment had arrived to offer Sadie's to the re-maining bidders, he found himself filled with jealousy at the prospect. Until now, that particular emotion had remained foreign to him.

"Well, Reverend?" one of the men in the thinning crowd prompted. "Whose is it?"

"It was prepared by Mrs. Bishop," he answered, then gently cleared his throat and asked, "Who will start the bidding?"

No one spoke.

"Come now. Who will bid twenty-five cents for what, I can assure you, is a meal fit for a king?" He held his breath, torn between the desire to see it fetch a high price and the more selfish hope that it would not sell at all.

"Twenty-five cents!" a gruff voice rang out.

Claire recognized it immediately. Her eyes lit upon Red, her own bunkhouse cook, who stood with two of Glorieta's other ranch hands near the doorway. She cast him a smile of mingled amusement and gratitude while linking her arm through Sadie's.

"If he wins, he'll probably ask you for the secret to your fried chicken," she whispered teasingly. "*His* tastes like old shoe leather."

Sadie's mouth curved up faintly as she looked back to Thomas. She, too, was disappointed that they would not be able to share the supper she had made. It was too bad he was a preacher. Nothing could ever come of their friendship. Nothing at all . . .

"I have a bid for twenty-five cents. Do I hear more, gentlemen?"

"Thirty!" declared Charlie Beadle, the youngest of Claire's employees.

"Thirty-five!" Red countered, glowering at his freckle-faced cohort.

"Forty!" This time, the bid was entered by Anne Denney's twenty-year-old son, Clay. His outraged mother sprang from her seat and virtually flew across the room to inform the hapless young man, in a furious undertone overheard by many, that she'd have to have one foot in the grave before she'd let him break bread with the likes of Sadie Bishop.

"Forty-five!" said Red.

"Fifty!" Charlie exclaimed rashly.

"One dollar!"

No one was more surprised than Thomas when those words fell from his lips. His gaze met Sadie's, and he gave her a smile that made her heart turn over in her breast.

"Can he do that?" a bewildered Red asked no one in particular.

"Why not?" Tate responded, with a wry grin. "His money's as good as the next man's."

"One dollar is the high bid," Thomas continued. "Would anyone care to offer more?" After a few tense seconds, he pronounced happily, "Sold to Reverend Mueller!"

"It ain't decent!" huffed Lydia Cassidy. But everyone was too busy eating or flirting or gossiping at the moment to second her opinion.

"Now, we have come to the last," the parson told the assembly when he lifted the box. Claire had forgotten to retrieve her shawl; she watched as it fell atop the table. "It so happens that this meal was brought by Miss Claire Parmalee. Who will—?"

"Twenty-five cents!" Red eagerly started the bidding.

"Fifty!" Tate was quick to double it.

"Fifty-five!" Charlie sang out in an admirable show of loyalty.

"One dollar!" said Tate, confident that it would require no more.

"You wouldn't pay that much if *I* had done the cooking," Claire murmured dryly.

"The hell I wouldn't," he parried, with a low chuckle.

"The high bid stands at one dollar," Thomas proclaimed, his eyes traveling about the room. "One dollar. Are there any further bids?"

Red and Charlie shook their heads in defeat. The handful of other men left muttered that the whole getup was too rich for their blood.

"Then, I suppose Mr. Jenner holds the winning bid. Sold to—"

"Ten dollars."

Claire's heart leapt into her throat at the sound of that familiar, deep-timbred voice. Her eyes widening with incredulity, she turned around to see Rand standing— tall and handsome and supremely confident—in the doorway. His dramatic (and suspiciously well-timed) entrance upon the scene was met with what seemed like a full minute of stunned silence.

"Ten dollars?" Thomas finally repeated, both astonished and pleased at this latest development. He smiled broadly, while noting, "A generous bid of ten dollars has been entered. Will anyone bid more?"

"Fifteen dollars!" Tate did not hesitate to rise to the challenge. His gaze, angry and intense, locked in silent combat with Rand's.

"Tate, no!" Claire said quickly, her hand closing about his arm. "That's much too—"

"Twenty," Rand offered in a calm, measured tone. He sauntered forward now, with only the ghost of a smile touching his lips. He was wearing a simple blue cotton shirt and denim trousers, yet he was without a doubt the most striking man in the room. *Or anywhere else for that matter,* the impudent voice inside Claire's brain saw fit to add.

"Twenty dollars!" a delighted Thomas echoed once more. "Perhaps we shall have enough left over to purchase new hymnals for the sanctuary. Are there any other bids?"

"Please, Tate. Don't do this!" Claire entreated. She was painfully aware of the fact that a battle was being waged—and before dozens of witnesses to boot. It was humiliating to have them fighting over her as though she were some sort of trophy to be won. Humiliating . . . and strangely thrilling.

"Twenty-five!" Tate upped the bid in spite of her protests.

"For heaven's sake! It's only supper!" she whispered. She looked to Rand now, but she knew that it was useless to try and reason with *him*. Her eyes flashed vengefully up at him as he drew to a halt beside her. Oblivious to her fury, he gave a curt nod toward the dais.

"Fifty dollars."

Another collective gasp filled the crowded hall. Claire caught her own breath and turned her fiery, expectant gaze upon Tate.

His indecision was all too apparent. For a moment, it seemed that he would come through for her, that he would do whatever it took to beat Rand. But her hopes died when he slowly shook his head.

"Sorry, Claire," he told her, his mouth turning up into a rueful little smile. "It's been a good year—but not that good."

"Fifty dollars is the bid," Thomas reiterated. "Fifty

dollars once, twice . . . *sold* to the gentleman in the blue shirt!"

Some of the younger men broke out in cheers. Some of the women allowed scarcely a second to go by before setting up a fleet-tongued discussion of the incident. Claire accepted her fate with an ill grace. Her color was high, her whole body fairly quaking with anger as her gaze sliced back to Rand.

"Just what the devil do you think you've gone and bought yourself?" she demanded in a low, ireful tone.

"Fried chicken, ma'am," he answered, with maddening equanimity. "And the pleasure of your company." He took her arm in a firm grip and started to lead her forward, but Tate moved to block their path.

"You won the bid fair and square, Parker," he conceded, though something in his voice promised that the victory would be short-lived. "You go ahead and have your supper. But remember—*I'm* the one who'll be takin' Claire home."

"The night's still young," Rand warned enigmatically. Brushing past the other man, he propelled Claire along with him to the dais. He handed over the exorbitant amount of money to Reverend Mueller. But instead of taking the box of food, he first retrieved Claire's shawl from the table and placed it, with all the familiar solicitude of a sweetheart, about her shoulders.

The gesture was small yet profound. Gossip sparked and blazed with even more intensity throughout the hall. Claire's transgressions were rapidly enumerated— first, she had had the audacity to come sashaying in, pretty as you please, on the arm of Tate Jenner; then, she had provoked two grown men to absolute foolishness; and now, she was obviously taking up with her new ranch hand.

Claire heard the talk. She had anticipated it to a certain extent, of course. But not because of Rand. His interference was something she hadn't counted on.

"If you think for one minute that I'm going to eat with you—" she ground out, forced to lean close in order to be heard above the music that had just started up again.

"I won you fair and square, remember?"

"You didn't win *me* at all!"

"Let's go outside." He took possession of her arm once more and caught up the box. His tone was one of mocking amusement when he queried, "Unless you'd care to dance instead?"

"I have every intention of dancing—but not with you!"

Although seething with outrage, she had little choice but to go along with him as he escorted her to the doorway. They emerged into the shadows of the churchyard, where a few more lanterns had been hung from the trees to ensure that every propriety was observed by the couples outside.

Rand chose a bench that was well away from the rest, in the semidarkness on the far side of the fellowship hall. Claire jerked her arm free, watching with absolute murder in her eyes while he set the box down and casually placed his hat atop it.

"What are you doing here?" she demanded at last, still taking care not to be overheard. She crossed her arms angrily against her chest and tilted her head back to confront him.

"Claiming my rights," he replied. His eyes strayed downward . . . to where her full breasts swelled enticingly above the rounded neckline of her gown.

"*What* rights?"

"You're my wife, Claire." His gaze met and held hers once more. "Like it or not, that's the way it is. Did you really think I'd stand by and do nothing while you made a fool of yourself with Tate Jenner—or with any other man?"

"I wasn't making a fool of myself," she denied hotly. "But even if I was, it's none of your business. If I want to strip off all my clothes and dance buck naked in the moonlight, there's not a blessed thing you can do about it!"

"Nor would I want to. So long as I'm the only one watching." His tone was laced with a combination of humor and desire, his eyes darkening at the vision her words conjured up. She swallowed hard and retreated a few steps in a futile, belated attempt to put some distance between them.

"You shouldn't have come here tonight," she charged, struggling to regain her composure. "It was wrong of you to bid against Tate like that. What in heaven's name did you think you were doing? You behaved like an extravagant fool. And you made *me* look like a fool as well. Everyone will be talking about this for—"

"That doesn't matter."

"Of course it does!" She felt her pulse give a wild leap when he moved closer again and smiled softly down at her. Even in the shadows, she could see the warm glow contained within his deep, gold-flecked gaze.

"You took in Sadie and Harmony. You hired Micah. By damn, you stood up to everyone in this whole town and showed them up for the narrow-minded jackasses they are." His expression grew quite solemn, his voice underscored by what sounded suspiciously like pain when he said, "You've got a heart of gold, Claire. Maybe someday, you'll find some forgiveness in it for me."

A sudden lump rose in her throat, and she caught her breath while her eyes fell beneath the penetrating steadiness of his. It was difficult to ignore the ache deep inside her . . . difficult to pretend she wasn't stirred by his remark. For a moment, she found herself battling the urge to tell him that forgiving was far easier than forgetting.

"I'm going back inside," she murmured tremulously, turning away now.

"Not yet." His hands came up to close gently, possessively, upon her shoulders. She was startled at her own lack of resistance when he urged her about to face him again. Only dimly aware of the music drifting along on the night wind and the presence of the other couples within what was commonly called spitting distance, she stared up at him as though transfixed. There was something different about him tonight, she thought, something that—once again—both frightened and excited her.

"I'd turn back the clock if I could," he declared quietly, his eyes burning down into hers. "I'd erase these past six years and every single thing that's happened since your father caught us out in the barn. But I can't do that. So we'll have to go forward. Starting here and now, Claire. Starting tonight."

"No!" she choked out. A flush crept up to her face; she cursed the way her insides melted. "How many times do I have to tell you—*it's too late!*"

"Not till one of us is dead." His mouth curved slowly upward again. "And I've got it in mind to live another fifty or sixty years."

He swept her close then. She was appalled to feel herself swaying against him, yet she allowed the kiss he gave her to last for several long, thoroughly intoxicating moments before she finally summoned the presence of mind to struggle free. Nearly upsetting the bench in her haste to escape his provocative touch, she jerked her shawl back up into place and stood proudly indignant while his gaze fell to her décolletage once more. Fiery color stained her cheeks; she felt an alarming heat as his eyes traveled boldly over the exposed curve of her breasts.

"Supper's over, Mr. Parker," she decreed in a strident whisper. Her eyes made a swift, furiously anxious scan of the churchyard. "Now go away. Go pay a visit to those new 'friends' of yours down at the saloon and leave me alone." She turned on her heel to leave, but his strong fingers closed about her arm in an iron grip.

"You're playing a dangerous game." His face had become a grim mask of determination, while his blue eyes had taken on the look of molten steel that she had come to know all too well. "I'm warning you, Claire. Even if you're only using Jenner to make me jealous, you won't like what happens if you forget—"

"Using him to make you jealous?" she echoed, disbelief instantly turning to outrage. Her emerald gaze sparked and blazed as she jerked away. "You can save your threats. *And* you can go straight to hell!"

She spun about in an angry swirl of blue silk and fled back across the grounds to the hall. Behind her, Rand muttered an oath and battled his own rising temper.

She had been right, in a way, he mused with a dark frown. He *was* a fool for ever thinking he could keep his duty and his personal life separate. The line between the two was growing perilously thin. Even so, he was making progress with the investigation. He was convinced that it was only a matter of time before the case broke wide open, before the one piece of incontrovertible evidence he needed finally surfaced. The robbers were far more cunning than the report had led him to believe. Still, they weren't clever enough to suspect that one of their own might turn informer. When and if that finally happened, all hell would break loose.

And Claire would be right in the middle of it.

No, by damn, he swore, while his eyes gleamed almost savagely, he wasn't going to let that happen. He wasn't going to let her get hurt. No matter what it took, he would see her safe. Even if that meant the line got blurred altogether . . . even if it meant he overstepped his bounds in the worst way possible.

Inside the fellowship hall, Tate was watching when Claire came scurrying breathlessly through the doorway. He wasted no time in making his way to her side. His brow creased into a frown of half worry, half anger when he took in the sight of her distress.

"What is it?" he demanded, his voice rising above the music. "What's wrong? And where's—?"

"Don't ask me any questions right now, Tate," she pleaded. "Let's just dance!" She gave him no opportunity to argue. Tugging off her shawl, she draped it across her arm and lifted her hand to his shoulder. He obliged by catching up her other hand with his own and drawing her close. They joined the other dancers in the center of the room while the energetic strains of "Oh! Susanna" reached a midway crescendo.

A few moments later, Tate was the recipient of a firm, commanding tap on the back of his shoulder. He stopped abruptly. While Claire gasped in startlement, he jerked his head around to meet Rand's steady and unfathomable gaze.

"I'm cutting in, Jenner."

"Oh, no, you're *not!*" Claire blurted out, then colored guiltily and dropped her own gaze to the floor before uttering, with an obviously forced politeness, "I'm sorry, Mr. Parker. I prefer to finish the dance with Mr. Jenner."

"You heard the lady," remarked Tate, his eyes glinting triumphantly. He pulled her close again—and would have resumed the dance—but Rand blocked his path.

"I said I'm cutting in."

"And *I* say you're a thick-headed wrangler who ought to learn to take no for an answer!"

"Tate, don't!" Claire entreated, panic knotting in her stomach. She didn't like the look in Rand's eyes. Why was he set on provoking Tate? It was almost as though he *intended* to start a fight. Hoping to avoid an unpleasant scene, she deemed it wisest to capitulate. "Very well, Mr. Parker," she told him coldly. "I will dance with you."

"You've already got a partner," Tate insisted. His hand tightened about hers; he turned his back on Rand again.

It was a mistake.

While Claire watched in horrified disbelief, Rand laid hands on her would-be champion and spun him around. His fist came up to land a punishing blow to the other man's unguarded chin. Tate staggered backward, ground out a vengeful curse, and launched himself at Rand.

Several of the ladies screamed. The music stopped, the dancers' feet stilled, and a crowd of onlookers immediately gathered around as Rand dodged Tate's retaliatory strike and hit him again. Reverend Mueller drew away from Sadie and hastened across to intervene, but his heartfelt pleas for a return to reason fell on deaf ears.

"Stop it!" cried Claire, furious with Rand. Although tempted to storm into the fray and pull him off Tate, she remained on the sidelines and looked desperately about for help. Red and Charlie had already taken themselves off to the saloons, and none of the other men except the parson seemed the least bit inclined to break up what promised to be a good (if short-lived) fight.

Someone yelled that the sheriff should be fetched. Someone else vetoed that idea and countered with the suggestion that the punch bowl be emptied on the two combatants to cool them off. In the end, however, there was no need for either course of action. Rand landed a third and final blow to Tate's chin, sending him crumpling, unconscious, to the damp wooden floor.

"Sorry, Reverend," offered Rand, directing a curt nod at the preacher. Without another word, he stepped forward and seized Claire's wrist.

"Mr. Parker—" Thomas worriedly protested.

"I'll see Miss Parmalee home."

An open-mouthed Claire was at first too stunned to resist. The room erupted into a boisterous roar as Rand propelled her outside to where he had left his horse tied in front of the church. She came to life again when he turned and grasped her about the waist.

"I'm not going anywhere with you!"

"You don't have a choice."

A sharp gasp broke from her lips when he tossed her roughly up into the saddle. She tried to scramble down, but he mounted behind her before she could do anything more than swing a leg across the saddle horn. His arm clamped like a band of steel about her waist while he gathered up the reins.

"Let me go!" she demanded hotly. "What do you think you're doing?"

"What I should have done a long time ago."

His reply struck a chord of very real fear in her heart. She gasped again when he pulled her back against him. Her hips came into intimate contact with his lean thighs. And the hardness between. A sudden shiver danced down her spine.

"You can't—"

"*I can.*"

He touched his heels to the stallion's flanks. Claire opened her mouth to give a belated scream. But her cry for help was lost in the darkness as the horse galloped away.

Chapter 8

The wild night ride across the deserted, starlit prairie was one Claire would never forget.

She could do nothing more than hold tight to the saddle horn as Rand spirited her away from town. In what seemed at once like an eternity and a fleeting moment in time, they had reached Glorieta.

Unbeknownst to either of them, Micah was walking outside near the corral when he heard their approach. Sully was fast asleep in the bunkhouse, and all the other hands had gone off to enjoy their Saturday night. As usual, he had stayed behind to keep himself out of trouble. Trouble was the one thing he'd already had enough of; truth be told, enough to last him a lifetime.

He stopped short when he saw that it was Claire and Rand who rode up before the house, their faces revealed by the glow of the lamp he had earlier hung from one of the porch columns. He frowned to himself, wondering what had happened to send Miss Claire back early—and why she hadn't come home with Tate Jenner. But something told him it was best not to interfere. Not yet, anyway.

Wolf sprang up from where he had been sleeping on

the front porch. Strangely enough, he did not bark. His tail began wagging, and he panted a happy greeting while Rand reined to a halt and swung down.

"Leave me alone." Claire ground out, so angry she could barely speak. She started to dismount on her own, but Rand caught her in his arms and whirled her about so that her feet met the bottom step. She jerked away, her eyes shooting green sparks as her hand clenched within the folds of her shawl. "What in blazes did you think you were doing tonight? You started that fight with Tate on purpose! Damn you, Rand Logan! You had no right to—"

"Shut up, Claire."

"What?" she said, her eyes widening in shock now.

His only response was to sweep her up hard against him and capture her lips in a kiss that was almost violent in its intensity. She moaned a protest, yet couldn't find the strength to offer more than a feeble resistance.

Across the yard, Micah smiled to himself and shook his head. He had seen enough, he thought as he headed back toward the bunkhouse. Miss Claire wouldn't be needing his help after all.

When Rand let her go again, she was flushed and breathless and so light-headed she nearly lost her balance. But one look at his handsome, softly smiling countenance was enough to send her crashing back to earth with a vengeance.

"I hate you," she seethed. "Dear God in heaven, how I hate you!" Spinning about, she flew up the steps and across the porch. Rand was hot on her heels.

She wrenched open the front door, then hurriedly tried to close it behind her and draw the bolt. But Rand was too quick for her. While she inhaled upon a gasp of dismay, he sent the door crashing back against the wall and stepped inside. She instinctively retreated toward the staircase, her legs unsteady beneath her as he advanced upon her. The house was still and dark, the only sound that of the ancient clock chiming off-key in the upstairs hallway.

"Get out!" she ordered, panic making her voice shrill. "Get out of my house!"

"No." That one word held an ominous significance. It foretold of what was to come, of a promise fulfilled at last.

With a faint, strangled cry of alarm, Claire turned and raced up the carpeted staircase. Her long skirts tangled about her legs, but she managed to reach her bedroom. She slammed the door shut. Her fingers trembled as she turned the key in the lock.

Raising a hand to her throat, she stared in fearful expectation at the door. She held her breath and backed slowly away, until her hips came up against the quilt-covered iron bed. The room was bathed in near total darkness; she hastily lit the lamp on the table beside the bed, never taking her eyes off the door.

Her ears strained to detect the sound of Rand's footsteps in the hallway. She heard nothing.

"He's gone," she whispered to herself, though she didn't yet dare breathe a sigh of relief. He must have realized that she could bring both Micah and Sully running at a moment's notice. Either that, or whatever sense of decency he still possessed had overruled his baser emotions. But the reason for his departure didn't matter. She was safe now. Safe from his damnably irresistible kisses. And from her own wicked, wanton response . . .

"Claire."

His low, deep-timbred voice reached out to her from the other side of the door. Her throat constricted anew, and she sank down onto the bed while her arm curled tightly about the white scrolled post of the headboard.

"Go away!"

"Open the door, Claire."

"If you don't leave right this minute, I'm going to scream for help!" she warned.

"Open the door, or I'll break it down."

Paling at his threat, she sprang from the bed and flew across to the window. She had done no more than throw it wide when Rand, true to his word, kicked the door open and crossed the room in two long, purposeful strides to scoop her up in his powerful arms. There was no time to scream now, no time to plead or reproach or even catch her breath as he swiftly bore her back to the bed and tossed her down upon the feather mattress. Her skirts and petticoat twisted up about her knees, revealing her slender, stockinged limbs and a hint of the lace on her open-leg drawers.

Before she could escape, Rand lowered his own body full-length atop hers and imprisoned both her legs with the forceful pressure of one of his. She cried out and squirmed in a mixture of panic and furious defiance beneath him, but he captured her wrists and forced her arms above her head. Still she fought him, striving valiantly to prevent what had always been inevitable between them.

"You're mine, Claire," he declared huskily, his eyes smoldering down into hers in the lamplit darkness.

"I hate you," she raged through clenched teeth. She arched her back, but it only made her more acutely conscious of his virile, hard-muscled warmth pressing her down into the mattress. Her gaze kindled with vengeful fire. "As God is my witness, if you do this, I'll never forgive you! I'll kill you! I swear, I'll kill you if you—"

"You probably *will* kill me," he conceded, with a faint smile of irony. "But I can't think of a better way to die."

"Get off me, damn you. Let me go!"

"Never."

Her heart turned over in her breast. She opened her mouth to scream, but found herself well and truly silenced when his lips came crashing down upon hers. The kiss was hard and demanding, almost punishing at first, and she moaned in protest while continuing to squirm beneath him. He was impervious to her struggles, his lips drinking deeply of hers while his hot, velvety tongue ravished the sweetness of her mouth. Six years of waiting, of longing and desire and the dream of this moment, made him impatient. His body burned to possess her. . . . *He would wait no more.*

He transferred both of her wrists to the steely grasp of his left hand, while his right moved to close upon her breast. Her eyes flew wide, and she was left gasping when his mouth suddenly trailed a fiery path downward to roam hungrily across the full, creamy flesh swelling above the rounded neckline of her gown. She trembled at his passionate assault, her senses reeling and her pulse racing violently.

His hand glided lower. With an alarming urgency, he raked her skirts and petticoat all the way up to her thighs. His warm, strong fingers moved toward the opening of her white cotton drawers.

"No," she said, her eyes filling with dread. "Stop it."

But he would not be denied. She shivered at the first touch of his hand upon that secret place between her thighs. His fingers delved within the triangle of soft golden curls, parted the silken flesh, and set up a gentle yet masterful caressing that almost immediately turned her blood to liquid fire in her veins.

She moaned again, her whole body aflame when his lips returned to claim hers. Passion blazed brilliantly between them, and she forgot everything but Rand as he released her wrists and kissed her with an urgency that made her compellingly, rapturously, light-headed. She entwined her arms about his neck, her legs parting wider of their own accord. Desire had built to a fever pitch within her; she was certain she would faint. She squirmed restlessly now, yearning for something she could not name, yet lost to all reason or guilt or blame as the husband she had vowed to forget reminded her—in the most effective way possible—of her womanliness.

Finally Rand could bear no more of the delectable agony. His hand moved to unfasten his trousers, then slipped beneath Claire's hips and lifted her slightly. He raised his head, his gold-flecked blue eyes gleaming hotly with desire.

"Easy, Claire," he murmured in a low, vibrant tone.

She stared up at him in bemusement, her own gaze soft with passion's glow and her beautiful face flushed.

Before she could ask him what he meant, he eased himself forward, then plunged all the way inside her. His hard, throbbing manhood sheathed with perfection within her honeyed passage.

She uttered a breathless cry of pain and startlement. Her hands grasped weakly at his broad shoulders. She felt as though she were being stretched far beyond the limit, as though she were being filled with a heat that would surely consume her. But the pain rapidly subsided, replaced by sensations so deep and pleasurable that she felt her passions spiraling heavenward once more. Her eyes swept closed, and she caught her lower lip between her teeth, her breathing erratic and her heart stirring wildly as Rand's hips began tutoring hers in the age-old rhythm of love.

His thrusts grew more intense. The sweet madness took hold of them completely, until Claire found herself lost in a fierce, blinding flash of emotion. She was unprepared for it; it was unlike anything she had ever experienced before. Another unintelligible cry broke from her lips. In the next instant, Rand stiffened above her and gave a low groan. She inhaled sharply when his seed flooded her with its potent, life-giving warmth.

And then it was over.

He rolled to his side in the bed and drew her close. She rested pliantly against him for the moment, too overwhelmed by what had just taken place to think straight. Her whole body tingled, and she was only vaguely aware of the night breeze drifting in through the open window. The cool air danced across her skin. Beneath her cheek, Rand's heart beat strong and steady.

It had all happened so fast. In a matter of minutes,

her whole life had changed. Nothing would ever be the same again. *She* would never be the same again. God help her, what had she done?

"I love you, Claire," Rand told her quietly. "I've never stopped loving you."

"Don't," she whispered, her voice fraught with emotion.

"What's wrong?" He frowned down at her while his hand slid possessively up her arm.

"How could you?" She raised up on one elbow to favor him with a wrathful, accusatory glare. "How could you do such a thing to me?"

"It wasn't that difficult." His eyes lit with roguish amusement. She resisted the urge to slap him.

"You forced yourself on me, you arrogant scoundrel! And now you expect me to—"

"That's not the way I remember it," he cut her off, all traces of humor vanishing. His fingers tensed about her arm, while his handsome face grew thunderous. "Damn it, Claire! When are you going to admit that you still care for me?"

"Care for you?" she repeated in stunned disbelief. Bristling, she pulled away from him and swung her legs over the edge of the bed. Although her head swam, she scrambled to her feet and jerked her creased skirts back down into place. Her long golden tresses streamed riotously about her face and shoulders, and her full breasts heaved beneath the tight bodice of her gown as she exclaimed, "I feel nothing for you but—but loathing and disgust!"

"Call it what you will," he replied, climbing from the bed now as well and fastening his trousers. Her eyes strayed with a will of their own to his movements. The ghost of a smile touched his lips when he noted the fiery blush staining her cheeks. "So long as you know I'll be back. I didn't want it to be like this the first time. But what's done is done."

"It's done, all right—and I'll never forgive you," she flung at him once more.

"Maybe not. But that won't keep me from doing it again. And it won't keep you from liking it."

"Oh!" she ground out. Infuriated beyond reason, she whirled and snatched up the loaded rifle she always kept propped in the corner near the bed. She wasn't given the chance to find out if she would really use it, for Rand was beside her in a flash. He wrenched it from her grasp and caught her up none too gently against him.

"Try that again, Mrs. Logan," he warned in a tone that was at once affectionate and mocking and dangerously level, "and you'll find yourself across my knee."

"You lay a hand on me, and I swear I'll make you sorry you were ever born," she countered, pushing at his chest.

"I've got a hand on you now." She suffered another audible intake of breath when his fingers swept downward to close upon the shapely, well-rounded curve of her bottom. He gave her a look that made her legs grow weak. "I love you, Claire. But that doesn't mean I'm going to let you run roughshod over me. No, by heaven—and I'm not going to stand for any more of your nonsense with Tate Jenner."

"You have no right to—"

"I have every right. Especially now that you're no longer a kissless bride."

She crimsoned anew, groaning inwardly at his words. They were all too true. He was her husband in every sense of the word now. Under the law, he could lay claim to everything she owned . . . and to her affections as well.

"You bastard!" she hissed, her eyes murderously ablaze. "If you think I'm going to let you come waltzing back in here after six years and take over Glorieta, you'd better be prepared for the fight of your life!"

"I don't want Glorieta." He reluctantly let her go and headed back across the room. Pausing in the doorway, he proclaimed, "I want *you*, Claire. And I'll have you. Body and soul."

"People in hell want ice water, too," came her acid retort.

But it was too late. He had already gone.

Feeling terribly confused and angry—yet also strangely contented—she sank down onto the bed and buried her face in her hands. She sat there for a long time, battling tears and cursing fate, before finally standing and crossing to the washstand. Her brow creased into a frown when she caught sight of her reflection in the mirror above. Surprisingly enough, even though she had only moments ago crossed the threshold between innocence and enlightenment, she didn't look any different. No indeed. She looked like the same Claire Parmalee who had tumbled out of bed that morning . . . *Claire Logan,* a tiny voice inside her brain amended.

A highly expressive malediction fell from her lips.

She poured water from the pitcher into the bowl, then stripped off every stitch of clothing she had on. Taking up the cake of lavender-scented soap, she set about trying to erase all vestiges of Rand's lovemaking. Such a thing was impossible, of course, and she knew it, but still she scrubbed at her skin until it was very nearly raw.

By the time Reverend Mueller brought Sadie and Harmony home, she had donned her nightgown and robe and taken herself downstairs to wait in the kitchen. She would have preferred to remain in her room, to avoid the challenge of facing Sadie altogether, but she realized that she'd have to offer *some* sort of explanation for what had happened that evening.

"Claire? Claire, where are you?" Sadie called anxiously as she and her daughter hurried inside the house.

"In the kitchen," directed Claire. She rose from her seat at the table and even managed a smile of welcome when they appeared in the doorway.

"Are you all right?" Sadie queried, her opal eyes brimming with concern.

"Of course," she lied. "I'm fine."

"Well then, I'd best go tell Thom—Reverend Mueller that you're safe. We were so very worried about you." She gathered up her skirts again and headed back outside—to where the parson stood waiting for her report.

"I saw the fight!" Harmony announced as soon as her mother was safely out of earshot. The ever-faithful Wolf was at her side, and he followed when she crossed the room to disclose in a conspiratorial whisper, "Mr.

Jenner was real mad when he found out you were gone."

"What—what did he do?" Claire stammered, her own voice unsteady. A knot tightened in her stomach as Tate's face swam before her eyes.

"Well," the little girl answered, "when he got up, he said he was coming after you." Her dark eyes fairly danced with excitement. "But, Reverend Mueller and some of the other men told him to go home. So he left. And then everyone started talking about how you'd caused such an awful lot of trouble, and how—"

"Harmony, it's time for bed," Sadie interrupted sternly from the doorway.

"Aw, Mama. Can't I finish talking to Miss Claire first?" pleaded Harmony.

"No. It's getting late. Now you go on upstairs. I'll be along in a minute."

Claire watched as the child, with the old cow dog trailing devotedly behind, trudged from the room. Sadie came forward then, her skirts setting up a faint rustle as she approached Claire with a lingering frown of disquietude.

"Are you sure you're all right?"

"Quite sure." She resumed her seat in the chair and affected a casual tone when she asked, "Has the reverend gone?"

"Yes."

"Did you have a good time?"

"I suppose so," replied Sadie, her gaze falling self-consciously. She took a seat on the other side of the table and released a sigh. "Thomas is a very kind man."

"I think so, too," Claire murmured. She reached for

the half-empty cup of coffee before her, her fingers tracing an absently repetitive pattern along the handle. "I'm sorry about what happened at the social tonight."

"It wasn't your fault," the other woman was quick to assure her, then gave a brief smile of irony. "But I don't think Mr. Jenner will be too quick to forget. And neither will anyone else."

"I'm used to being the talk of the town."

"That doesn't make it any easier." She hesitated, noticeably uncomfortable when she ventured, "Claire, about you and Mr. Parker . . ."

"Mr. Parker will be leaving Glorieta soon," Claire pronounced in a tone with a definite edge to it.

"Will he?"

"The sooner the better."

"I know who he is, Claire," Sadie now confided gently.

"You *do*?" Her eyes widened in surprise, and her fingers tensed about the cup. "How long have you—"

"Almost from the first. A person would have to be blind not to see there's something between the two of you."

"Is it really that obvious?" she asked, coloring at the thought.

"Well, it is to me. And Harmony *did* confirm it, in a way. But I don't think any of the others have guessed. I expect Sully already knows, doesn't he?"

"And Micah, too," Claire admitted. She pulled herself up from the chair and began pacing distractedly back and forth, folding her arms against her chest while the lamplight played across the stormy beauty of her countenance. "I'm sure you must have heard all about my own 'scandalous past.' How could you help but hear, when people keep dredging it up at every turn?"

"You don't have to explain—"

"I never believed I'd see him again, Sadie." She heaved a long, ragged sigh and shook her head. Her eyes clouded with painful reminiscence. "When he ran out on me six years ago, I thought he'd stay gone for good. I resigned myself to the fact that I was an abandoned bride. And I did what I could to get on with my life. Great balls of fire, I never dreamed that he'd show up one day with a badge in one hand and the absolute, unmitigated gall to plant himself here at Glorieta!"

"A badge?" Sadie echoed in puzzlement.

Too late, Claire realized what she had blurted out. Now, she had little choice but spill the whole story. Or at least *most* of it, anyway.

"You might as well know the truth." She sat back down and wearily raked a hand through the unbound thickness of her hair. "He's a Texas Ranger. And he insisted on this little charade so that he could investigate the train and stage robberies."

"That explains a lot," noted Sadie. She had wondered why Rand had wanted to keep his identity a secret. And why he hadn't tried to claim his wife. "So he'll be moving on as soon as he catches the robbers?"

"I want him out of here *now*!"

"What about Mr. Jenner?"

"Mr. Jenner doesn't know, either." Her eyes kindled at the memory of Tate lying unconscious on the floor of the fellowship hall. "It never occurred to me that Rand would turn up at the social. He warned me not to go. But if I had thought for one minute . . . Poor Tate. His pride must be hurting something awful." She sprang from the chair again and swept across to take up a furious stance beside the stove. It was still warm, but there was such a blaze within her that she wouldn't have noticed if it had been burning hot to the touch. "Damnation, I could *kill* that man!" There was little doubt which man had drawn her wrath.

"If there's anything I can do to help—" Sadie offered earnestly.

"No one can help," she murmured, her voice quavering with a combination of fury and perplexity. "Rand Logan doesn't let anything stand in the way of what he wants." Her body could certainly attest to that. She blushed hotly, recalling with vivid and mortifying clarity, the things he had done to her.

"Maybe you should talk to Reverend Mueller," Sadie suggested. She hadn't failed to notice Claire's heightened color, yet she was reluctant to pry. "He might be able to think of something."

"No," said Claire. The corners of her mouth curved into a brief, bitter smile. "The good parson wouldn't approve of what I plan to do. The church tends to take a pretty dim view of divorce."

"Divorce?" echoed Sadie, visibly shocked. "Oh, Claire. You don't really mean to—"

"I do. I've been a fool, Sadie. A cowardly little fool. I should have done something years ago. I would have, too, if my father hadn't been so dead-set against it. But he's gone now, and there's nothing to prevent me from ridding myself of a husband I neither need nor want." Again, she was taunted by memories of Rand's devilishly irresistible lovemaking. She meant what she'd said. She would never forgive him. And she would never forgive herself, either. *You've made your bed, now you'll have to lie in it,* the old saying went. That was the problem; she didn't want to lie in it at all. . . .

"Do you think Mr. Logan will agree to a divorce?" asked Sadie, interrupting her turbulent reverie.

"I don't need his consent." She returned to the table and sat down again. Her chin lifted to a stubbornly defiant angle when she added, "In any case, I'm not going to ask for it. I can't do anything until after he's completed his investigation, but as soon as that's done, I intend to make the necessary inquiries. It so happens that an old friend of my father's practices law over in Dallas. I'm sure he would agree to handle things for me."

"It might not be that simple," Sadie commented, with a pensive frown. "The two of you were married legal and proper, weren't you?"

"Rand Logan deserted me on our wedding night six years ago. I heard nothing from him in all that time. For heaven's sake, what difference does it make if the preacher spoke a few words over us?"

"Still, he did come back."

"Yes, but not for *me*!" Another lie, at least a partial one.

"Wouldn't it be possible for you to get an annulment then?" Sadie pointed out. "I don't know much about the law, but it seems to me the church would have to agree that a woman shouldn't be bound by a marriage in name only." She was surprised to witness the telltale color flaming in the smoothness of Claire's cheeks, and even more surprised by the confession that followed.

"An annulment is out of the question."

"Oh, I see." Averting her gaze, she searched for words, but Harmony's voice suddenly rang out from above.

"Mama, I can't get my dress unbuttoned!"

"Well, I—I'd best be getting upstairs," Sadie said. She gave Claire an apologetic half smile and stood up. "I can come back down if you want to talk some more. I'm not much good at advice. But I can listen. Sometimes it can help to share your troubles."

"No, that's all right." Claire was quick to decline. She'd said too much already. "This is something I'll have to work out for myself." She watched as the pretty widow turned and started from the room. "Sadie?" she called impulsively after her.

"Yes?"

"The reverend *is* a good man."

"Yes, he is," the other woman affirmed quietly. The sadness had come back to her eyes. "But all the goodness in the world can't make some things right."

It wasn't much later when Claire, catching up the lamp, climbed the stairs to her own room. She frowned darkly at the sight of the splintered wood on the doorway's inner frame. It was yet another reminder of Rand's unpardonable—and irreversible—transgression.

Closing the door softly behind her, she took off her robe, blew out the lamp, and climbed beneath the covers of her bed. She closed her eyes and listened to the breeze rustling through the trees outside, listened to the monotonous, peaceful serenade of the crickets and the faint lowing of the cattle. But it did no good. Chaos reigned supreme within her. The memory of Rand's kisses and caresses, of his fierce yet ultimately tender conquest of her body, would not be pushed to the back of her mind.

She flung the covers aside and slid from the bed. Padding barefoot across to the window, she frowned and lifted a hand to the high-necked bodice of her nightgown, while her troubled gaze drifted toward the bunkhouse. She could scarcely make it out in the darkness.

With an eloquent sigh, she folded her arms tightly beneath her breasts and tried, without success, to forget the way her heart had soared when Rand had told her he loved her.

He hadn't meant it, she told herself dampeningly. He had only said it because—because that's what men did when they wanted to take advantage of women. And he had certainly wanted *that*.

She closed her eyes and turned about to lean back against the wall. The years fell away, and she remembered how she had sneaked out of the house to meet Rand on the night her whole world fell apart. If her father hadn't discovered them, she might well have given herself to him there in the barn. Would he still have taken flight if she had? Would he have stolen her maidenhood and then deserted her?

The thought prompted her eyes to fly wide and gleam like twin pools of liquid green fire. She returned to the bed and lay down. Punching at the unresisting softness of her pillow, she pulled the covers all the way up to her chin and stared at the ceiling.

Her life, she reflected miserably, had gotten far more complicated than she would ever have believed possible. In the space of that single evening alone, she had become embroiled in a new scandal, Tate Jenner had been knocked out cold, and Rand Logan had finally claimed the rights he had been granted six years ago.

I'll have you. Body and soul. His parting words still echoed throughout her mind.

"Never!" she whispered. She would draw strength from her mistake. Yes, by heaven, she would remember it well. And she would never again let down her guard. No matter how damnably seductive she found his kisses. No matter how much her traitorous flesh had delighted in his every caress. . . .

Chapter 9

She thought it was nothing more than a dream.

Yet, momentarily trapped in that hazy, enchanting world between sleep and wakefulness, she could have sworn she was not alone.

She moaned softly, her arms tightening about the pillow beneath her head as she turned on her side and stretched out in the familiar comfort of the bed. A faint sigh of contentment escaped her. And then she felt the covers being pulled back, felt the hemline of her white cotton nightgown being eased slowly upward. A pair of warm lips brushed lightly, provocatively, across her cheek while a strong arm slipped about her waist. She was pulled back against the heat of an undeniably masculine body.

It was no dream.

Her eyelids fluttered open at last, and she saw that the room was bathed in the light of a single candle burning on the table beside the bed. She inhaled sharply, her every muscle tensing in alarm.

"I told you I'd be back," Rand murmured close to her ear in a low, resonant tone that sent chills down her spine. Startlement turned to indignation.

"What are you doing here?" she gasped. She tried to scramble from the bed, but he easily held her captive against him. "Get out! Get out before Sadie hears—"

"It's past midnight, Claire. Sadie and Harmony are sleeping. And I intend to take full advantage of the hours left to us before dawn." His fingers moved purposefully to the buttons on the front of her prim, white cotton nightgown.

"Stop it." She squirmed in his embrace, but her actions only served to bring her thinly covered backside fanning across the lean hardness of his thighs. His arousal was all too evident. Her face flushed when she realized that he was completely naked.

"Careful, Mrs. Logan," he warned huskily. "I don't want to hurry this time."

"There isn't going to be a 'this time'!" she whispered in furious defiance. Struggling as vehemently as possible with his arm tightening like a vise about her waist, she attempted to force his hands away from her bodice. In spite of her efforts, however, he managed to liberate the buttons. She suffered another sharp intake of breath when he suddenly rose to his knees on the mattress, tugged her up to face him, and yanked her nightgown all the way off. He sent it flying to land in a discarded heap on the floor.

Claire was shocked into immobility. Her eyes grew enormous within the delicate oval of her face. She glanced down, saw that she was every bit as naked as Rand now, and peered back up at him. His gaze, smoldering and highly appreciative, raked over her exposed curves with a thoroughness that made her tremble. She swallowed hard, then was unable to prevent her own eyes from traveling over the bronzed, hard-muscled expanse of his chest and arms, down across a flat stomach and narrow hips, and lower still to where his manhood sprang from a tight cluster of dark curls between his thighs. Although her knowledge of such things was rather limited, she knew he was a truly magnificent specimen of a man. There wasn't an ounce of fat on his body. And as her fascinated gaze lingered on the instrument of his passion, she couldn't help wondering if all men were so splendidly equipped.

A fiery blush crept up to her cheeks. Another involuntary shiver ran the length of her spine. She gave a strangled little cry, whirled off the bed, and bolted to the door. Rand was upon her in an instant, scooping her up in his arms as though she weighed no more than a babe.

"You're beautiful, Claire," he told her, his deep-timbred voice laced with such warmth that her heart began pounding wildly within her breast. "And you're mine."

"No!" She flashed a desperate glance back at the door, but instinctively suppressed the cry of help that rose to her lips. She didn't want Sadie to find her like this. She certainly didn't want to risk treating Harmony's innocent eyes to such an unwholesome spectacle. Micah and Sully, of course, were still only a scream away. Yet the thought of their intrusion upon the scene was more embarrassing than she could stand. Dear heaven, what was she to do?

The answer was one she would have preferred to ignore.

While she continued to fight Rand like a veritable tigress, he tossed her back down to the bed and lowered himself atop her. This time, however, he proved himself a man of infinite patience—and skill.

Claire gasped when bare flesh met bare flesh. His eyes burned down into the wide, luminous depths of hers. And then he kissed her. Deeply, provocatively, his mouth claiming hers with such sweet, sensuous persuasion that she felt her head spinning.

It was like touching fire to a powder-keg. Her eyes swept closed. She moaned in passion, not protest, while her arms stole across the gleaming hardness of his back. Her mouth welcomed the captivating assault of his, and she offered no resistance when his hand swept downward to set up a gentle yet bold exploration of her supple, trembling curves. She kissed him back, stirred by a rapidly intensifying desire as time stood still and the world receded.

By the time his mouth finally relinquished hers, she had forgotten all about her vow to kill him if he touched her again. He slid down her body until his head was level with her breasts. His mouth roamed hungrily across the satiny fullness, then closed about one of the rose-tipped peaks. His tongue flicked and swirled about the delicate nipple with tantalizing slowness, while his lips sucked gently, seductively. She gasped again and again, her back arching while her fingers clung to his shoulders. He paid loving tribute to her other breast as well. Her head tossed restlessly on the pillow, her whole body aflame.

The next thing she knew, she was being turned facedown in the bed. Her eyelids fluttered open, and her brow creased into a frown of bewilderment as she raised her head. But before she could ask Rand what he was about, she felt him sweeping her long golden tresses aside, felt his warm lips trailing a fiery, imaginary path downward, along the curve of her spine.

Rosy color flooded her face when he dropped a kiss upon her bare bottom. Embarrassed, she wriggled in protest then, but he merely caught her about the hips and held her captive for his pleasure. *And her own.* She released a long, shuddering breath and closed her eyes again. Her head fell back upon the pillow while his lips and tongue wandered across her firm, rounded flesh. He explored every hill and valley. Her arms tightened about the pillow, a delicious heat spreading over her skin. The way she moaned and squirmed left little doubt that she was well past the point of no return.

But Rand was not yet through with her. Determined to make her want him as much as he wanted her, he urged her onto her back once more. His mouth lowered audaciously to the soft blond curls at the juncture of her thighs.

"No—don't!" gasped Claire, her eyes flying wide in shock. She tried to sit up, but he pressed her back down. His hands delved beneath her buttocks, bringing her closer to the enchantment of his moist, delectably tormenting caress. She told herself that what he was doing was wrong, that it was wicked and most assuredly a sin . . . but it was also sheer heaven. Her fingers threaded almost convulsively within the dark richness of his hair. Desire streaked through her like wildfire now.

"Rand, please," she whispered brokenly, certain she could bear no more. She forgot her pride as she begged

him for mercy, forgot all else save the white-hot blaze of pleasure and yearning that threatened to consume her.

Rand's blue eyes gleamed in loving triumph. With passion thundering hotly in his own blood, he slid back up on her body. His hands gripped her about the hips, and he plunged full to the hilt inside her readied, inviting softness.

There was no real pain this time—only a dull ache that quickly gave way to ecstasy as she felt him move within her. Although this was only the second time they had been together in such an intimate way, she met his thrusts with a well-matched eagerness. And when the blending of their bodies reached its ultimate and wholly satisfying conclusion, she could not prevent a soft scream from escaping her lips. The sound of it was like music to Rand's ears as he tensed above her and sought his own release at last.

In the aftermath of their tempestuous union, he cradled her in the strong, warmly protective circle of his arms and brushed her damp forehead with his lips. The gentle breeze stirred the lace curtains at the window and swept lightly across their entwined bodies, while the candle, burning low, flickered in the quiet darkness. Claire listened for any sounds that might indicate Sadie or Harmony had been awakened by her cry of pleasure—the memory of which made her groan inwardly—but she heard nothing. She heaved a sigh of mingled relief and contentment, while in the next instant her eyes clouded with angry self-reproach.

Incredibly, she had done it again. Yes, by heaven, she was damned twice over now. Doubly guilty . . . and doubly branded by her husband's fiercely rapturous possession.

"Claire"—he spoke her name in a low, vibrant tone, as if it were an endearment in itself—"I love you."

"You—you don't even know me anymore," she stammered breathlessly. Her head still swam, and she couldn't deny the deep feeling of satisfaction lingering within her.

"I know you better than you think."

"How can you say that?" Her brows drew together in a frown of confusion, and she took a slightly uneven breath before reasserting, "I'm not the same person you left behind six years ago. Things change. People change."

"Some things stay the same." Tenderly sweeping several wayward strands of hair from her face, his hand wandered downward to rest upon her silken hip. "I loved you even then, though I hated like hell to admit it. I was used to my freedom. I guess I had enjoyed it too long to want to give it up without a fight. But the first time I set eyes on you, I was done for. If only I'd had more time—"

"Time?" she echoed. Her gaze kindled with resentment. "You had more than enough time to decide you wanted to try and seduce me, remember?"

"I could never forget that," he murmured, a wry smile briefly touching his lips. "Damn it, woman. I was no saint. Still, I never meant to hurt you. I'd have married you, Claire. In my own good time. But your father didn't give me the chance to realize how much I wanted that until it was too late."

"He did what he had to do." The note of anguish in

her voice sent a twinge of remorse slicing through his own heart.

"In his place, I probably would have done the same." He frowned; then his eyes suddenly glowed with a touch of ironic humor. "I've got a feeling I'll find out someday."

"What do you mean by that?"

"Only that we'll probably have a daughter of our own, maybe two or three. And if they're half as beautiful as their mother, I'll have to worry that some randy, hot-blooded young son of a bitch like I was—"

"You still *are*!"

"—will come along," he continued blithely, "and lure them out to the barn. They'll have brothers to watch over them, more than likely, but it will fall to their father to make sure they're treated with respect."

"I don't know what the devil you're talking about," she muttered in exasperation.

"Children, Claire. Yours and mine."

"Children?" She hastily pushed up on one elbow and stared down at him with eyes that were very round and full of startled disbelief. "Why, I'm not going to—"

"Not yet, maybe. But I'd say the odds are in our favor." His mouth twitched, and the look he gave her was disarmingly roguish. "I intend to make certain of that."

Warm color flooded her face. She drew away from him and sat up, only to inhale upon a gasp when she observed the way his gaze, darkening with renewed appreciation, drank in the sight of her naked breasts. She snatched up the quilt in a belated attempt to cover herself, but he tugged it aside and pulled her masterfully back down, into place beside him.

"Daylight's still a long time away," he pointed out.

"Don't you think you've done enough?" she accused, tilting her head back to eye him narrowly.

"No. I don't." With another ghost of a smile playing about his lips, he suddenly swept her atop him. She suffered a sharp intake of breath as her soft curves molded to perfection against his lean, hard-muscled warmth. Her honey-gold tresses cascaded down about her shoulders and teased at his chest.

"But, we just—" she tried to object.

"You underestimate the both of us, Mrs. Logan," he drawled, then quickly sobered. His penetrating blue eyes caught and held the sparkling virescence of hers, and his tone was very low, almost wistful, when he said, "I don't think all the time in the world can make up for the nights I spent dreaming about you . . . wanting you so bad that nothing could ease the pain. I tried, Claire. God knows, I meant it when I said I was no saint."

She paled, wondering why it hurt so much to hear that. A sudden lump rose in her throat, and she frowned as she found herself taunted by visions of other, faceless women lying with him as she was now.

"Maybe I am solely to blame for what happened," he allowed gravely. "But I've paid for my mistakes. I can't do anything about what's past. I can only do my best to make sure you'll never be hurt again."

"It isn't that easy," she whispered tremulously, her pulse racing from more than just the shocking intimacy of her current position. She attempted to pull away again, but his arms tightened about her until she could scarcely breathe.

"It can be," he decreed. It seemed that his gaze bored into her very soul. "If we both want it bad enough."

"I—I don't know *what* I want anymore." It was true. She had never felt so terribly disordered before. And anyway, it was impossible to consider the situation in a clear-headed manner while she was being held captive in his embrace. "I don't know what to think or feel."

"That's a start, I guess." He smiled ruefully up at her. She felt her stomach do a strange flip-flop, while her mind's inner voice noted that he looked even more appealing by candlelight.

"Please, just let me go," she said.

"I love you, Claire," he repeated, his hand moving up to take her chin in a firm grasp. "And I'm going to keep on loving you for the rest of my life. You can hold me to that promise."

"I don't want any promises from you."

"You will, once you let go of your anger."

"Will you please *leave*?" It was more of a demand than a request, of course. Either way, it would have evoked the same response.

"When daylight comes," he vowed. She had no sooner opened her mouth to argue when he rolled so that she was beneath him again. His mouth descended upon hers, his hand gliding boldly downward to explore all her feminine secrets once more.

Claire moaned low in her throat as she felt the familiar, provocative heat spreading throughout her body. She knew she would hate herself afterward. She knew she would curse the surrender of her flesh and the weakness of her spirit. But heaven have mercy on her soul, it was no use trying to fight against the delectable agony Rand was provoking within her. His very touch set her afire. And he was certainly touching her now. . . .

When she awoke the next morning, he was gone.

Just like a thief in the night, she mused with more than a hint of indignation. He was a thief, all right. First he had stolen her peace of mind, and now he had stolen her virginity as well. Yet, her conscience saw fit to challenge, wasn't she at least a little bit to blame for both?

Frowning darkly, she pulled herself up into a sitting position on the feather mattress and looked down to see her well-loved breasts shining naked and pale in the soft golden sunlight that filled the room. She muttered an oath and abruptly covered herself with the quilt. Her gaze drifted to where the spot beside her still bore the faint indentation of Rand's tall, muscular frame. She remembered falling asleep in his arms, her heart beating in unison with his while passion gave way to a peacefulness like no other.

Heaving a sigh, she climbed from the bed. Her body was plagued by an embarrassing soreness; she crimsoned at the memory of all that had happened since Rand had crept into her room at midnight. He had claimed his "husbandly rights" with a vengeance. She would probably ache for days to come.

Unwilling to think about the more permanent repercussions of the night, she hurried to wash and dress. Her fingers worked to fasten the top two buttons of her white blouse when she slipped from the room a few minutes later. She paused before the old grandfather clock in the hallway, only to see that its hands indicated a time well past what she had expected.

"Ten-thirty?" she whispered in disbelief. Sudden, guilty color washed over her when she recalled Tate's promise to take her to church that morning. Had he already come and gone? she wondered anxiously. Even worse, was he waiting downstairs for her right now? The prospect of facing him was not a happy one. Not after she had been stolen away from him with such pride-stinging ease. Not after she and Rand—

"Don't!" she commanded herself sternly. Gathering up her long brown skirts, she hastened down the stairs. When she arrived in the parlor, she was relieved to find that it was empty. A quick search of the front porch also yielded nothing. The sound of two voices—male and female—beckoned her to the kitchen, where she discovered Sadie sharing a pleasant, easy conversation with Micah.

"Mornin', Miss Claire," he said, politely rising to his feet when she stepped through the doorway. He had come inside at Sadie's invitation a short time earlier, accepting her offer of a cup of coffee and the chance to talk about his plans to surprise Harmony with a tree house down by the creek.

"I—I overslept," Claire stammered by way of explanation. She could feel another dull flash staining her cheeks, and her gaze fell beneath the fond amusement of theirs.

"I don't see how," Sadie replied, with a soft, crooked smile. "Between the two of them, Harmony and Wolf have been raising enough of a ruckus out back to wake the dead." She stood and crossed to the stove, inquiring, "Would you like some breakfast?"

"No. No, thank you. I'm not hungry."

"Well now," observed Micah, "that's something you got in common with the boys. Red wasn't set to cook this morning, and they weren't set to eat. They came dragging back from town at first light, looking like they'd all been rolled hard and put away wet."

"I've never understood why men get such enjoyment out of filling themselves with whiskey," Sadie remarked dryly.

"Has Mr. Jenner been by yet?" Claire asked. She tried to conceal the lingering stiffness of her muscles as she accepted the cup of coffee handed to her. There were faint, telltale shadows beneath her eyes. She would have been truly mortified if she had known that Sadie was aware of their cause.

"No."

"He was supposed to take us to church this morning."

"It's too late for that now," the other woman noted, without a trace of reproach in her voice. "I did wonder if he and his brothers would still be coming for dinner today."

"Dinner?" echoed Claire, then frowned again. She had forgotten about that, too.

"Sunday or no Sunday," Micah said on his way to the back door, "we'd best be getting those repairs done while the good weather holds."

"Micah?" Claire detained him on sudden impulse.

"Ma'am?"

"Did you—did you see or hear anything out of the ordinary last night?" Why the devil had she asked that?

"Out of the ordinary?" He shook his head, his dark eyes aglow when he answered truthfully, "No, ma'am. Nothing I didn't expect to be seeing."

"Oh." Not at all certain what to make of his response, she gently cleared her throat and moved to take a seat at the table. "Please tell Sully I'll be out to have a word with him as soon as I've finished my coffee."

"Yes, ma'am. I'll do that." He raised his hat to his head and strode outside. Once the door had closed behind him, Sadie cast a quick, maternal glance out the window to make sure Harmony was still in sight.

"Should I go ahead and make enough dinner for the others?" she then asked, turning back to face Claire.

"I suppose so. The last thing we need on our hands is a house full of hungry men and no food."

"We haven't had the Jenners over in quite a while." Her own brow creased into a slight frown. "They're a strange lot."

"Strange?" Claire echoed in surprise. "Why do you say that?"

"Well . . . take young Will, for instance." She went on with her chores while she talked, her hand grasping the handle of the pump at the sink. "He's full-grown, but those brothers of his treat him like he's still only a boy. Zeke and Harmon, they're likable enough, though hot-tempered and prone to trouble. They're the sort who go looking for a fight. I came across plenty of men like them when I was working at the saloon." A shadow of painful remembrance crossed her face. Filling the sink with water and adding soap, she began washing the stack of dishes left over from breakfast.

"What about Tate?" Claire prompted quietly.

"He's the hardest one to figure out. One minute, you could swear he's as nice and gentlemanly as he seems to be. But the next, he's like an overwound clock, all tight and ready to spring. He was that way at the box social last night."

"Are you warning me away from him, too?"

"No. You're able to make up your mind about him either way."

"At least *you* credit me with some sense," Claire murmured underneath her breath.

Her eyes flashed when she thought of Rand's high-handedness. If she let him, he would rule the roost. But there was no real danger of that, she reflected. He would be gone soon. . . .

"I'd better go and talk to Sully," she announced, mentally and quite firmly shaking herself as she stood and carried her empty cup to the sink. "I'll come back inside to help you with dinner once—"

"There's no need for that," Sadie assured her. "I can manage just fine by myself. And if the Jenners don't show up after all, I guess the hands will be glad to finish off the extra."

"I'm sure even Red will welcome the chance to sample someone else's cooking," Claire opined in a wry tone. She headed back through the house, emerging onto the front porch and allowing her gaze to make a broad, encompassing sweep of the sunlit grounds. She spied Sully near the corral. Moving down the steps, she crossed the yard to join him, all the while determinedly keeping her eyes away from the bunkhouse.

"Glad to see you up and about," Sully remarked when he caught sight of her.

"And just what do you mean by that?" she demanded, folding her arms beneath her breasts and lifting her head to a defensive angle. She watched as he took off his worn leather work gloves, slapped them against his denim-clad thigh, and glowered at her.

"Only that we got a ranch to run." He raked off his hat, then lifted his arm to wipe the sweat from his brow with his sleeve. "You're so damn busy playin' female these days, you ain't had time to give much thought to anythin' else."

"Playing female?" she repeated, her eyes bridling with outrage. "Why, you old—"

"Rant and rave all you like," he broke in, with another accusatory scowl. "But if you don't stop twitchin' your hips at those two young bucks, you'll bring trouble down on us all."

"I haven't the faintest notion what you're talking about. I don't go about 'twitching my hips' at anyone, and I certainly haven't been neglecting things here at Glorieta."

"I heard about what happened over at the church last night." He fixed her with a hard stare, his eyes seeing far more than she would have wished. "Hellfire and damnation, girl! Don't you know what it is you're stirrin' up? You got a husband who's come back and don't seem too likely to be leavin' again anytime soon, another poor bastard that's been sniffin' around you for nigh on to a year now, and you're right square in the middle of the whole sorry mess."

"It *is* a mess, I suppose," she begrudgingly acknowledged, then refuted in another burst of spirit, "but it's none of my doing! And you're wrong about Rand. He'll be leaving just as soon as his investigation——"

"If you think that, you're a fool."

She gasped as though she had been struck. Her mind searched for an appropriate rejoinder, but could find none. She watched now in stunned, turbulent silence while Sully turned on his booted heel and sauntered away.

"We'll get the roof fixed today," he tossed back over his shoulder. "You'd best be takin' Micah and ridin' out to have a look at the herd. There ain't a hell of a lot of trouble you can stir up out there. Do you good to get away. Might clear your head a bit." He continued talking until he disappeared inside the stock barn.

Claire frowned in his wake, battling the urge to go after him. But there was no use in trying to argue with someone as bullheaded and ornery as Sullivan Greene, she mused with a long, exasperated sigh. No use at all.

Contrary to Sully's advice, she spent the remainder of the morning setting the account books in order and showing an eager-to-learn Harmony how to weed the garden. There was no sign of Rand. She could only surmise that he had gone off in pursuit of information connected with the robberies. Surely, she told herself, his investigation would yield results soon. She had no earthly idea how good he was at being a lawman—but she was all too cognizant of his abilities in other areas.

The thought of facing him again in the cold light of

day provoked such chaos deep within her that she found it difficult to concentrate on Harmony's engaging chatter. The two of them were enjoying a brief, well-earned respite in the cool shade of the porch, waiting to see if they would have guests for dinner, when Tate Jenner and his brothers rode up to the front of the house.

The four of them dismounted and tied their reins to the hitching post. Tate was the first to climb the steps. It was impossible not to notice the bruises on his face, but Claire made no mention of them as she greeted him with an only slightly self-conscious smile.

"I'm glad you could come."

"Sorry I didn't make it for church," he apologized, sweeping the hat from his head. "Something came up."

"Howdy, Miss Claire," said Will, the next to reach the porch.

"Miss Claire." Zeke and Harmon each nodded politely at her in turn. Both were fair-haired and attractive, though neither possessed quite as much charm as the eldest Jenner.

"Sadie's made beef stew," she told them, her smile easier now that she had faced Tate and managed not to make a fool of herself. "Why don't you all come inside to the parlor, and I'll see if she's ready for us yet." They were perfectly willing to let her lead the way. Behind her, Zeke and Harmon exchanged a knowing, amused look that they took pains to hide from Tate.

"You grown any more, Little Bit?" Will paused to ask Harmony, his gray eyes full of a teasing light as he swung the child up in his arms. She giggled, but grew solemn in the next instant.

"Mama says you won't really wait to marry me."

"Well now, maybe that's because she doesn't know me well enough yet."

"You still promise?" Her brown eyes sparkled with a hope that went far beyond her years.

"I promise. Just you see you don't go off and marry someone else before then," he warned, making her laugh again as he carried her inside the house.

Dinner was a surprisingly pleasant affair. Claire had feared that the atmosphere would be a trifle stilted. She was certain Tate's brothers had heard of his humiliating defeat at the social by now; surely, she had thought, they would place at least some of the blame at her feet. But not a one of them gave any indication of it. The conversation remained lively and flowing as each brother proved himself entirely capable of holding his own in the arena of "leisure parley." Sadie was in her element as well, serving up platters of stew, steaming bowls of mashed potatoes and buttered carrots, and freshly baked corn bread muffins to the appreciative men. Harmony was content to sit at the end of the table beside Will and cast him adoring glances in between bites of the food her mother had piled on her plate.

Afterward, the three younger Jenners took themselves off with the stated intention of finishing up repairs back at their own place. Tate stayed behind, leading Claire outside once Sadie had refused her latest offer of help.

They strolled together along the path leading to the creek. It had turned out to be a particularly lovely afternoon—bright and warm and lazy, except for the sound of hammering that filled the air. At least, Claire told herself wryly, Sully had been thoughtful enough to wait until after dinner to begin work on the roof.

"I'm glad we're alone," Tate remarked, with uncharacteristic gravity as the two of them made their way through the trees. With Harmony and Wolf back at the house with Sadie, and the hands busy either pounding shingles into place or thumbing their noses at Sully's authority by sleeping on the job, the fragrant coolness beside the creek afforded them almost complete privacy. "We need to talk."

"About what?" Inwardly, she tensed, for she knew what was coming.

"Last night."

"Oh, Tate. There's—there's nothing to talk about." She stopped at the water's edge now and turned back to face him. "I'm sorry about what happened. Jake should never have come. What he did was unforgivable." *In more ways than one.* "Let's just leave it at that."

"I can't." He stepped closer to her, his gaze drifting out toward the rippling surface of the pond while he toyed absently with the hat in his hands. "There's something goin' on between you and Parker. I want to know what it is."

"I don't know what you're talking about." She lied smoothly, though her face paled.

"Why do you keep him on, Claire? He's a cocksure son of a bitch, that's for damn sure. And after last night—" He broke off and rounded on her to demand, "Did he try anything when he brought you home?"

"Try anything?" She shook her head in a vehement denial. "Of course not!"

"Because if he did, I'll kill him!"

"Don't be ridiculous," she retorted, then tried to temper it a bit. She even managed a smile, albeit a weak one. "You're a good friend, Tate, but I don't need you or anyone else to—"

"Marry me, Claire!"

While she drew in a sharp breath and blinked up at him in astonishment, he unexpectedly wrapped his arms about her and pulled her close.

"Marry me," he urged, the light in his eyes almost feral, "and I swear I'll keep you safe!"

"Safe? Safe from *what*?" She struggled within his embrace. "For heaven's sake, what's gotten into you? Please, we've been through this already. Surely you—?"

"I'm in love with you, Claire."

Her struggles abruptly ceased. Rand's declaration of love echoed anew in her ears, inviting a comparison she would rather not have made. Strangely enough, his words had rung much truer than Tate's. He hadn't said "in love" as if it were simply a state of mind, or something temporary that could be overcome with time and patience. No indeed, she recalled dazedly, he had proclaimed it to be a deep, everlasting emotion that gripped the very heart and soul . . . *his* heart and soul.

"You're in love with me, too," Tate went on. His mouth curved into a smug, confident smile. "You're just gun-shy because of that husband of yours."

"No!" She shook her head again, her eyes brimming with both remorse and a very real apprehension as she brought her hands up to his chest. "I—I do care about you very much, but not in that way. And Rand has nothing to do with it. Nothing at all." She met his gaze squarely and told him in all truthfulness, "I'm sorry, Tate. But I don't love you."

"Then I'll have to make you!"

Before she could reply, he tightened his arms about her and brought his lips slanting down hard upon hers. She moaned in protest and squirmed against him, but he threatened to cut off her breath as his mouth sought a full, greedy possession of hers.

The kiss was nothing like those she had shared with Rand. There was no answering spark of passion within her, no pleasure or longing or even indignation. She felt nothing but a desperate need to escape. It occurred to her that she could strike out at him, that she could tear her lips from his and scream for help and thereby ensure that he found himself facing the business end of Sully's gun.

She had no real desire to see him hurt, of course. Yet, at the moment, he didn't seem like the Tate she knew. She remembered the way Sadie had described him only that morning—"all tight and ready to spring." He had sprung, all right. Dear Lord, how could she make him understand? Why couldn't things be the same as they were before? Why did his embrace cause her to yearn for the fiery enchantment of Rand's?

Once more, she struggled against him. But he would not let her go. She instinctively raised her knee, preparing to bring it up against his manhood.

And then suddenly, *she was free*.

She staggered backward, a loud gasp breaking from her lips as she lost her balance and fell to the grassy earth. Landing in an inglorious swirl of skirts, she jerked her head about. Her wide, startled gaze flew to where Rand had just sent Tate crashing forcefully back against a tree.

His blue eyes were filled with a savage gleam; there

was a grim, dangerous expression on his face. A tremor of fear shot through Claire. She scrambled up to her feet again, blanching as she watched Tate suffer another bruising uppercut to the chin.

"No!" she cried out, horrified. "Stop it!"

Just as before, however, her protests did no good. Tate tried to defend himself. He managed to land a blow or two, but Rand possessed a superior strength and skill. Giving the other man no quarter, he hit him again and again, until Tate collapsed down onto the ground. He lay there, his nose streaming blood and his breathing painfully labored, while Rand stood over him.

"For God's sake, that's enough!" Claire charged. She raced forward now and dropped to her knees beside Tate. But she found herself hauled roughly to her feet in the next instant. The look Rand turned upon her was enough to provoke her into shocked, trembling silence. His fingers relaxed their steely grip upon her arm before he turned his attention back to Tate.

"Get up," he ordered.

With considerable difficulty, Tate complied. He winced as he dragged himself slowly upright. Bracing a hand against a tree, he shook his head in an effort to clear it, then sliced Rand a narrow, vengeful glare. In spite of the fact that he had just suffered another humiliating defeat, he wasn't ready to cry uncle.

"Damn your eyes, Parker! This wasn't any of your business!" he snarled, angrily lifting his arm and wiping the blood from his face with his sleeve.

"Touch her again," Rand warned him in a tone of deadly calm, "and I'll kill you."

"Why, you interferin' bastard," Tate ground out. Fury

driving him to recklessness, he reached for the gun holstered low on his hip.

In one lightning-swift motion, Rand thrust Claire protectively behind him and whipped out his own six-shooter. He beat his opponent to the draw, but he did not pull the trigger. His mouth curved into a faint, humorless smile while a surprised—and once again outmaneuvered—Tate muttered an oath and wisely decided to call it quits.

"Next time," promised Rand. There was little doubt what he meant.

"I won't forget this, Parker," Tate vowed malevolently. "Someday, I'll put a bullet in that thick head of yours." His harshly lit gaze shifted to Claire when she stepped from behind Rand. There was a stricken look on her face, and her eyes were clouded with a mixture of pity and remorse.

"Tate, I don't . . ." she murmured, her voice trailing away as words failed her.

"Remember what I said, Claire," he advised. "I'll be back." He shot Rand one last contemptuous scowl, then turned and strode quickly away.

Left alone with her husband, Claire wavered between outrage and trepidation. An awful silence filled the air, a silence that alarmed her far more than an immediate tongue-lashing would have. Finally Rand pivoted about to face her. She had expected his anger. But she had *not* anticipated the form it would take.

"By damn, woman, I ought to wring your neck," he told her, his tone so low and underscored by barely suppressed violence that she shivered. His eyes smoldered down into hers.

"I did nothing wrong," she asserted. She folded her arms beneath her breasts and raised her chin to a proud, defensive angle. "Not a blasted thing!"

"You're my wife, Claire." He stepped closer, battling the impulse to lay hands on her then and there. "I've never hit a woman in my whole life. But if I ever catch you in another man's arms again, so help me God, I'll gladly make an exception."

"I wasn't in his arms! Well . . . I *was*, I suppose," she amended, while hot, guilty color stained her cheeks. "But it was none of my doing. And don't you dare threaten me, Rand Logan! You don't *own* me. I'm a grown woman, fully capable of taking care of myself."

"Is that what you were doing?" he challenged, angry and mocking. His blood still boiled at the memory of the intimate little tête-à-tête he had interrupted. If not for his training as a lawman, he would have killed Tate Jenner with his bare hands. "If I really believed you had been a willing victim, I'd tan your hide here and now."

"Why, you insolent, overbearing son of a—" stormed Claire, her beautiful eyes filling with green-sparked outrage. She planted her hands on her hips and tossed her head in a gesture of even more furious defiance. "Tate is in love with me. Yes, and if I were the slightest bit tempted to take him up on his offer of marriage, I certainly wouldn't let *you* stand in the way!"

The words had no sooner left her mouth than his arms captured her with their powerful, sinewy warmth. He swept her up hard against him, his gaze raking over her upturned face.

"Once and for all, Claire—you're mine," he reminded her tersely. *"Now and forever!"*

She thought he meant to kiss her. In fact, she held her breath and waited for the inevitable. But his lips didn't descend upon hers as she had expected. Instead, he suddenly scooped her up in his arms and tossed her into the pond.

A startled cry escaped her just before she hit the water. When she came up to the surface again, she drew in a deep, ragged breath and struggled to find her footing.

"Damn you, Rand Logan!" she sputtered indignantly. Her long hair tumbled down from its pins, her white blouse and chemise clung with near transparency to her heaving breasts, and her wet skirts tangled heavily about her legs.

His only response was to lift his hands and begin unbuttoning his shirt. Claire's eyes grew round as saucers, and she felt her heart leap into her throat.

"What do you think you're doing?"

He said nothing. While she watched in ever-increasing dismay, he removed his shirt, flung it aside, and took a seat on a large, flat-surfaced rock in order to tug off his boots and socks. His movements were sure and unhurried. When he stood again, his fingers moved to the front of his denim trousers.

"No!" Claire gasped. She gathered up her skirts and hastened to make her way out of the water. But it was no use. Rand stripped off his trousers and waded into the pond, advancing on her with a look that could best be described as tenderly wolfish.

She caught her breath at the sight of his naked and magnificent body. Her wide, sparkling gaze strayed to where his desire for her was all too evident.

"I wanted to join you for a swim that first day I saw

you," he confided, his voice still edged with anger. "Maybe I should have."

"What are you—? Someone will see us!" she stammered in alarm, retreating back toward the center of the pond until the water swirled up about her thighs. She knew he had more than swimming on his mind. The prospect of what was to come sent hot color flying to her cheeks. "It's the middle of the day, for heaven's sake! This is *indecent*!"

"Just the way I like it." He reached for her now, his arm snaking about her waist, and, none too gently, drawing her close. She inhaled sharply when her wet, tingling breasts came into contact with the hard warmth of his naked chest. "By damn, Claire! You're a stubborn little wildcat," he murmured, his tone quiet and splendidly vibrant. His glowing eyes caught and held hers. "You've got more courage and spirit than any woman I've ever known. But it's time you learned something about obedience. Only one of us can be the boss around here. And it sure as hell isn't going to be you."

"Let me go!" She pushed at him and tried to wriggle free, but his arms merely locked about her.

"There'll be no more walks with Tate Jenner," he decreed. "Or any other man."

"I'll do as I please," she countered defiantly, then was rewarded with a hard, punishing slap upon her bottom. Her eyes narrowed and blazed. "Why, you—"

"From here on out, you're to stay clear of Jenner. Understand?"

"You go to the devil!"

This time, she suffered the indignity of being thrust

beneath the water's surface. When she was pulled back up into the chilling air again, she coughed and spluttered and shot Rand a glare that spoke volumes.

"If it's a strong hand you need, then it's a strong hand you'll get," he promised.

"I hate you!" she fumed.

"Do you?" He gave her a slow, thoroughly disarming smile that set her traitorous pulse to racing again. His mouth came down upon hers at last. She moaned low in her throat and swayed against him in spite of herself.

By the time he raised his head, she was flushed and breathless. But *still* far from submissive.

"I want you to promise not to see Jenner again," he demanded authoritatively.

"I can't do that." She was dunked again. A highly expressive curse fell from her lips when she was hauled back up to confront her handsome tormentor.

"Promise me, Claire."

"How—how can I?" She blinked against the water streaming down her face and raised her hands to push at his chest once more. "Tate has been a good friend to me this past year. Where the devil were *you* during that time? Gallivanting all over Texas, doing God only knows what, letting me go on wondering whether you were alive or dead."

"So you did think of me," he drawled, with maddening complacency.

"How could I help it?" she countered. "Every time I turned around, someone was reminding me of my 'poor, unfortunate state.' I didn't mind so much being the talk of the town. I didn't care when people speculated about your whereabouts and my chances of ever becoming anything more than a tainted woman. But it bothered the ever-living daylights out of me, Rand Logan, to find myself caught in a no-man's land of uncertainty these past six years! And now, here you are, bent on upsetting my whole life . . . when I've managed to do just fine without you—"

"Like hell."

Her eyes flashed at his presumption. She would have launched another verbal barrage at him, but his mouth resumed its fiery, mesmerizing possession of hers. While the kiss deepened, he swept her up in his arms and carried her to the edge of the pond. He tenderly lowered her to the cushion of grass. The moment she felt the ground beneath her back, however, she embraced resistance once more.

"No!" she cried. "Not again!"

Squirming wildly, she rolled to her stomach and scrambled up onto her hands and knees. Rand easily caught her again and pulled her back toward him. Holding her captive with one arm, he entangled a hand within the drenched folds of her skirts and raked them above her waist. Her face flamed as he suddenly yanked her wet, lace-trimmed drawers all the way down to her knees.

"*Rand!*" she said, gasping in shocked protest.

"You've got a beautiful backside, Mrs. Logan," he pronounced, his voice brimming with both amusement and passion. Her eyes flew even wider when she felt his warm lips roaming boldly across the pale, naked curve of her bottom.

"Don't," she objected tremulously, though she knew it was useless. He would have his way with her. And she would delight in every wonderful, wicked minute of it. . . .

His hand wandered around to the secret place between her thighs, and her eyes swept closed while his gentle, oh-so-skillful fingers stroked her silken flesh. The flames of desire spread throughout her body; she forgot her embarrassment as he knelt behind her. His other hand crept up to her breasts. He caressed her through the thin, clinging layers of cotton, prompting her to gasp and moan and shudder with passion. His lips teased at the graceful curve of her neck, and she could not prevent her hands from stealing upward to thread within the dark, sun-kissed thickness of his hair.

When the delectable torment became too much to bear, he plunged into her from behind. She gave a soft cry of ecstasy, her feminine passage welcoming the hot, throbbing fullness of his manhood. Instinctively she strained back against him. Her hips followed the fiercely loving motion of his, while his hands returned to her breasts. The climax of their fiery union was like heaven on earth, leaving them fully sated and marveling at the perfect match of both their bodies and their passions.

Afterward, Rand stretched out on his back, naked and unashamed in all his masculine glory, while Claire lay pliantly against him. For the moment, at least, she had neither the strength nor the inclination to stir. She could still hear the sound of hammering in the near distance. Her mouth curved into a faint smile of irony when she recalled Sully's warning about "twitching her hips" at Rand and Tate. There was nothing the least bit funny about what had happened, of course. And by heaven, it still wasn't her fault. . . .

"You haven't given me your word about Jenner yet," Rand pointed out, breaking the silence now. His fingers wandered to the pearl buttons running along the front of her blouse.

"What difference does it make?" She released a long, troubled sigh and frowned. "Once your work here is done, you'll be on your way again." A sudden shadow crossed her face at the thought, and she did her best to ignore the sharp twinge of pain slicing through her heart.

"Will I?"

"You're a Texas Ranger. I find it difficult to believe you'd receive any sort of permanent assignment to a town the size of Parmalee."

"True enough. But I might just surprise you."

"I've had all the surprises I can take, thank you very much." She shivered at the sound of his quiet, mellow chuckle.

"One thing's for sure," he said, his arms gathering her close again. "I'll never let you go."

"And I'll never leave Glorieta!"

"Then I guess I'll have to take up ranching."

"What?" She tilted her head back and peered quizzically up at him. "You're not really serious, are you?"

"I've been roaming a long time, Claire," he remarked, his rugged features sobering. "Maybe it's time I turned in my badge."

"You mean you—you'd give up the law?" she stammered in disbelief.

"Not give it up, exactly. Just steer it in a different direction." He smiled briefly, then grew serious again. "I never thought I'd get the chance to settle down with you. And now that I've got it, I'd be a fool to risk losing you again."

"But you can't stay on at Glorieta," she protested, her head spinning. She abruptly drew away from him and sat up. "I don't *want* you here. Besides, Sully would never agree to work for you, and neither would Micah."

"You want me," he disputed confidently. "Sully can be persuaded. Micah and I have already reached an understanding. And Sadie and Harmony are welcome to stay on as long as they like."

"This is *my* ranch! If you dare to try and take it from me—"

"I told you before, I don't want the ranch. But I'll be damned if I'll continue sleeping in the bunkhouse after all this is over." He sat up as well now. His hand closed gently yet firmly about her wrist while his blue eyes filled with a devilish light. "Unless you'd care to join me there."

Claire did not share his amusement.

"Our marriage was a mistake." It was her turn to reiterate. "And I'll do whatever it takes to see it dissolved."

"Try anything," Rand parried, with deceptive equanimity, "and you'll find yourself standing for a week."

"Go to hell!"

"I've been there."

She endeavored to rise, but he pulled her back down. In spite of her struggles, he proceeded to strip off every stitch of clothing she had on. She hesitated to scream for help—once again, she rationalized, it would be hu-

miliating in the extreme to be caught fraternizing so in-
timately with a man she had professed to despise—and
she knew that the outcome of her "wrestling match"
with Rand would provide her with more than enough
pleasure to make up for the blow to her pride. Like it or
not, she found his touch irresistible. Completely,
damnably—*inflamingly*—irresistible.

He made love to her a second time, then scooped her
up in his strong arms again and carried her back into the
pond. They got on with the business of swimming at
last. Claire was both surprised and secretly captivated
by Rand's playfulness as he splashed about and dived
beneath the water's surface to pull her down as well.
She made more than one halfhearted attempt to escape,
but he would always seize whatever part of her body
was most convenient to his reach and "punish" her with
a long, wet, slow kiss. . . .

By the time he finally allowed her to leave and return
alone to the house, her clothes were only slightly damp.
She avoided Sadie and Harmony and went straight up to
her room. Catching sight of her reflection in the mirror,
she blushed crimson. Guilt, embarrassment, and a
whirlwind of other emotions made her head spin anew.
She wondered if Rand had meant what he'd said about
staying on.

The Sunday afternoon had turned out to be one she
would not soon forget. And when she finally climbed
beneath the covers of her bed that night, her slumber
was deeper and more restful than it had been in a long,
long time.

Chapter 10

Life settled into a relatively normal routine for the next three days. Once again, Claire saw little of Rand. Half expecting him to come sneaking into her room each night, she was torn between relief and indignation when her privacy remained undisturbed. It galled her to think that he found it so easy to stay away. Especially when *she* tossed restlessly in the loneliness of her bed, her dreams so vivid and downright shameless that she groaned at the memory of them in the morning.

She offered neither complaint nor comment about the fact that he took to disappearing from the ranch for hours on end. Even Sully kept quiet about it—a true rarity, she mused with wry indulgence. Recalling Rand's assurance that the crusty old foreman could be persuaded to accept him on a permanent basis, she frowned and staunchly turned her thoughts elsewhere . . . just as she had been doing ever since that "mischief" at the pond on Sunday.

Tuesday afternoon found her out riding the range with Harmony and Micah. The little girl had formed a real attachment for the former buffalo soldier, and it was obvious to Claire that he returned Harmony's affection. The two of them rode together atop his horse, talking companionably about the birds and animals and insects they spied, while Claire allowed her gaze to sweep across the rolling, cattle-dotted plains. Several new calves had been born in the past few weeks; come fall, the herd would be a healthy size indeed.

Come fall, her mind repeated. Would Rand still be there in the fall? Would she have gotten up enough courage by then to contact that lawyer friend of her father's down in Dallas? She certainly couldn't put it off forever. Not if she ever hoped to regain her independence. Not if she hoped to remove temptation (in the form of a tall, blue-eyed scoundrel with all the charm of the devil himself) and see her life return to its usual orderliness.

Back at the ranch, Sadie gathered in the last of the sun-freshened sheets from the clothesline. The repairs to the roof had taken longer than Sully had anticipated, making it necessary for her to postpone the washing for an entire day. She hadn't really minded the change, since it had provided her with the opportunity to be alone with her thoughts.

And her thoughts, just as they had been more and more of late, were centered around Reverend Thomas Mueller.

Thinking of him brought her a contradictory mixture of pleasure and pain. It was difficult to convince herself that she didn't find him attractive. It was even more difficult to believe that she, a one-time "saloon angel," could ever hope to dream of a future with a man of the cloth.

Not that he had declared his intentions, of course. More than likely, she told herself, he was interested in nothing more than the friendship she was prepared to offer him. There was little doubt that he liked her. She could still remember the way his blue-green eyes had glowed with genuine warmth and affection on the night of the box social. He had been so kind, a true gentleman . . . yet every inch a *man* at the same time.

"You're a foolish woman, Sadie Bishop," she declared scornfully. Flinging the last of the sheets into the large wicker basket, she straightened and raised a hand to sweep a few wayward strands of long, silky black hair from her face while the wind set her gingham skirts flying up about her trim ankles.

"I do not think you foolish."

She started at the sound of that pleasant, familiar masculine voice. Her eyes flew wide, and her hand fluttered nervously to her throat as she turned to find Thomas surveying her from a few feet away. He looked very handsome in his black suit and white shirt, the sun lighting fire in his thick blond hair. The smile he gave her was so appealing that she felt her heart quiver.

"Reverend! How long—?" she started to ask, only to break off and hastily look away.

"Do you often talk to yourself, my dear Mrs. Bishop?"

"No." Dismayed to feel her cheeks growing warm, she bent to take the laundry inside. He was beside her in an instant, gallantly appropriating the basket while his eyes twinkled down at her.

"I am told there is no harm in it. So long as one does not prolong the conversation."

"Then maybe there's hope for me yet," she murmured, her pulse leaping alarmingly at his nearness. She hastened to put some distance between them, and she even managed a wan little smile while asking, "What brings you here today? I'm afraid both Harmony and Claire are away at the moment, but—"

"I came to see you." He held the basket underneath one arm now.

"Oh." Her color deepened. She started toward the back door, but his hand suddenly closed about her arm.

"You did not attend church on Sunday."

"No, I . . . we weren't able to make it."

"Because of what happened at the social?" he probed gently.

"No. That is, not exactly." She shook her head and tried to ignore the way her skin tingled beneath his fingers. Even through the fabric of her sleeve, his touch felt warm and strong and—God forgive her—*right*. "I doubt if I'll be coming anymore," she announced on sudden impulse. "There's always so much work to be done, and the townfolk don't want me there."

"Ah, but they will accept you in time."

"If only that were true." She gazed wistfully up at him. "Some things never change, Reverend."

"Thomas," he corrected. He set the basket down and smiled again. "Please, can you not think of me as a man instead of a minister?"

"I could," she conceded, "but I won't." Gently but firmly, she disengaged her arm from his grasp and took a step backward.

"I see. You do not like me, then?"

"Oh, no. It isn't that at all," she blurted out. Another

dull flush crept up to her pretty, wide-eyed countenance. "But there's no getting around the fact that you're a preacher and I'm a—a woman with a past."

"Everyone has a past," he pointed out, undeterred.

"Not like mine."

"I am glad for your past, for without it you would not be who you are." Although his eyes danced anew at her astonished expression, he declared with some formality, "I realize, of course, that we have been acquainted for a very short time. I am also well aware of the fact that, as a widow, you cannot help but retain a certain devotion to your late husband. Nevertheless, perhaps you will allow me to court you."

"Court me?" she echoed, even more incredulous than before.

"In a proper manner, my dearest Sadie." He drew closer, his voice brimming with tenderness and a thoroughly flesh-and-blood desire when he said, "And I hope that you will, indeed, be my dearest. In a few months' time, we can be wed. I offer you my solemn oath that little Harmony will become as my own daughter, even if we should find ourselves blessed with a dozen others."

"But you don't even know me!" Her head swimming, she raised her hand to tuck her wind-teased curls back into place again and averted her opal gaze from the beguiling ardor of his.

"Is that not the purpose of a courtship?"

"Yes, but I— Good heavens, I didn't expect this!"

"No doubt, you are shocked at my haste," he remarked contritely. "Please, I ask that you forgive me for my selfishness."

"Forgive you?" The look she turned upon him was anything but reproachful. "You've done nothing wrong. Why, *I'm* the one—"

"I will not allow you to speak ill of yourself." His tone was one of quiet, loving authority. "To me, you are all that is good and kind and beautiful. I would not have thought it possible that an affection so strong could grow in only a week's time, yet it has. And if you will but grant me the honor of nurturing that affection, I will count myself the most fortunate of men."

"I can't," she choked out. Hot tears suddenly sprang to her eyes, and she shook her head again in a futile denial of her own secret longings. "You'd be throwing your whole life away."

"I do not understand," he replied, a slight frown of bemusement creasing his brow.

"It's hard enough for the people here to accept me as Claire's housekeeper. They'd never accept me as the parson's wife!"

"I am confident that you can win their approval. Once we are man and wife, they will look upon you differently."

"You really *are* naive, aren't you?" She was exasperated by his persistence, yet also filled with a joyfulness of spirit that had nothing whatsoever to do with his professional calling.

"Perhaps you will help me gain wisdom," Thomas parried, delighting in the acceptance he glimpsed in her eyes. "There are, however, some things even a parson does not need to be taught." His arms came up about her, and she did not resist as he pulled her tenderly against him. He proved his point most effectively, his lips claiming hers in a warm, sweetly passionate kiss that left her flushed and breathless and not at all certain she wanted to wait for a proper courtship.

"I—I don't know anything about being a preacher's wife," she protested weakly.

"You shall have a lifetime in which to learn." He kissed her again.

"What about Claire?" she asked when he finally, reluctantly, let her go. "She's been so good to Harmony and me. I owe her more than I can ever repay."

"She will rejoice in your happiness," he assured her. Retrieving the basket, he took her arm and began leading her toward the house. "But, if you prefer, my love, we can keep our courtship a secret for a while. Not too long, mind you," he insisted, his turquoise gaze softening with both humor and passion once more. "I have never been particularly adept at concealing my true emotions—a definite disadvantage for a man in my position, would you not agree?"

My love. The sound of it made her heart soar. Dear God, could she let him love her? Could the world be that forgiving?

"Thomas, are you really sure you want to—?" she queried once more, her own feelings of unworthiness planting doubt in her mind.

"More than anything in the world."

And so it was agreed. They sealed their betrothal with a kiss, their eyes still warmly aglow when Harmony and Claire came upon them in the kitchen a short time later. Claire suspected the cause of their mutually high spirits, but she said nothing about it. Harmony, as usual, saw more than anyone gave her credit for.

That same night, long after everyone had gone to bed, Claire tossed her dressing gown about her shoulders and slipped out of the house. The moon, only a sliver in the starlit blackness of the sky, bathed the wild, rugged beauty of the landscape in a pale silvery light, while the air was stirred by only a hint of the ever-present Texas wind. The ranch was quiet, the stock bedded down for the night and the hands fast asleep in their bunks.

Claire wandered restlessly across the yard. Her emerald gaze strayed (as it always did now) toward the darkened bunkhouse. She had abandoned her solitary nighttime walks of late; the prospect of encountering Rand had prompted her to turn coward. But she was determined to regain her courage. Yes, and by heaven, she vowed silently, to regain her peace of mind as well.

An audible, disgruntled sigh escaped her lips. She tied the belt of her dressing gown and raked her shimmering, unbound tresses away from her face. *Rand.* For more than three days now, he had kept his distance. She should be glad of it. She should get down on her knees and thank the good Lord above that her "husband" had apparently decided he'd done enough damage. Why, then, did she feel this awful sense of disappointment, of something too dangerously akin to frustration? And why the devil couldn't she stop thinking about his proposal—serious or not—to stay on at Glorieta?

She sighed again and continued her wandering, only to draw up short when she suddenly detected the sound of voices. Both low, and both obviously male, they drifted to her from the direction of the springhouse.

"Who on earth . . .?" she whispered, her brows knitting together into a frown of perplexity. She gathered up the folds of her nightgown and robe and crept forward to investigate, her bare feet tiptoeing across the ground until she had reached the front corner of the small stone building. She stopped and listened. Her eyes widened in startlement, for she easily recognized the voices when they spoke again.

"You got to keep your word," said Will Jenner.

"Consider it done," Rand assured him grimly. "But I can't promise to hold back if something goes wrong."

"I know," the younger man acknowledged, his tone fraught with obvious worry.

"Go home, Jenner. And don't come here again."

"You think anyone's suspicious?"

"It's a liability to think too much in my line of work," Rand drawled sardonically, then sobered again. "If you need to talk to me, leave word with the sheriff."

"I'm not sure he can be trusted."

"Neither am I."

"Dammit to hell, Parker—"

"Do you want the deal or not?" snapped Rand.

"I don't have much of a choice, do I?" Will shot back angrily. Although Claire was afraid to venture a glance around the corner, she could tell that he was mounting his horse. She heard the soft creak of the leather as he swung up into the saddle, and the grinding of the metal bit in the horse's mouth when he pulled the reins taut. "You tell those Ranger friends of yours that all bets are off once the shootin' starts."

"Then you'd better make sure you don't get caught in the crossfire."

Will said nothing more before he rode away. Claire

held her breath, still motionless and silent as the sound of hoofbeats grew faint.

All bets are off once the shootin' starts. What was going on? she wondered, her mind racing as a result of the mysterious exchange she had just overheard. The thought of Rand in some kind of danger provoked a sharp, disturbing twinge of apprehension within her. What kind of deal had he made with Tate's brother?

She pivoted stealthily about and started back toward the house. Without warning, a hand suddenly clamped across her mouth. She gasped as she was imprisoned by a strong, sinewy arm from behind and hauled roughly inside the springhouse.

"Were you looking for *me*, Mrs. Logan?" Rand challenged in a mocking undertone. He released her, closed the door, and moved to light the lamp. In a matter of seconds, the cool, single-room structure was filled with a soft golden glow.

Claire's eyes bridled with resentment as she watched him. Although her every instinct told her to flee—just like the last time she had been alone with him here—she allowed curiosity to overrule caution.

"What was Will Jenner doing here this time of night?" she demanded, yanking the belt of her robe tight. "And what kind of deal have the two of you made? Does he know something about—?"

"All in good time." He cut her off with maddening evasiveness. He negligently tugged the hat from his head and hung it on the peg beside the door. His handsome face was inscrutable, his gaze fathomless as he slowly advanced upon her.

"What do you mean, 'all in good time'?" Folding her

arms beneath her breasts, she raised her head proudly and argued, "For heaven's sake, Rand Logan. This is *my* ranch, and I have a perfect right to know what's going on."

"Keep quiet about Will."

"I will, so long as you explain——"

"I mean it, Claire." His hands seized her about the shoulders, and he frowned sternly down at her. "He made a mistake in coming here. And you're going to forget you ever saw him."

"He *does* know something about the robberies, doesn't he?" she said, her own gaze lighting with triumph.

"Yes," he relented enough to confirm. "And his life would be in danger if it became public knowledge."

"Do you really think me such an idiot?" she scoffed, acutely conscious of his hands upon her, yet unable to make herself move away. "Besides, I want those men caught every bit as much as you do."

"And why is that?"

"For the same reason I stated before——because once they're arrested, you can be on your way."

"I'm not going anywhere. Not without you."

"You'll go." Her voice quavered with raw emotion. "Just like you did before."

"Damn it, Claire! When are you going to stop punishing the both of us?" he ground out, his fingers clenching with near bruising force about her shoulders. His eyes seared compellingly down into hers. "I'm here to stay for good. No more running away, no more broken promises or broken dreams. *I'm here to stay.*"

She would have offered a reply, but he never gave

her the chance. He gathered her close, his mouth branding hers so hotly and completely that, with a low moan, she swayed against him in unspoken surrender. For the past three long and lonely nights, she had secretly yearned for his touch. She had been taunted by the memory of his every kiss and caress, by his words of love and her heart's wild flight at the sound of them. And now that she was in his arms again, she found herself an eager, wanton participant in the embrace.

His hunger was even greater than her own. He kissed her fiercely, soul-stirringly, his arms crushing her to his hard and virile warmth while she clung to him. His hand stole within the edges of her dressing gown and closed upon the ripe, thinly covered fullness of her breast. She gasped in pleasure against his mouth.

And then he was urging her back against the wall of the springhouse, his other hand impatiently raking up the folds of her nightgown so that he could claim the tiny bud of femininity between her pale, slender thighs. He stroked her gently yet provocatively, his touch setting her afire. She clutched at his shoulders and gasped anew while he virtually tore open the buttons on the front of her gown and allowed his mouth to wander fiercely downward, along her neck. In the next instant, he had bared her rose-tipped breasts. His lips and tongue paid moist, loving tribute to her satiny flesh, sucking and swirling and teasing until she was certain she could bear no more of the exquisite torment. Her gasps and moans only served to send his own white-hot desire blazing higher and higher.

Her eyelids fluttered open when he suddenly made it clear that he meant to take her standing up, but she was beyond caring about the shocking unfamiliarity of her position. She offered not a single protest as his hands clasped her about the hips and lifted her slightly.

He brought her down upon his waiting hardness. Her honeyed, velvety warmth accepted the whole pulsing length of him. She could have sworn he touched her very womb.

"Rand!" She breathed sharply, her eyes sweeping closed while deep tremors of passion shook her. She wrapped her arms about his neck as his mouth crashed down upon hers once more. Only dimly aware of the hard, cool stones against her back, she met his thrusts boldly and returned his kisses with an equal ardor.

The fulfillment was downright earth-shattering. Claire cried out softly in the lamplight, certain that her very soul was soaring heavenward. Rand spoke her name in a hoarse whisper as he tensed and flooded her with his hot seed.

Once the delectable madness had yielded to reality once more, he reluctantly drew away, watching as she pulled her clothing back down into place and buttoned her nightgown. His eyes glowed with affectionate humor.

"At this rate, Mrs. Logan, I'll be old before my time," he teased. She blushed and refused to look at him.

"My back will probably hurt for a week." Though she spoke it querulously, she couldn't deny that she shared equal blame for any bruising she might have suffered.

"Let me know if you want me to tend to it for you." He retrieved his hat and settled it on his head. "I'll be glad when we can stop all this sneaking around. Not that I'm complaining about the variety."

"Is that what you've been doing these past three nights?" she impulsively demanded, tying the belt of her dressing gown while her eyes sparked with resentment. " 'Sneaking around' in Parmalee?"

"There's no reason for you to be jealous," he drawled, with an ironic half smile. "I finished sowing my wild oats a long time ago."

"I'm not jealous!" She knew it was a lie. God help her, she knew it.

"I've been to a saloon or two," he readily confessed, "but that was business."

"I'll just bet it was."

"So long as I've got you waiting for me, sweet hellion, I'll be hanging my hat right here at Glorieta." His mouth twitched again as he opened the door and blew out the flame.

"You're feeling awfully pleased with yourself, aren't you?" she accused, bridling at the look of wholly masculine satisfaction on his face.

"Damn straight." He caught her up against him when she tried to step through the doorway. His eyes gleamed warmly down at her in the darkness, and his voice brimmed with a captivating earnestness when he declared, "I feel whole again, Claire. For the first time in six years, living's a pleasure instead of a chore."

"It—it's purely physical." Her argument lacked any real conviction, even to her own ears.

"You've got a lot to learn."

"And I suppose you think *you're* the one who's going to teach me." She tried to pull free, but he held fast.

"You've already proven yourself an apt and willing pupil," he pointed out.

"Why, you—"

"I know. I'm an arrogant, overbearing, cocksure son of a bitch." His tone became little more than a whisper as he slowly, purposefully, lowered his head toward hers. "But I love you more than life itself. And there's not a blasted thing you can do about it." The kiss he gave her was so tender and beguiling that, once again, she felt her blood turn to liquid fire in her veins.

When he finally released her, she spun about and raced almost frantically back across the yard to the house. She couldn't have said what frightened her most—Rand's feelings or her own. But either way, she knew the moment of truth had come.

Procrastination would only yield regret. And if there was one thing she'd had her fill of, it was regret.

A plan took shape in her mind as she climbed beneath the covers of her bed and heaved a long, ragged sigh. "Come tomorrow," she whispered. It was a vow she meant to keep . . . even if her heart ached inexplicably at the thought of what lay ahead.

Chapter 11

Gathering up the full skirts of her two-piece traveling suit of robin's egg blue, Claire allowed the driver to assist her into the stagecoach. The morning sunlight streamed in through the open windows on either side of the battered old Concord as she sank down upon the worn leather seat. A sharp frown creased her brow, and her gaze brimmed with mingled impatience and apprehension while it flickered across the bustling, dust-choked width of Parmalee's Main Street.

Confound it, she swore inwardly, if only she had been able to travel to Dallas via the rails. It would have been faster and a dozen—no, a *hundred* times more comfortable. But there wouldn't be another train coming through until Saturday. And she couldn't wait that long. Not after she had made up her mind to go. Not after she had finally called forth the devil-may-care gumption to do what she should have done six years ago.

She had confided her true plans to no one except Sadie, who had in all good conscience warned her against such "rashness." To Sully, she had simply announced her intention to pay a visit to an old friend for a couple of days. He had raised no further questions when she tied her carpetbag behind her saddle and mounted up to ride off alone. Yet he had briefly detained her with a startling and—in his view, at least—quite generous proposal.

"You want me to get rid of him while you're gone?"

"Who?" she asked, feigning ignorance.

"Who the gol-durned hell . . . *Logan*," he clarified, with his usual irascibility.

"Leave it be, Sully." Her eyes clouding in secret guilt, she battled the sudden impulse to tell him everything. "He'll be gone soon enough."

"Sometimes, you ain't got the sense God gave a mule."

"And *you're* just too mean to live." She abruptly reined about.

"Females," he muttered in her wake. But his peppery tone had been tempered with a deep and genuine affection.

Luckily there had been no sign of Rand as she had ridden away. She had arrived in town a full quarter of an hour before the stage was scheduled to depart. Graham Cooper had agreed to stable her horse while she was away, although the outrageous amount he was charging her for the privilege had made her regret declining Micah's offer to ride along with her that morning.

She had left Sadie and Micah with instructions to fetch the supplies on Saturday if she hadn't returned by then. It was difficult to predict how long her business in Dallas would take; she could only hope that the attorney, Mr. Templeton, would be able to expedite things a bit. The sooner the whole thing was over with, the better.

Leaning back against the seat, she released a sigh and closed her eyes for a moment. Why did her heart feel so heavy? She was doing the right thing . . . wasn't she? Rand Logan would bedevil her to the end of her days if she let him. It would be impossible to trust him after all he had done. Even if she *were* inclined to give him the second chance he was so all-fired determined to take, there was no way she could ever be sure of him. How could she believe his love—or whatever it was he felt for her—would last forever? She could end up just like before. Only, it would be worse this time. *Much worse.*

Why, oh, why was she still plagued by this strange, accursed temptation to scramble down out of the coach and ride hell-bent for leather back to Glorieta?

"Well, I'll be—" Lydia Cassidy's snappish voice suddenly broke in on her reverie. "If it isn't Claire Parmalee!"

Claire's eyes flew wide. She watched as Lydia, with Jane Willis hot on her heels, flung open the door and hoisted herself inside. They were both dressed in their Sunday best, their hair pinned up tightly beneath their bonnets and their eyes widening in surprise at the sight of her.

"My goodness, Claire. What a coincidence!" remarked Jane, her voice holding at least a small note of pleasure. "Are you on your way to Denton, too?"

"No." She gave an inward groan. *Of all people,* she silently lamented. It was beyond belief that these two women would just happen to be traveling on the stage that day. Fate was toying with her again.

"We're callin' on my sister," Lydia proclaimed, settling her calico-clad bulk on the seat opposite. "She's got five daughters, and not a blessed one of them willin' to help her when she's feelin' poorly. Where are you headed?"

"Dallas." She swept her skirts aside in order to make room for Jane, forcing a polite little smile to her lips. Although she could tell they were waiting for her to elaborate, she did not.

"You weren't at church on Sunday," Jane noted, closing and latching the wooden door.

"I know," she replied. Her eyes lit briefly with wry amusement. She lifted a hand to readjust the simple straw hat perched atop her head. The driver gave the last call just then and cracked the whip above the horses' heads.

The three passengers clutched at the leather straps hanging from above. The stagecoach moved forward with a sudden lurch, a cloud of dust following as the wheels bounced and rolled over the street. Horses and pedestrians scattered like so many chickens. In no time at all, the town was only a speck in the distance.

"I heard tell Reverend Mueller was seen drivin' back from your place yesterday," said Lydia, raising her voice to be heard above the creak and rattle of the coach. Her pale blue eyes narrowed angrily when Claire offered no comment. "It ain't proper, him payin' so much attention to that Bishop woman."

"He was *dancing* with her at the social!" Jane exclaimed, obviously still scandalized.

"What would you rather he had been doing with

her?" Claire retorted impulsively. Jane gasped and turned beet red.

"You're a fine one to be talkin' so bold, Claire Parmalee," Lydia admonished, with a derisive glower. "You and that new hired hand of yours. In *my* day, it would've been downright indecent for a girl to go ridin' off into the night alone with a man like that!"

"Yes, but this isn't your day. And I'm no longer a girl, remember?" She smiled to herself, wondering again how they would react if they knew just how far she had left girlhood behind. "Besides, what I do—and with whom—is my own business. It's high time you and everyone else in Parmalee realized that."

"You've changed of late," accused Lydia. "And I swear, it's been gettin' worse ever since Jake Parker—"

"Mr. Parker has nothing whatsoever to do with it," Claire denied, almost too emphatically.

"Well then, that's a good thing," Lydia countered. Her mouth curved into a smile of knowing, malicious satisfaction. "Seein' as how Graham Cooper came across him down at the saloon the other night with one of those painted floozies sprawled all over him like ants on sugar."

Claire tensed, her eyes kindling while hot color sprang to her cheeks. *It's only business,* Rand had assured her. She offered up another silent curse and tightened her hold on the small floral-embroidered bag in her lap.

"A man like that can't ever be trusted." Jane sighed, unaware that she was echoing Claire's thoughts exactly.

"Tate Jenner's the steady type, all right," Lydia pronounced. Her opinion of him had undergone a sudden and remarkable transformation. "'Course, I don't suppose it matters none. You're still married to that other feller, even if he did up and run off. Don't go thinkin' everyone around here's forgotten about *that*."

"Maybe he'll come back someday," Jane suggested hopefully. "Or maybe he'll turn up dead. Then you can—"

"Then you can finally settle down and stop making such a spectacle of yourself," the plump, gray-haired matron interjected, lifting her chin to a stern and queenly angle. "Folks have had just about enough of your tomfoolery. All that carryin' on at the social the other night. You ought to be ashamed, goadin' those two young roosters to fightin' over you that way!"

"Mr. Parker might be something of a rascal," Jane murmured thoughtfully, "but he sure is a good-looking one. I wonder if he's set his sights on anyone yet. There's a lot of women in this town who'd be more than happy to spend time with him, even if he is the sort who'd leave them none the wiser."

"You wouldn't have to look far to find one of those women," Lydia opined, casting a significant nod in Claire's direction.

Claire did not rise to the bait. She turned her fiery, preoccupied gaze toward the passing countryside and tried to ignore the doubts that were plaguing her with more intensity than ever. She should never have come. . . . But no, she had to do *something*. She had certainly threatened to often enough this past week. Whether or not Mr. Templeton would agree to help her seek a divorce, she must at least try and ensure that Glorieta remained under her control alone.

Husband or no husband, she'd be hanged if she'd let Rand Logan take over. *Only one of us can be the boss,* he had said. No doubt, he would rule her and everyone else with an iron hand if he got the chance. The prospect of answering to him day in and day out made her see red. Yet, the prospect of falling asleep in his arms every night was anything but disagreeable. . . .

"We're slowin' down," Lydia suddenly observed, with a frown. "Why are we slowin' down?"

"It might be that one of the horses has thrown a shoe," offered Jane.

"We'll be late gettin' in, as usual!"

"Don't worry, Lydia. I've brought a whole basket of food."

Drawn back to the present, Claire hastily ducked her head out the window and was startled to see three riders blocking the road. Their faces were concealed by white cotton hoods. And they were brandishing rifles.

She drew in her breath upon a gasp, her eyes widening and her heart leaping in alarm as the stagecoach driver slowed the team to a halt.

"Throw down your guns!" one of the three horsemen shouted tersely. His voice was muffled by the fabric of his hood, but Claire could have sworn she had heard it before.

"Lord have mercy! what—?" Lydia started to question.

"A holdup!" Jane said harshly, her own horror-stricken gaze flying toward the front of the coach.

"Now the strongbox!" came the order from outside.

There was no time for discussion. In the next instant, the door was flung open.

"Out!" the hooded robber directed, punctuating his command with a jerk of the revolver he had just drawn from his holster.

Terrified, Jane began screaming. Lydia clamped a protective arm about the younger woman's shoulders and glared defiantly at the man.

"Can't you see there's only us three women in here?" she charged.

"Shut up, *Grandma,* and get out!"

"Do as he says," Claire advised. Her outward composure belied the fear deep within her. Failing to notice the way the robber's eyes shot to her in surprise, she gathered up her skirts and climbed down from the coach. While Lydia and Jane wisely followed her example, she looked about. Her anxious, searching gaze lit upon the man who still sat astride his horse.

He stiffened at the sight of her, his eyes narrowing to mere slits beneath his hood.

"Let's go!" he ground out. His voice sounded much lower than before.

"But we ain't—" protested the gunman who was trying to hoist the strongbox onto his horse's back.

"I said let's go!"

The other two obediently mounted up now. Leaving the strongbox behind in their haste to be off, they reined about and spurred their horses into a frenzied gallop across the sunlit prairie. The guard riding in the "shotgun" position atop the stagecoach immediately scrambled down to retrieve his weapon, but it was too late.

Claire released a long, pent-up breath and leaned back against the coach while her heart pounded erratically. She gazed toward the spot where the robbers had disappeared, wondering why they had left in such a hurry.

"Don't you dare faint, Jane Willis!" Lydia's shrill-toned voice rose in the air. She slapped lightly at the younger woman's flushed cheeks and scowled when Jane's legs gave evidence of collapsing beneath her.

"You ladies all right?" the driver twisted about to ask.

"Yes," Claire hastened to assure him. "We're all right."

"Speak for yourself!" snapped Lydia. Motioning to the guard, she instructed him to lift the swooning Jane back up into the coach. "Set her down. Careful now!"

"I'll fetch some water," Claire offered.

The driver quickly secured the reins and climbed down to join her at the rear of the coach. He untied the dusty canvas tarpaulin over the boot, frowning as he rummaged about for a canteen.

"What in tarnation spooked 'em away like that?" he muttered, half to himself. He had been a whipster for nigh on to eight years; he was well accustomed to the hazards of the job. Yet today was the first time anyone had held him up and then changed their minds about the whole thing. His eyes suddenly moved to Claire's face. "Seems to me it was when they saw you they decided to hightail it out of here."

"Me?" Claire replied in astonishment. "Why on earth—?"

"Maybe they got a soft spot for a pretty woman. Whatever made 'em leave, I thank God for it. I didn't fancy havin' my box stole and my carcass shot full of holes." He handed her the canteen and strode away to have a word with the guard.

Claire stared after him for several long moments, then hastened back up into the coach with the water. Jane was soon revived, and they were on their way once more.

They rolled into the busy little town of Denton only twenty minutes behind schedule. Lydia, with a pale and sniffling Jane trailing close behind, marched into the stage office to complain loud and long about the ordeal they had just been through. Claire accepted her carpet-bag from the driver, assured him once more that she had suffered no lasting damage, and stepped into the small, cluttered office. Frowning at the realization that the connecting stage to Dallas would not depart for half an hour yet, she sank down onto a bench near the front door and took off her hat.

She was more shaken by the attempted robbery than she cared to admit. It had all happened so fast. The voice of the man who had apparently been the leader of the trio kept echoing in her mind. . . .

"The sheriff'll want to talk to you before you leave," the guard said, approaching her with a somber expression. He was a big, burly man who looked entirely capable of holding his own against anyone. Yet he hadn't been able to hold his own when facing down the barrel of a Winchester rifle.

"But why?" Claire asked in puzzlement. "You saw a good deal more than I did."

"I know. But he said I was to fetch you down to the jail just the same."

She nodded mutely in acquiescence, rising to her feet

and taking up her carpetbag as she followed the man out of the office. Behind her, Lydia continued to harangue the young, pale-faced clerk while Jane threatened to faint again.

The jail lay only a short distance down the boardwalk. Claire's eyes were wide—and filled with more than a hint of trepidation—when she swept through the doorway. She told herself there was no reason to be nervous, but she couldn't help feeling uneasy.

Once inside, a tall, auburn-haired man not much above thirty smiled at her as he rose from his seat behind an old oak desk. He gave her escort a silent nod of dismissal. The guard left them alone, closing the door on his way out.

"I'm John Malone, the sheriff."

"Claire Parmalee," she murmured in response. Her gaze made a quick, encompassing sweep of the interior. She caught a glimpse of the iron-barred cells that lay through a locked door in the center of the wall. There was another door, narrower than the other, in the right-hand corner.

"Parmalee," the sheriff repeated. His eyes lit with immediate recognition of the name. "Why, you're—"

"Yes. My father was Samuel Parmalee."

"Please, Miss Parmalee, have a seat." He indicated the chair on the other side of the desk. She sank gratefully down into it, set her carpetbag on the floor, and watched as he resumed his own seat. His eyes shifted toward the corner doorway before returning to meet hers again. "What can you tell me about the attempted robbery?"

"Not very much, I'm afraid," she replied, her hands

clasping the straw bonnet in her lap. "I'm sure you've already heard that there were three men, all of them wearing hoods. They left without taking anything."

"The guard said they lit out in a hurry once you and the other two women stepped down from the coach."

"Yes. I suppose they were struck by a sudden attack of gallantry." Her mouth curved into a faint smile of irony at the thought.

"Did you hear any of them speak?"

"Yes, I did. But they didn't say much."

"And is it possible you'd recognize their voices if you heard them again?"

"No," she answered, shaking her head. A dull flush crept up to her face; she hastily looked away.

"Tell me, ma'am—why were you traveling from Parmalee to Denton?"

"I'm on my way to Dallas, actually. I—I have business to attend to there."

"Personal business?"

"I fail to see what that has to do with—"

She broke off as the door in the corner suddenly swung open. Her eyes flew across the room, only to widen in stunned disbelief at the sight of the man who stood so tall and handsome—and forebodingly solemn—while staring back at her.

"What are *you* doing here?" she asked indignantly. Her color deepened to a fiery, guilty red. Springing to her feet, she instinctively moved behind the chair and squared her shoulders.

"The sheriff and I are old friends," Rand told her, with deceptive nonchalance. He sauntered forward, an unfathomable little smile playing about his lips while his gaze, glinting like cold steel, caught and held the emerald luminosity of hers. "Malone, it seems you've just had the pleasure of meeting my wife."

"Seems that way, all right," the other man drawled. He, too, had pulled himself upright and now surveyed the two of them with a perplexed frown. "Would you mind telling me what's going on, Logan?" he appealed to Rand.

"Maybe Claire can enlighten us." He stopped directly before her, the look in his eyes promising retribution for her defiance. "Personal business in Dallas?"

"Yes," she confirmed with a spirited toss of her head, then quickly turned the tables on him. "But never mind that. How is it you just happen to be here in Denton when—?"

"I got word there might be a robbery."

"You got word?" She gaped up at him in further surprise.

"Evidently, I was misinformed," he conceded, his eyes darkening.

"Not exactly—" Malone began. Claire shot the sheriff a look. He stopped in mid-sentence.

"That informer of yours must have been mistaken," the sheriff remarked dryly.

"Maybe. It won't take long to find out."

"I don't understand," Claire uttered, rounding on him accusingly once more. "You're supposed to be back at the ranch."

"So are you."

"Maybe I should leave you two alone to sort this out," Sheriff Malone suggested, with a grin. "Just be sure and keep your voices down." He gave a curt nod back toward the cells while adding, "Ol' Jed Harwell's still sleeping off a bender, but he might come to and find whatever it is you have to say to each other mighty interesting."

"Point taken," said Rand. "I'll be back." He reached for Claire at last. "Come on."

"Where are we going?"

"To have a talk. Your plans have changed," he decreed, his fingers closing like a vise about her arm. She opened her mouth to argue, but thought better of it and allowed him to lead her toward the doorway.

"I might have some more questions for you later, Mrs. Logan," the sheriff cautioned.

"I prefer 'Miss Parmalee,' " she tossed back at him over her shoulder. Rand exchanged a significant glance with his old friend before propelling her outside and closing the door. "My carpetbag," she cried, suddenly remembering that she had left it on the jail house floor.

"I'll get it later," Rand promised. She suddenly jerked free, her eyes ablaze as she faced him on the boardwalk. Fortunately there was no one within easy earshot at the moment.

"I don't want to talk," she declared in an emotion-charged undertone. "There's nothing to say. I've made up my mind, Rand Logan. And I'll be hanged if I'll let you stop me."

"I'll provide the rope," he parried, although there wasn't so much as a trace of humor in either his manner or his voice. He seized her arm again and urged her along with him toward the other end of the main street. It was nearing time for the noonday meal. The shops and offices were for the most part empty, the air filled with the mingling aromas of wood smoke, coffee, and horses.

"Where are you taking me?" Claire demanded furiously.

"To the hotel."

"If you're not going to allow me to continue on to Dallas, then you could at least take me home."

"I could. But I won't."

"Will you please let go of me? I have a perfect right to—"

"The only rights you have are the ones I choose to grant you. And as it stands now," he warned in a low voice edged with barely controlled fury, "I'm not in the mood to be generous."

Her expression was downright murderous in response, but he paid it no mind as he led her inside the whitewashed, two-story building with a sign proclaiming it to be THE BLUE STAR HOTEL. She had stayed there once before; it was where she had first met Sadie. Instead of choosing a secluded corner of the spacious, red-carpeted lobby as she had expected, Rand started up the staircase.

"Where . . . ? I thought we were going to talk," she pointed out in angry confusion.

"We are. In my room."

"You have a room here?" Her eyes widened in surprise once more.

"I do." His mouth twitched briefly. "I keep one just in case." With no further explanation, he unlocked the door, opened it, and pulled her inside.

"What do you mean, 'just in case'?" Finally released, she rubbed at her arm and watched as he closed the door. There was an air of perilous calm about him. She swallowed a sudden lump in her throat, cursing the fear gnawing at her as she awaited the inevitability of his wrath.

The room in which they stood was small yet charmingly decorated. Red-checkered curtains hung at the open window, a patchwork quilt covered the mattress of the carved, four-poster oak bed, while the bare wooden floor had recently been polished with beeswax. A pitcher and bowl sat atop the washstand in the corner, with a mirror hanging above. The bathroom, Claire knew, lay only a short walk down the hall. *All the comforts of home,* she mused resentfully.

"By heaven, Claire—" Rand ground out, turning to confront her now.

"Is this where you conduct your business whenever you're down this way?" She cut him off with biting sarcasm. Her gaze kindled at the thought. Jealousy overrode the apprehension she had felt only a moment ago. "I've heard of your popularity at the saloons back in Parmalee. Maybe you have an equal number of 'associates' here in Denton."

"You're the only one I care to associate with," he avowed grimly. Then he went on to demand, "What the hell were you doing on that stage?"

"I thought it preferable to walking all the way to Dallas!"

"You were going to see that lawyer friend of your father's." It was a statement, not a question.

"Perhaps," she retorted.

"I told you—*there will be no divorce.* Once and for all, get that through your thick, pretty head and stop acting like a fool." He strode forward to tower ominously above her, his handsome face thunderous and his cobalt blue eyes smoldering down into the green fire of hers. "Damn it, woman! You might have been killed!"

"How the devil was I supposed to know what would happen? You might have told me. For heaven's sake, Rand Logan. You might have bothered to confide in me a bit. If I'd had any notion at all that someone was planning—"

"If you'd stayed put where you belong, you wouldn't have been in danger," he ground out. His hands closed about her shoulders, and he yanked her up hard against him while battling his more violent instincts. "I could beat you for disobeying me, Claire."

"Why do you have to be so all-fired mysterious about everything?" she shot back, undaunted. Her eyes narrowed, searching his face. "It was Will Jenner who told you about the holdup, wasn't it? That's why he was at the ranch last night."

"Yes." His grip relaxed a bit, and he frowned again. "Until now, I'd hoped he would keep his part of the bargain."

"What bargain?"

"Information in exchange for a certain degree of immunity."

"Immunity?" She swallowed hard. "You know who those men are, don't you?" she asked, though she feared the answer. "Oh, Rand. Is Tate—?"

"He is."

"Dear Lord!" she gasped, the color draining from her face. She suddenly felt very sick at heart. *Tate*. It was difficult to believe he could be ruthless enough—he had always been so kind and helpful—and yet, she told herself numbly, the Tate Jenner she had seen lately was different from the one she had known these past several months. Maybe it was the real man coming out from behind the facade he had created. Maybe, just maybe, she had *wanted* to be deceived all this time.

She recalled the first day, more than a week ago, when Rand had arrived at Glorieta with his badge and his questions. Even then, she had thought of Tate. And that voice she had heard today . . . it had sounded very familiar.

"He's been the prime suspect from the very beginning," Rand went on to confide. His hands fell away from her shoulders; his gaze softened with compassion at the evidence of her pain. "He and his brothers. But we didn't have enough proof to convict them. We still don't."

"But what about Will?" Her head spinning, she made no mention of her own suspicions. "Wouldn't his testimony be enough?"

"It will take more than his word." He turned away, wandering across to the window and sweeping aside the curtain to stare down at the virtually deserted street below. "He's not exactly a willing informer. It required a bit of 'persuasion' to make him cooperate. In short, I offered him a deal he couldn't pass up."

"I—I still can't believe he would turn against his own brothers like this," she murmured ruefully.

"He had no choice," explained Rand, facing her again. His gaze burned across into hers. "And he's trying to save them, Claire. He doesn't know who I really am. But he does believe I have highly placed connections back at the Rangers' headquarters. Once I told him that an order had gone out to bring in the robbers dead or alive, he agreed to help. He decided it was better to see them behind bars for a few years instead of six feet under the ground."

"But what if you're wrong?" Her voice held a desperate hopefulness. "What if Will is lying?"

"Why would he do that?" He shook his head and asserted quietly, "No, he isn't lying. It's them. They've covered their tracks pretty well. Even Will didn't know until after the last robbery. He's been kept in the dark. I guess Tate's trying to protect him, in his own misguided way. But as soon as Will discovered what was going on, it didn't take him long to start talking."

For Claire, the horrible realization had begun to sink in. Tate Jenner was a cold-blooded thief, a man who had nearly killed a guard during a robbery a few days earlier. What else was he capable of doing? she wondered, shuddering at the thought.

"What will you do now?" she asked Rand unevenly.

"Wait for them to make their next move."

"And when will that be?"

"Soon, I hope." He closed the distance between them once more, his hands lifting gently to her arms. "I'm sorry, Claire. I know it must hurt to find out Jenner's not the friend you thought he was. I would have told you everything before now, but—"

"—you didn't trust me," she finished for him. Her eyes clouded with both sadness and reproach.

"In a way," he admitted. "I wasn't sure how far you'd go to protect him."

"And you're sure now?" She couldn't prevent a note of bitterness from stealing into her voice.

"I'm sure."

"He asked me to marry him," she recalled, half to herself. "I wonder if he ever meant it at all."

"He meant it," said Rand. His gaze darkened anew. "You were never part of the plan. I don't think he counted on falling in love."

"Did you keep warning me away from him because of what he's done, or because you were jealous?"

"Both." He glimpsed the sudden shadow crossing her face.

"Would you—would you still have come back if you hadn't been assigned to the investigation?" she said, her voice faltering, her breath catching in her throat. It had nothing to do with Tate Jenner or the robberies, of course. Nothing at all. And she had asked him once before. Yet she felt an urgent need for reassurance, an urgent need to hear that she was more important to him than duty or honor or anything else.

"I'd have crossed through hell itself," he declared, his tone wonderfully low and vibrant in the stillness of the room.

She read the truth in his eyes.

Her heart stirred wildly. She trembled, flooded with warmth and a lightness of spirit that cast out all but the most persistent of doubts. For the first time in six long years, she felt that Rand Logan might just have meant it when he'd said that he would never stop loving her.

"Claire." Her name was an endearment upon his lips. She gazed up at him, her eyes wide and glistening with sudden tears.

"Oh, Rand. I—" she whispered, only to break off when a sob rose in her throat. She offered no resistance as his arms encircled her with their hard warmth. He pulled her close while the tears spilled over to course down the flushed smoothness of her cheeks. She wasn't sure why she was crying. Maybe it was because of Tate Jenner. Maybe it was because she was so very tempted to throw caution to the winds and expose herself to the danger of heartbreak once more. Whatever the reason, she rested within her husband's strong, comforting embrace and let the tears come.

She didn't weep for long. And when she finally raised her head and withdrew a handkerchief from the pocket of her skirt, she saw that Rand was smiling softly down at her.

"I've gotten your shirt wet," she murmured, feeling uncomfortable beneath his tender gaze.

"It'll dry." He grew serious in the next instant, his deep-timbred voice sending a shiver down her spine when he asked, "Why did you do it, Claire?"

"Do what?"

"Light out for Dallas."

"I—I was going to talk to Mr. Templeton about the ranch," she stammered evasively. She drew away now and moved to the window. "I wanted his advice."

"Glorieta is yours. I'll make no claims upon it."

"How do I know I can trust you about that?" she countered. "Or about anything else, for that matter?"

"I've never lied to you."

"Haven't you?" She whirled to face him, her own gaze stormy again. "What about those vows you took six years ago?"

"I'm keeping them." The merest hint of a smile tugged at his lips. "You promised to obey me, remember?"

"Yes, but that was before—"

"No 'buts' about it." He cut her off authoritatively. "I warned you to forget about a divorce, Claire."

"Yes, and I warned *you* that I wouldn't let you come waltzing back into my life after all this time and take up right where you left off!"

"I've already done that."

Her face flamed at the implication in his tone—and the light of devilment in his eyes.

"I've got to have a word with Malone again," he suddenly announced, crossing to the doorway. "I'll fetch your carpetbag while I'm there."

"And what am I supposed to do while you're gone?"

"Stay put."

"Absolutely not," she proclaimed. "I'll take the next stage back to Parmalee. There's one leaving at two o'clock. I should get home in time for—"

"We won't be heading back until tomorrow," he told her quietly.

"You mean you intend for us to spend the *night* here?" The prospect sent a chaotic whirl of emotions— most of them quite pleasurable—racing through her.

"I do." Opening the door, he paused to give her an intense, cautionary look. "Do as I say, Claire. You're free to go about the town. But don't even think about leaving."

"So I'm supposed to play the meek and adoring little wife, waiting for her man to come home from a hard day's work?" she demanded, with angry sarcasm. "Will you want me to have supper ready from here on out as well?"

"No." His smile this time was devastating. "I've tasted your cooking before."

If she'd had something handy, she would have thrown it at him.

Once he had gone, she surrendered to the temptation to take a long, soothing bath. And after that, she ventured forth to wander along Denton's main street. Her entire world had consisted of Glorieta and Parmalee; it was a refreshing change to spend a day elsewhere. Or it *would* have been, if not for the fact that she was still greatly troubled about Tate.

How would it all end? she wondered, heaving a ragged sigh. On the one hand, she wanted to see justice done. But on the other, she couldn't bear the thought of someone who had been such a good friend suffering through years of incarceration—or worse. He deserved it, of course. He and his brothers would certainly reap what they had sown. Nevertheless, her throat constricted painfully at the thought of what was to come.

When her stomach reminded her that she had eaten nothing since early that morning, she turned her steps toward a small, homey restaurant only a short distance from the jail. She muttered an oath underneath her breath when she spied Lydia and Jane walking farther down the boardwalk. Hoping to avoid them altogether, she hastily turned away. But it was too late. They had seen her.

"Claire!" Jane called out, lifting a hand in greeting.

There was no escape now. She had little choice but to speak to them. Tensing, she watched as they advanced upon her at a brisk, determined pace. Their skirts swayed to-and-fro, their high-top laced boots thumping atop the dusty wooden planks.

"You missed your stage," Lydia observed unnecessarily.

"I know. I—I decided not to go."

"Is it any wonder?" said Jane, visibly shuddering at the memory of their shared ordeal. She clutched her drawstring bag close to her bosom, as if hooded robbers were standing ready to pounce on her there and then. "Lydia and I are taking the two o'clock stage straight back to Parmalee. I don't care if I never travel more than a mile away from home again my entire life!"

"You'll be going with us, I expect," Lydia remarked, her features looking sour as ever beneath the stiff brim of her bonnet.

"No," Claire replied evenly. "I'm staying on here for a night or two."

"In Denton? Why on earth would you—?" Jane started to ask, only to fall abruptly silent and widen her eyes in astonishment when she saw Rand approaching them. Claire tossed a quick glance back over her shoulder, then groaned inwardly.

"Mrs. Cassidy. Miss Willis. Miss Parmalee," Rand offered, tugging off his hat and favoring the three of them with a brief, amiable smile.

"Where'd you come from?" Lydia demanded sharply.

"Aren't you supposed to be back at the ranch, *Mr. Parker?*" Claire hastened to intervene. Her eyes held a silent warning.

"Yes, ma'am." His outward manner was impeccably respectful. "But I had some business to take care of."

"It looks like you came prepared to stay awhile, Mr. Parker," Jane noted, her curious gaze falling toward the carpetbag he carried in one hand.

"It looks that way all right," came his noncommittal response.

"Now that's a right strange coincidence"—Lydia sneered—"seein' as how our Miss Claire's suddenly taken it in mind to do the same."

"Well then, maybe we'll run into each other again." He settled his hat atop his head once more.

"Oh, Claire," whispered Jane, anxiously drawing her aside, "you can't stay on *now*! Why, what will folks say if they hear you and Mr. Parker—?"

"I wasn't born yesterday, young man," Lydia told Rand scathingly. Her eyes narrowed to mere slits as they shot to Claire and back.

"No, ma'am. I can see that," he replied. Claire was the only one who caught the note of unholy amusement in his voice.

"Matter of fact," Lydia continued, while her suspicions took root in fertile ground, "that bag you're holdin' looks an awful lot like the one Miss Parmalee brought with her on the stage this mornin'."

"Why, it most certainly does!" Jane seconded, her scandalized gaze flying to Claire again.

"She's a married woman, Mr. Parker," Lydia saw fit to inform him.

"Oh, for heaven's sake!" Claire cried in exasperation. "It isn't what you think." That was true enough, she thought, her temper flaring. "But even if it *were*, it's my affair and not yours."

"I couldn't have put it any better myself," the older

woman commented with a look of smug, malicious satisfaction.

"Why, Lydia!" Jane gasped.

"Good day," Claire ground out. She whirled about and—on a sudden and regrettably wicked impulse—snatched the carpetbag from Rand's grasp. With her back proudly erect, she marched toward the hotel.

"Ladies," Rand said, with a curt nod at Lydia and Jane. Neither of them spoke. Shocked into uncharacteristic silence, they stood with their mouths wide open as he strode away in pursuit of Claire.

He caught up with her just before she sailed through the lobby's front doorway. His hand closed about her arm, gently pulling her to a halt.

"Forget about them, Claire," he said, his eyes glowing down into the fiery depths of hers. "They don't matter."

"Maybe not to *you,* they don't," she shot back. "You're a man. You'll allowed to do as you please. Yes, by heaven, you're allowed to do whatever you want and damn the consequences!"

"We don't have to stay on in Parmalee. We can start over someplace else."

"Are you out of your mind?" Recalling that they were in far less than private surroundings, she lowered her voice before asking, "Do you really believe I'd leave Glorieta and everything I've worked so hard for all these years?"

"What I believe," he declared somberly, "is that one day you'll realize you've got something even more important."

"And what the devil is that supposed to mean?"

"You'd have to search high and low for a man who loves you as much as I do. And you'd never find him. Not in a million years."

A sudden weakness of the knees struck her. She might well have attempted a response, but Rand turned on his booted heel and left her alone. After staring after him for several long moments, she gathered up her skirts and disappeared inside the hotel.

Darkness had already fallen by the time he returned.

Claire sat in a chair beside the window, reading from an old, leather-bound volume of poetry she had discovered on the bedside table. She had visited nearly every shop in town, had finally procured a meal in the hotel's own restaurant, and had still found herself with an abundance of time on her hands.

She leapt to her feet when the door swung open. Rand stepped into the lamplit room and closed the door again. Without a word, he removed his hat, hung it on one of the wall pegs, and bent his tall frame down upon the edge of the bed to tug off his boots.

"Where have you been?" Claire demanded, sounding every bit like a wife.

"Don't tell me you were worried?" His mouth curved into a faint smile of irony as he stood and unbuttoned his shirt.

"As a matter of fact, I *was*." The words tumbled from her lips before she could stop them.

"I'm glad to hear it."

"Your hair is wet," she noted, frowning.

"I took a bath." His eyes filled with a roguish light when he offered, "I'd be more than happy to take another one if you'd share it with me."

"Hellfire and damnation, Rand Logan! Don't you ever think of anything else?" Coloring hotly, she folded her arms beneath her breasts and hurried to change the subject. "I still don't see why we had to stay here tonight." It had occurred to her to defy him, to hire a mount from the livery stable and head back to Glorieta on her own. But her instincts had warned against it. "It's ridiculous to waste perfectly good money this way."

"Sometimes, 'Miss Claire,' you're a bit slow on the uptake," Rand teased softly, peeling off his shirt. He was clad only in his denim trousers now. His hard-muscled chest and arms gleamed bronze in the lamplight.

Claire felt a delicious warmth stealing over her. She quickly sought refuge in anger once more.

"According to Lydia Cassidy, you were seen enjoying the company of a 'painted floozy' down at the saloon the other night. What the devil makes you think I'd ever let you touch me again after hearing that?"

"You know better than to listen to rumors." He moved toward her, his gaze traveling boldly, significantly, over her clothed form. She took an instinctive step backward.

"So you're denying it then?"

"No."

"No?" Incredulous, she stared up at him and tried to control the jealousy burning in her again. "Do you mean to tell me—?"

"What I mean to tell you, Mrs. Logan," he broke in, with another ghost of a smile, "is that appearances can be deceiving."

"I'll never be able to trust you," she charged, her wayward pulse leaping as it always did whenever he was near.

"You can do anything if you want it bad enough."

"You've said that before!"

"And I'll keep on saying it until you believe it." He drew her against him now. "Just as I'll keep doing this," he murmured huskily, his warm lips descending upon hers for a long, passionate kiss. When he raised his head again, she was flushed and breathless. "And this." His hand closed gently upon the fullness of her breast. "And this." He knelt before her, raking up her skirts and pulling her forward until his mouth was level with the triangle of delicate blonde curls between her thighs.

"Rand!" she gasped, profoundly shocked—and delighted—at the realization of what he meant to do.

Her fingers threaded within the damp brown thickness of his hair, her eyes sweeping closed and her moans urging on his hot, tantalizing caresses.

Finally he swept her up in his powerful arms and carried her to the bed. And before the night was through, she had secretly concluded that, whatever the cost of the hotel room, it had been money well spent.

Chapter 12

They headed back to Glorieta the next morning.

"What are you going to do about Will?" Claire asked, her arms holding Rand securely about the waist as she rode behind him. He had insisted that the two of them share his mount. She was happy to comply, since the day had dawned cool and damp, and she had neglected to bring a wrap. The warmth of his body against hers was a comfort. In more ways than one.

"Young Jenner and I are going to have a serious discussion," he announced wryly. He directed a quick glance up toward the cloud-choked sky before tugging the front brim of his hat lower. "There's always an outside chance his mistake wasn't intentional."

"Do you think Tate suspects him, then?"

"Maybe. Either way, this whole damn thing is about to bust wide open. Until it does, you're to keep quiet about everything I told you—understand?"

"I *do* have a brain, Rand Logan," she reminded him severely.

"Yeah, I know. That's the second thing I noticed about you." There was no mistaking the undercurrent of humor in his deep-timbred voice, but Claire chose to ignore it.

"I'm not at all certain I can behave in a normal manner toward Tate from now on," she admitted, frowning pensively. It seemed strange to think of exchanging pleasantries with someone so ruthless and unprincipled. God help her, why did it have to turn out to be Tate who had committed the robberies?

"You'll just have to do your best," advised Rand. His tone became quiet and commanding when he pronounced, "I don't want you mixed up in this any more than you already are, Claire. If Jenner says or does anything suspicious, you're to let me know. And under no circumstances are you to be alone with him again. Is that clear?"

She nodded mutely and heaved a sigh. Gazing about at the endless stretches of green, rolling plains, she found her thoughts drifting back to her confrontation with Lydia and Jane the day before. Her cheeks reddened faintly, and she cursed herself for having allowed her temper to get the better of her—again.

"The news of my latest 'indiscretion' is probably all over town by now," she lamented, scarcely realizing that she had done so aloud.

"They'll know the truth soon enough." He smiled, his hand moving to cover the both of hers. "There's no shame in spending the night with your husband."

"Yes, but as it stands now, I'm being branded an adulteress." She sighed again before remarking, "At least no one will call me a kissless bride anymore." Her insides melted at the sound of his low, resonant chuckle.

"You're far from that."

"At first," she impulsively confided, "everyone assumed my father had good reason for that shotgun wedding. But after a few months had passed, people stopped waiting for the anticipated evidence of my sins and started focusing on the fact that I had been abandoned on my wedding night."

"Better late than never."

"What do you mean?" She peered up at him, leaning forward to search his face.

"I mean, Mrs. Logan, that it's high time we gave the good people of Parmalee what they've been waiting for."

"How can you possibly suggest that?" she exclaimed indignantly, green eyes ablaze. "Why, I don't even know if you'll still be around tomorrow, much less in another year's time! And besides that, if I . . . if we . . . if there ever *were* to be a baby, it would have to be conceived in love!"

"My sentiments, exactly," he quipped, glancing back at her.

"You can get that look out of your eye, Rand Logan." Trying her very best to disregard the sudden lightheadedness plaguing her, she pulled herself primly erect and frowned once more. "Yes, by heaven, you can get it out right now, because I have no intention of starting a family until things are settled between us." In truth, the prospect filled her with a sweet inner warmth. *A child.*

"If memory serves me correct," he pointed out, "we've already tempted fate more than a few times. And in theory, at least, it only takes once."

"You'd like that, wouldn't you?" she accused, her

gaze narrowing. "Indeed, if I were to be kept barefoot and pregnant, you'd still be free to tomcat around!"

"Is that what you call it?"

"I don't know what *you* call it, but—"

"You'll have to learn to trust me, Claire," he maintained, sobering. "When this is all over with, I'll tell you everything you want to know. But, for now, you'll have to believe me when I say you've got no reason to worry."

"No reason to worry?" she echoed in disbelief. "You disappear from the ranch for hours on end, you frequent known hellholes, you're in a line of work that's notorious for making widows, and yet you expect me to sit back and forget about what's going on underneath my own nose?"

She had no idea how much her concern made his spirits soar. His blue eyes gleaming with both tenderness and triumph, he urged her arms more tightly about him.

"I never thought I'd be able to say it, Claire," he told her, his voice sounding wonderfully vibrant to her ears, "but I'm looking forward to the day when I can hang up my guns."

"No doubt, you'll find the life of a rancher too sedate after so many years of excitement and adventure," she argued weakly.

"Not a chance."

For the first time since his return, she found herself believing him. Not just *wanting* to believe him, but actually taking his words to heart. The realization threw her into further chaos. More than ever before, she felt torn. Torn between the past and the present . . . between the secret desire to dream of a future with him, and the fear that history would repeat itself.

Once they had reached Glorieta, Rand left her to explain her earlier-than-expected return to Sadie while he took himself off to town. She was surprised when she learned that Micah had ridden along with him, but she offered no comment about it when Sully brought her the news.

No one at the ranch had heard about the attempted stagecoach robbery yet. Claire related the whole story to Sadie (though she made no mention of Tate) before going about her chores for the day. The hours passed in a flurry of activity—cleaning, hoeing, organizing, and the like. After supper, she sat on the front porch with Sadie and Harmony and Wolf while twilight stole leisurely over the countryside. Her eyes lit with interest when she spied a familiar, canvas-topped buggy approaching the house.

"You didn't tell me the reverend was coming to call this evening," she teased Sadie.

"I—I wasn't sure he'd be able to make it," the pretty brunet stammered honestly. Blushing, she rose to her feet and raised a hand to pat at her softly upswept hair. She had donned her prettiest gown (just in case), and had even dared to put a bit of vanilla behind her ears.

"He probably just wants to tell us to come to church again," opined Harmony. Sitting on the top step, she did her best to drag a curry comb through the dog's thick and perpetually burr-spotted coat. "That's his job."

"True enough," Claire replied. She cast an affectionately knowing glance at the other woman. "But I don't think he's here on official 'preacher's business' this time."

Thomas, meanwhile, had driven the buggy to a halt in front of the house and climbed down. His gaze made immediate contact with the opal warmth of Sadie's. He swept the hat from his head as he started forward.

"Good evening, ladies. I hope you do not mind that I have dropped by unannounced once more."

"Of course not," Claire assured him. Her own eyes missed little of what was going on. "As a matter of fact, you're quite welcome to make a habit of it."

Gratefully accepting her offer to take a seat, he chose to settle himself on the porch swing beside Sadie. He was soon made comfortable with a glass of lemonade; he was further honored when Wolf shuffled across to sprawl at his feet.

"Did you come to invite us to another box social?" Harmony queried, hastening to retrieve the comb which was still tangled in the dog's thick brown fur.

"No. I am afraid not. But perhaps we will have another one soon."

"Were you visiting some of your flock out this way?" asked Claire. She watched as his eyes glowed with ironic amusement.

"Old Man Arbuckle conveyed a special greeting to me but an hour ago. Indeed, I am surprised I did not come to you with my poor trousers full of buckshot."

"Didn't anyone bother to warn you about him?" Sadie demanded, visibly appalled at his brush with disaster.

"Yes. But I am not a man easily deterred." His voice was brimming with such regard that she colored anew.

"Can we go for a ride in your buggy?" the little girl at his feet put forth boldly.

"Harmony!" Sadie was quick to admonish.

"An excellent idea, Miss Bishop," Thomas blithely encouraged. He smiled again as he turned to Sadie. "Perhaps, Mrs. Bishop, you yourself would care to accompany us. We will not travel far afield."

"There isn't enough room for the three of us," she protested lamely. "And it's getting dark."

"Still, I must insist." Setting aside his glass, he bent down, lifted a giggling Harmony in his arms, and rose to his full height. "This young lady will fit very nicely between us. As for the lateness of the hour—nothing would give me greater pleasure than to view the miracle of another sunset with two such fine companions."

"But what about Claire?"

"Go," Claire exhorted, standing and folding her arms across her chest. Her mouth curved into an arch smile. "For heaven's sake, go and have a good time. I'm more than accustomed to my own company by now. Sometimes, I even prefer it."

"Well, if you're sure . . ."

"That miracle won't wait forever."

Green eyes sparkling, she watched as the three of them climbed into the buggy and drove away. They had no sooner disappeared from view than Sully materialized at the right-hand corner of the porch.

"Been meanin' to talk to you all day," he proclaimed.

"What about?" She wandered back to the swing and sank down, her hand falling instinctively atop Wolf's shaggy head.

"Logan." He sauntered around to the front steps now,

his movements sure and easy in spite of his advancing years.

"Great balls of fire, Sullivan Greene," Claire muttered in exasperation, "I *told* you—"

"Let me have my say before you light into me." He cut her off testily.

"There's nothing more to say!"

"Then sit quiet and listen." He dragged the sweat-stained hat from his head and climbed up to lean against the porch column. His craggy, weather-beaten features took on an expression that Claire couldn't recall ever having seen before. If she didn't know him better, she'd have sworn he looked contrite about something. "When Logan first came back, I'd've just as soon put a rattle-snake in his pocket and asked him for a match."

"I do seem to recall a certain bit of 'unfriendliness' on your part," she remarked sarcastically.

"There's no need to go takin' that tone of voice with me," he scolded, with all the authority of someone who had known—and loved—her for nearly two decades. His eyes narrowed to mere slits, and he scowled darkly before confessing, "Dammit all to hell, girl—what I'm tryin' to tell you is I don't think that husband of yours is the yellow-backed rounder he used to be."

"And what happened to change your mind?" She sprang to her feet and charged forward to confront him squarely. "Why, only yesterday, you were still offering to get rid of him for me!"

"That was before I got me a report from the boss of the Rangers hisself."

"What do you mean, you got a report?" Her eyes grew round with incredulity, and she took a step backward while a slow, crooked smile spread across the old wrangler's face. "What kind of—?"

"Think you're the only one around here knows how to get things done?" he taunted in self-satisfaction. "I sent a telegram on down there to headquarters in San Antone. Took some time to get an answer, but it finally came."

"When?"

"Yesterday. After you'd lit out for wherever it was you were in such an all-fired hurry to get to."

"But . . . you hardly ever go into town anymore," she said, her head spinning.

"I made an *ex-cep-tion*," he enunciated, with another burst of ornery humor. "Don't you want to know what was in the report?"

"I'm sure you're chomping at the bit to tell me."

"All right then, I won't beat around the bush. He's not the same worthless son of a bitch who turned tail and ran six years ago." He paused for a moment, noisily cleared his throat, and slapped his hat against his leg. "Seems he's turned out to be a damn fine lawman. A real straight shooter, Claire. God's truth, I never thought he'd come to any good."

"Neither did I," she murmured, a faint smile tugging at her lips as her gaze met his again.

"That adjutant general feller says he's one of the best in the whole outfit."

"I see." Frowning thoughtfully, she turned away and crossed back to the swing. "So, all of a sudden you're ready to forgive and forget?"

"I didn't say that."

"Then what *are* you saying?" she challenged, whirling to face him again.

"Just that I'm not aimin' to short his stake rope."

"Sparing his life and accepting him as a permanent fixture here at Glorieta are two entirely different things."

"You plannin' to let him stay on?" he demanded sharply.

"Is the ranch big enough for the two of you?" she shot back. Before he could offer a reply, she heaved a long, quavering sigh and found herself confiding in him the way she had when she was a child. "To tell the truth, Sully, I don't know what I'm going to do. Rand claims he *wants* to stay on, to turn in his badge and settle down here, but I'm not at all certain he can do that. He's been on his own for so long. He's used to his freedom. How can a man like that be expected to put down roots?"

"I've heard it said it's better to wear out a couple of saddles before picking out a corral." In a rare display of affection, he lifted a dirty, rope-calloused hand to her shoulder. "Could be, Logan's already worn out his share of saddles. And there ain't a better corral in all of Texas."

"Your opinion's a bit slanted," she accused, her eyes shining softly while a sudden lump rose in her throat.

"Hell, yes." He drew away, pulled on his hat, and started back down the steps in the gathering darkness. "Decide what you will," he said, and continued talking as he headed toward the bunkhouse. "Just don't go tryin' to boot me out. I been here too damn long to start over somewheres else. Took me nigh on to twenty years to get you broke in."

"I still say nobody else would be fool enough to take you on!" Claire called after him in mock annoyance. She smiled again and gave an indulgent shake of her head before going inside the house.

Alone with her thoughts, she put some coffee on to boil, sat down at the kitchen table, and took off her shoes and stockings. It was only a short time later when the back door suddenly flung open. Startled, she jumped to her feet and watched as Micah strode inside.

"You've got to come with me, Miss Claire," he said, his features alarmingly grim.

"Why? What's happened?"

"Mr. Logan's been shot."

"Shot?" she echoed, her eyes growing very wide and filling with horror. Her heart seemed to stop; she could literally feel the color draining from her face.

"He's waiting at the camp over on the west line," Micah told her. His own dark gaze brimmed with worry. "I didn't want to leave him, but he was bleeding like a stuck pig and I thought it'd be best if he stayed put while I came to fetch you." He didn't add that Rand had nearly passed out from both the pain and the loss of blood before he could get him to the cabin. "You'll need to bring along some iodine and bandages, and maybe a bit of whiskey while you're at it. He took a bullet in the shoulder, but it looks like it went clean through."

"I'll send Sully for the doctor," she announced tremulously. Although she was trying to remain calm, she found herself battling a flood tide of panic and dread.

"All right. But we've got to go now, Miss Claire."

"Yes. Yes, I—I'm coming!"

There was no time to think, no time to question or even offer up more than a quick prayer on Rand's behalf. She hastily gathered up the things Micah had suggested and followed him outside. Sully was waiting for them out back. He assured her that he would find the doctor no matter what it took. Nodding dazedly, she mounted Rand's horse, looped the handles of the canvas supply bag over the saddle horn, and reined about.

The ride across the night-cloaked prairie seemed to take forever. She urged the animal beneath her into a full gallop, her pulse matching the frantic pace as she and Micah sped toward the line camp.

Mr. Logan's been shot. Those four words continued to burn relentlessly in her mind, along with stark, agonizing visions of Rand—lying alone while the very life drained out of him.

Hot tears stung against her eyelids. A sob rose in her throat. And in that same fateful moment, the truth of her feelings for the man whose betrayal had once cost her so dearly struck like a bolt of lightning.

She loved him.

In spite of everything, in spite of all the pain and loneliness and humiliation she had suffered these past six years, she had never stopped loving him. There was no use in trying to deny the secret locked away in her heart any longer. Just as he had said, she was his. She would always be his. Body and soul.

And now, fate had played yet another cruel trick. Dear God, she wondered fearfully, what if it was already too late? The thought of losing him was more than she could bear. . . .

"Almost there!" Micah announced, nodding to indicate the small cabin standing perched on a distant hillside in the moonlight. Her bright, anguished gaze followed the direction of his.

Within a matter of seconds, they were drawing their mounts to a halt before the door. Micah looped the reins over the hitching post, then led Claire inside. He immediately lit the lamp. Her eyes made a swift, anxious search of the sparsely furnished room. She caught her breath, her heart twisting when she spied Rand lying atop the narrow bunk in the far corner.

"Rand." She whispered his name brokenly. Flying across the room, she dropped to her knees on the floor beside him while her stricken gaze fell to the bloody, bunched-up shirt he still clasped to his injured shoulder.

"Barefoot and pregnant," he murmured. Although his blue eyes reflected his pain, they were also full of loving irony. "I'm halfway there."

"What?" Frowning in bemusement, she glanced down and saw that, in her haste, she had forgotten to put on her shoes. Micah moved to her side, kneeling as well and handing her the bag.

"First thing's to get it cleaned out," he told her gravely. She nodded in silent agreement and opened the bag to withdraw the medicine and bandages while he hurried outside to fetch a bowl of water.

"What happened?" she asked, with a composure that belied her trepidation. Carefully peeling back the shirt, she paled at the sight of the gaping wound. He had been shot in the back. The bullet had gone in clean just below his shoulder blade, only to tear through the flesh on its way out.

"Someone decided to use me for target practice."

"Ambushed us from behind on our way back from town," Micah elaborated as he returned with the water. She took the bowl from him, set it on the floor, and poured some of the iodine into it. "There were two of them," he continued, watching her soak a cloth in the mixture. "They were too far away for me to get much of a look. I fired off a couple of shots myself, but it did no good. I kept thinking maybe they meant to come on in and finish the job."

"They might have, if you hadn't been there," Rand pointed out. He tensed, clenching his teeth in the next instant when she began dabbing at the wound with the wet cloth.

"I know it must hurt terribly, but there's a chance of infection if I don't get it clean."

"You've not had much practice at this, have you?"

"No, and I don't intend to make a habit of it, either." A shadow crossing her face, she looked to Micah. "If the bleeding doesn't stop, we'll have to cauterize the wound." She had watched her father use that particular treatment a long time ago when one of the hands had come home with a busted head. The memory of it made her shudder anew.

"Anxious to put your brand on me, Mrs. Logan?" teased Rand, though his voice was hoarse and uneven.

"I'm sorry," she murmured, her stomach knotting at the awful prospect, "but you've already lost so much blood. The doctor won't be here for some time yet, and—"

"Do what you have to do," he ordered quietly.

"I—I don't know if I can," she said anxiously. Her hands trembled as she pressed a thick fold of dry bandages to the wound.

"You can do anything you have to do." His eyes seared up into hers. Something passed between them in that moment, something so deep and powerful that she knew she would never be the same again. Drawing courage from him, and praying with all her heart that she was doing the right thing, she nodded silently.

"I'll start a fire," said Micah.

"Why would anyone try to kill you?" Claire wondered aloud, her own voice raw with emotion as she continued trying to staunch the flow of blood.

"I've got a pretty good idea," murmured Rand.

"Do you think Tate—?"

"Nobody has a better reason."

"Because of Will?" Casting a surreptitious glance toward Micah, she lowered her voice even further. "Do you think Tate found out about that?"

"No." The ghost of a smile played about his lips; he raised a hand to cover hers. "You're what he wants more than anything else in the world, Claire. And the way he sees it, I'm the one who's keeping the two of you apart."

"Don't you dare die, Rand Logan," she whispered on sudden, desperate impulse. Her eyes filled with tears once more, and she choked back a sob.

"You can't get rid of me that easily," he promised.

"I'll hold you to that!"

The bleeding would not stop. Finally they had to face the inevitable. Micah set about heating the iron poker in the fire, while Claire endeavored to spare Rand as much pain as possible.

"Here. Drink some of this." She caught up the bottle of whiskey she had brought, uncorked it, and held it to his lips. He took it from her, raising up a bit so that he could take a long draw.

"It's about ready," Micah announced soon thereafter. He squatted before the fireplace, slowly twirling the poker around in the flames.

"You'd better drink some more," Claire advised Rand.

"Gladly." He emptied half the bottle this time, his eyes sweeping closed as he lay back upon the bunk. "Get to it."

Micah turned and came forward with the poker now. The end of it was glowing red-hot. Claire swallowed hard, dreading what was to come.

"Hold him down as best you can," Micah instructed her solemnly. To Rand he said, "I don't have to tell you this is going to hurt something awful, Mr. Logan. You'd best put a wad of those bandages between your teeth. And hang on. Whatever you do, don't come off that bunk."

The torment that followed, while mercifully brief, was so intense as to make even the stoic Micah look troubled. The smell of burning flesh filled the cabin. Fighting down a wave of nausea, Claire watched as Rand arched his back and gripped the edges of the bunk so hard that his knuckles turned white. He groaned low in his throat, but uttered no other sound. Afterward, he collapsed upon the blanket, his breathing labored and his brow dampened with perspiration.

"That ought to take care of it," Micah pronounced, viewing the fused and blackened edges of the wound with satisfaction. The bleeding had slowed to a mere trickle now, yet there was still a danger of infection.

"Dear heaven," Claire whispered, sharing Rand's pain. She fell weakly back down to her knees on the floor and listened to her heart thundering in her ears. Rand drifted into unconsciousness at last, his taut features relaxing and the rise and fall of his chest growing more steady.

"The best thing for him now is to sleep," said Micah.

"Yes." She climbed to her feet and wearily smoothed several wayward strands of hair from her forehead. "He shouldn't be moved. I'll stay here with him for tonight. God willing, the doctor will arrive before morning."

"Meantime, I'll ride back to the ranch for some supplies." He took up his rifle and headed for the door, then paused and looked back at her with a worried frown. "You sure you'll be all right while I'm gone, Miss Claire?"

"Of course." The corners of her mouth turning upward a bit, she bent and retrieved Rand's gun from where he had positioned it within easy reach beneath the bunk. "I wouldn't hesitate to use it if necessary."

"No, ma'am . . . I don't guess you would." His eyes met hers in silent understanding, and he gave her a brief, slightly crooked smile of his own before slipping into the darkness outside.

Bolting the door after him, Claire returned to her vigil. She drew an old ladder-back chair close to the bunk, took a seat, and stared down at the man who had haunted her dreams for so very long.

He looked incredibly vulnerable at the moment, even younger than his twenty-seven years. He was so strong and vibrant. Surely he would make a rapid recovery, she told herself, blinking back tears once more. It was impossible to imagine life without him. Impossible to think of facing the months and years ahead without this stubborn, infuriating, devilishly appealing rogue at her side. He had fulfilled his vow to win her back. If only he could be aware of his victory . . .

A second chance. It had taken a near tragedy to make her see what he had been trying to tell her all along. He had known. He had always known. Dear Lord, she entreated as she closed her eyes and took a deep, ragged breath, please let him pull through. Please.

He still had not stirred by the time Micah returned with the food and other provisions. For the next two hours, they sat together in the stillness of the cabin, listening to the soft crackle and hiss of the fire—and for any sounds of approaching riders. Occasionally they would talk about the ranch or the progress of the herd, but mostly they remained lost in their own thoughts while keeping watch over Rand. He woke a few times, asked for a drink of water, and drifted back to sleep.

It was nearing ten o'clock by the time Sully arrived with the doctor. Claire felt light-headed with relief when they stepped inside the cabin, and she hastened forward with a report on Rand's condition.

"He's been shot, Dr. Harrelson. I'm afraid he's lost a great deal of blood. We—we decided to cauterize the wound. He's mostly been unconscious since then."

"Well now, let's have a look," the doctor murmured. A slender, gray-haired man of fifty, he was originally from Boston. He had been tending the inhabitants of Parmalee for more than ten years. Carrying his trademark black bag in one hand, he knelt beside Rand and carefully exposed the wound. Another low moan rose from Rand's throat, but he did not open his eyes. Claire hovered close by while the examination was being performed. Sully and Micah each stood, grim-faced, a few feet away.

"He seems to be holding his own well enough for the moment," Dr. Harrelson concluded when he stood again. "You did the right thing, applying heat to the wound like that. He'll require complete rest for a few days."

"Should we take him back to the house?" asked Claire.

"Not just yet. Perhaps tomorrow, if he's not in too much pain and there are no signs of infection."

"Will he make it?" Sully demanded tersely, his gaze narrowing as it flickered to Claire.

"I believe so. He's young, and he appears to be in excellent general health. Of course, the final decision rests with a higher authority than myself." He donned his hat and started for the door, all the while instructing Claire, "Keep him as still and quiet as possible. A poultice might help alleviate some of the soreness. See that he gets plenty of fluids, clear broth for a day or two, and absolutely no more strong spirits."

"I will. Thank you for coming," she told him in genuine, heartfelt gratitude.

"In truth, my dear young lady, you managed just fine without me," he opined, flashing her a somewhat paternal smile.

"I'll see you get back to town," said Sully.

"I appreciate the offer of an escort, Mr. Greene, but there is no need for you to trouble yourself further," Dr. Harrelson assured him. "Only a short time before your summons, I received word that Mrs. Brown has gone into labor. It is her first child. I would not be at all surprised if I were to be kept from the comfort of my bed for the duration of the night." With that, he was gone.

"You can head on back to the ranch now, Miss Claire," Micah told her, his eyes full of compassion. "I'll stay with Mr. Logan."

"No. Thank you, but I—I can't leave him."

"And I'll be damned if I'll leave *you* here alone," Sully rasped out. "Whatever bastard took a potshot at him might just take it in mind to try again." His gaze darkening at the thought, he lifted his gun and took up a protective stance near the doorway.

"Stay then," Claire agreed, with another sigh. Feeling drained, both physically and emotionally, she looked back to Micah and said, "You might as well go home and get some sleep. There's no sense in all three of us staying. Besides, Sadie will need to know what's happened."

"I'll be back first thing in the morning," he promised. Although reluctant to leave, he consoled himself with a secret plan of disobedience. He'd ride on back to the house and tell Mrs. Bishop what was going on, all right. But he'd be spending the night underneath the stars, a short distance from the cabin. And like Sully, he'd be standing guard with a rifle in his hands. "Miss Claire?"

"Yes, Micah?"

"Mr. Logan's a fine man. And he's tough. He'll come around just fine."

"I'm counting on that."

She gave him a wan smile before turning back to resume her seat beside Rand. Sully, closing the door after Micah, insisted that she eat something. She managed to down a little bread and water, but nothing else. Worry gnawed at her insides, making it impossible for her to rest. The same prayer echoed in her mind over and over as she watched her husband sleep. Visions of the past, present, and future whirled together in her mind. But just as Rand had said, all that really mattered was the here and now. He had to pull through. He had to. The alternative was unthinkable.

The long night wore on. Sully bent his wiry frame downward to sit on the floor, keeping his back ramrod straight against the wall, while Claire finally leaned forward across the foot of the bunk and lowered her head upon her arms. The fire burned down into a glowing pile of embers. Outside, the sky had darkened to the color of ink before the subtle, flame-colored rays of the new sun set the horizon eerily aglow.

"Daylight's come, Mrs. Logan."

Claire's eyes flew wide. Jerking her head up, she was startled to realize that she had fallen asleep. And even more startled that it was Rand's voice she had just heard. Her gaze shot to where he lay, smiling softly up at her in the half-light of the cabin.

"Rand!" Flooded with mingled joy and relief, she hastened to kneel on the floor beside him. She clasped his hand with the both of hers, then anxiously pulled one free in order to check for any evidence of fever. His forehead felt cool to the touch. And his eyes were clear. Wonderfully, heart-stirringly . . . clear. They brimmed with loving amusement as they traveled over her rumpled clothing and the wild, tangled mass of honey-gold curls tumbling down about her face and shoulders.

"You look like hell," he murmured, with no conviction whatsoever.

"So do you." She smiled archly before sobering again. "Are you in any pain?" she asked, her own eyes falling toward his bandaged shoulder.

"Some." He tried to sit up, but she firmly pushed him back down.

"The doctor says you're to have complete rest for a few days." A shadow crossed her features, and there was a discernible catch in her voice when she told him, "You lost a great deal of blood, Rand. You can't—"

"So," Sully muttered behind them. "You're awake." He climbed to his feet and frowned when his gaze met Rand's. For a fleeting moment, it appeared he might actually inquire after the younger man's health. But he said instead, "Damn cold in here this mornin'," and moved forward to start a fire.

"The old sidewinder's been here all night," Claire informed Rand, her tone both low and indulgent.

"Well then, I guess he's decided to let me live."

"You'll live." She settled a gentle hand upon his forehead once more, her green eyes shining with hope and the love she intended to declare when the right time came. "But you do have to follow the doctor's instructions and take it easy for a while."

"I'll be up and about by tomorrow," he vowed.

"Perhaps." She knew it was of little use to argue with him.

"I can make it back to the ranch now." In truth, he was thinking of her welfare instead of his own.

"Well . . . I *could* look after you better there," she allowed, battling indecision. The words had scarcely left her mouth when he pulled himself into a sitting position and flung back the covers. He winced at the throbbing pain in his shoulder, yet still managed to rise from the bunk. Although he would never admit it, his head swam.

"We leavin'?" Sully asked gruffly.

"We are," confirmed Rand. His mouth twitched as Claire drew close and slipped her arm about his waist for support. He still wore no shirt; the feel of her soft, curvaceous warmth against his naked skin did more to boost his spirits than any tonic could have. "I might just enjoy being an invalid," he teased after Sully had doused the fire and marched outside. "So long as I get to lie in the boss lady's bed."

"You're probably still delirious," she retorted, though her heart soared at his banter. He sounded entirely like his old self now. Gone was the man who had frightened her with his pallor and his restless mumblings the whole night long. Though she cautioned herself against believing the fight completely won just yet, she sensed that the tide had already turned. "For heaven's sake, Rand Logan," she complained in mock exasperation, "will you never think of anything else?"

"Never." The look he gave her belied his present weakened condition.

Though she was surprised to find Micah waiting for

them when they stepped into the gathering light of the dawn, she did not ask him how he came to be there at so early an hour. And he offered no explanation as he stood grasping the reins of the horses.

The four of them rode back to the house. Once there, Rand insisted on getting himself upstairs without assistance. In no time at all, Claire had him tucked securely beneath the covers of the iron bedstead, his shoulder swathed in fresh bandages and his thirst satisfied with an entire pitcherful of water. He also ate some clear broth, though he protested that he would starve to death if he didn't get some "real" food before long.

He agreed to remain abed—for that one day only. Claire proved to be a capable and devoted nurse, making certain he was as comfortable as possible. She applied a poultice of ground elderbush bark to his wound, and washed his upper body with warm soapy water and a sponge. His lower body would have enjoyed the same cleansing, save for his insistence that he had endured enough "torment" by then and would perform any further duties himself.

As afternoon finally drifted into evening, it became apparent that the patient would make a truly remarkable recovery indeed. Claire slipped into the room once more, bearing a wooden tray laden with yet another bowl of broth and a cup of Sadie's special chamomile tea.

She had taken a bath and changed into a pretty, sprigged cotton gown. Her long silken tresses cascaded freely about her face and shoulders, and there was a newfound sparkle in her eyes as she closed the door behind her.

"How are you feeling?" she asked, lowering the tray to the bedside table.

"Lonely." His own eyes warmed at the sight of her.

"Harmony would like to come up and see you."

"That's not quite what I had in mind." He eased himself up into a sitting position and raked a negligent hand through the sun-streaked thickness of his hair before challenging dryly, "What are the other hands going to say when they find out you've got me up here in your bedroom?"

"Probably that I've gone loco," she retorted, folding her arms beneath her breasts.

"And have you?"

"I nearly did." There was a telltale catch in her voice, and her gaze fell involuntarily beneath the penetrating tenderness of his. "When I heard you'd been shot, I—I felt like my heart had stopped." The confession wasn't at all what she had planned, yet she couldn't regret having offered it.

"Then I guess it was worth getting shot."

"Worth it?" she repeated, her eyes bridling with indignation as they flew back up to his face. She uncrossed her arms and planted her hands on her hips. "For heaven's sake, Rand Logan! Do you have any idea what you've put me through? I thought you were going to die! And if you had, I'd—"

"Claire." He spoke her name in a low, resonant tone that sent a beguiling tremor through her. She broke off, swallowed hard, and tried to ignore the soft smile tugging at his lips. It was impossible. "I was beginning to think I'd never hear you say it."

"Say what?" she murmured, pretending ignorance as she turned to pick up the bowl of soup.

"That you love me."

"I didn't say that." It seemed a rather perverse argument under the circumstances, but she was determined to pay him back in kind, at least a little, for all the times he had taunted and teased her.

"Then say it now." His hand closed about her wrist, and she gasped when he suddenly pulled her down onto the bed beside him.

"Rand, stop it!" she protested in breathless astonishment, attempting to rise. "Your shoulder!"

"To hell with my shoulder." He slipped his good arm about her waist and swept her up against the naked hardness of his chest. A shiver danced down her spine while his eyes bored hotly into hers. "I've waited six years to hear you say it, Claire. I've waited long enough."

He was right, she conceded with an inward smile. It was time. She took a deep breath and lifted a hand to rest gently upon his rugged, slightly bristly cheek, all the while rejoicing that fate had thrown such a man into her path. Where there had once been darkness, there was now only light. *There was only Rand.* Nothing else mattered. Nothing else ever would again.

"I love you," she told him at last.

The words were the sweetest and truest she had ever spoken. And with them came a freedom that was so empowering, so exhilarating and pleasurable, that she knew she had finally left the horrors of the past behind.

"I didn't think it possible to feel this way, not after everything that happened," she admitted, her eyes shining softly into the vibrant-hued steadiness of his. "I tried to stop loving you. I almost managed to convince myself that I hated you. In the end, of course, it was no use. I suppose I never really had a chance." She released a sigh and allowed a faint smile of irony to touch her lips. "I don't know if you're any more trustworthy than before. I don't know if I'll ever be able to go to sleep without wondering if you'll be gone in the morning. But I love you, Rand Logan. Body and soul, just the way you wanted. And as God is my witness, I'm yours until the day I die."

Rand felt his heart take flight, felt it stir with the pure, never-ending love that had sustained him through the loneliness of the past six years. The second chance had been heaven-sent after all. His punishment was at an end. Whatever he had done, whatever sins he had been forced to atone for, Claire was his forever.

"You'll never have cause to doubt me," he vowed, his arm tightening about her.

"Just bear in mind that I've got a fearsome temper. There's no telling *what* I'm liable to do if I catch the scent of another woman's perfume hanging about you." She frowned and decreed sternly, "No more visits to those 'friends' of yours at the saloon. No more taking unnecessary risks. And no more disappearing without letting me know where you're headed."

"Reining me in already, are you?" Though his tone was mocking, his eyes glowed with an irresistible combination of love and triumph and desire.

"Damn straight."

Delighting in the sound of his quiet chuckle, she closed her eyes and swayed closer against him. Her hands curled about the corded muscles of his neck as she pressed her mouth to the firm, thoroughly captivating warmth of his.

The kiss was a promise of their future together. They had weathered so many storms while apart, had found themselves facing a test that only the strongest of loves could ever hope to survive. No matter what lay ahead, the bond between them could never be shattered now.

"Your soup is getting cold," murmured Claire, her senses reeling by the time she lifted her head once more.

"Let it." He captured her lips again. She summoned all her strength of will to put a stop to the sweet madness before it got completely out of hand.

"Oh, Rand. We mustn't!" She pulled away, hastily composing herself as she started to rise. "You need to rest."

"By damn, woman! I'm winged—not dead!"

He proved it by tumbling her back down beside him and kissing her a third time. If not for a timely interruption on Harmony's part (by virtue of a loud and insistent knock at the bedroom door), he might well have risked further injury. With obvious reluctance, he allowed his blushing wife to scramble to her feet and answer the summons.

"Supper's almost ready in case you're hungry," the little girl imparted. She craned her neck in an effort to catch a glimpse of Rand, for Claire was blocking the better part of her view. "Is Mr. Parker going to come downstairs now?"

"Not tonight. But perhaps you'd care to keep him company for a while."

"Wolf, too?" asked Harmony, glancing down at the panting, huge-footed beast beside her.

"Wolf, too," Claire readily consented. She turned and smiled at Rand, her emerald gaze lit with fond amusement. "Mr. Parker, I am entrusting you to Harmony's care until I return."

"Where are you going?" he demanded, his brow creasing into a frown of disgruntlement. His shoulder ached like hell, but it was the lingering fire in his blood that made him curse inwardly.

"I've got a few things to see to," was all she would tell him. She knew what his reaction would be if she revealed anything more. "I won't be long."

"I can look after him just fine, Miss Claire," the child assured her earnestly.

"I'm sure you can." She paused to catch up the blouse and skirt she had left folded atop a chair, then cast Rand one last affectionate—and significant—look before slipping from the room.

"Don't leave the ranch!" his deep, authoritative voice followed her out onto the landing. She smiled to herself, blithely intent upon disobedience as she continued downstairs.

The smile had faded by the time she reached the kitchen. On one hand, she felt as though a terrible weight had been lifted from her shoulders; on the other, she was plagued by an awful uneasiness. Someone had tried to kill Rand. Would they try again?

Chapter 13

It didn't take her long to change and secure her hair into a single long braid. Declining Sadie's offer of a meal, she hastened outside to saddle her horse. Micah insisted upon going with her, but she charged him with the duty of keeping watch over things—Rand, in particular—while she was gone.

"Nothing will happen to him, Miss Claire," promised Micah, holding the reins for her as she swung up into the saddle. "I'll see to that. But you shouldn't be riding off alone. Sully can—"

"No." She shook her head and took the reins from him. "I'm only going to the line camp and back. I'll be back before it gets too dark."

"It can wait till tomorrow."

"Maybe. But I want to clean up before . . . well, before anyone else finds out about what happened. The fewer people who know right now, the better chance we stand of finding the black-hearted coward who did it. I don't think any of the hands will talk." Pulling her father's battered old hat low upon her head, she managed a brief, reassuring smile while pointing out, "Besides,

I've been riding on my own since I was a child. I know my way around this country better than anyone."

"Mr. Logan won't like it," he observed gravely.

"Mr. Logan doesn't have to know."

She reined about and touched her booted heels to the mare's flanks, heading westward across the twilight-cloaked plains. The line camp was only a few miles' ride away. Once there, she dismounted, retrieved the cleaning rags from her saddlebag, and swept purposefully inside the cabin.

She lit the lamp, then paused a moment to survey the damage. The floor was stained with blood, as was the bedding. She wasted little time in fetching water from the pump outside and setting to work. Kneeling, she scrubbed the telltale crimson marks from the floor. Since she had no way to wash the bedding, she stripped it from the bed and rolled it tightly, securing it with a length of rope so that she could tie it behind her saddle. The feather mattress, she concluded with a sharp frown, would have to be burned.

To that end, she crossed to the fireplace and quickly struck a match to the waiting stack of half-burned wood left from the night before. The flames soon danced to life. The soft, flickering golden light played across her face as she stood and turned back toward the bed.

"What are you doin' here?" A familiar voice spoke from the open doorway behind her.

Starting in alarm, Claire caught her breath and spun about. Her heart leapt into her throat, her eyes widening in dismay when she saw that it was Tate Jenner who stood regarding her closely.

"I might ask you the same thing," she retorted, her voice uneven.

"I saw you ridin' this way. Thought I'd make sure nothin' was wrong."

"Why should anything be wrong?" She watched as he sauntered inside, closed the door behind him, and tugged the hat from his head.

"I've never known you to make a habit of payin' visits to the line camps. Especially when night's drawin' in." His pale blue eyes seared across into the wide, wary green depths of hers.

She did her best to conceal the anxiety she felt at being alone with him. But it was difficult to push aside what she had learned about him recently . . . difficult to forget that he might be responsible for Rand's injury. The possibility filled her with a vengeful, white-hot rage that made her want to confront him with her suspicions there and then. Yet, she forced herself to betray nothing of the emotions boiling within her.

"It was high time to do some cleaning up, that's all," she murmured stiffly, pushing several wayward locks of hair from her face. "The hands have been too busy, what with the repairs and—"

"Somebody hurt?" he broke in to ask. He directed a curt nod toward the bloodstained mattress.

"One of the hands, a long time ago." She struggled to keep her tone casual. "I've been meaning to—"

"Looks fresh to me." He cut her off again. While she tensed, he strode forward and subjected the stains to a closer examination. His eyes glinted and narrowed when they met hers once more. "What happened, Claire?"

"I don't know what you're talking about." She started to move past him, but his hand shot out to close with near bruising force about her arm. "Let me go!" she demanded, trying to pull free.

"Not until I get the truth." His features reddened with an inordinate fury, and he yanked her up hard against him. "I want to know what the hell's goin' on!"

"Nothing." Fear gripped her. This was a different Tate than the one she had known. Gone was the kind, amiable man who had been her friend; in his place was a man who looked all too capable of the worst kind of violence. Rand's face suddenly swam before her eyes. She felt her stomach knot in growing dread.

"It's Parker, isn't it?" demanded Tate, his harsh tone underscored by jealousy as well as anger.

"Parker?" she echoed. She ceased her struggles and blinked up at him. Dear God, she wondered numbly, was he actually confirming her suspicions? "How could you know—?"

"Just a wild guess." A cold, cruel smile touched his lips. "And I can see by the look on your face that I'm right. Is he dead?"

"No. No, he's ... It was little more than a scratch," she lied on sudden impulse.

"Was it? Too bad."

"Why do you say that?"

"I've thought of nothin' but you since that day at the pond," he bit out. "And about how that cocksure, no-account bastard butted in! Damn it, Claire! Do you think I don't know how bad he made me look? Do you think I'm blind to what's goin' on between the two of you?"

"There's nothing going on," she was quick to deny.

"That's not what I heard." He released her arm as though the contact had burned him. But his gaze still glittered with a feral light. "It's said the two of you were in Denton together a couple of days ago."

"And you believed the talk?" By heaven, she should have known Lydia would waste no time in spreading the latest gossip. She cursed her own troublesome temper once more and said coolly, "You know I've always been a convenient target for rumors in Parmalee."

"Rumors or not, everythin' was fine till Parker came along. You and I were headin' on just find."

Folding her arms beneath her breasts, she schooled her countenance to a deceptive composure again. "Jake Parker has nothing to do with us, Tate. Even if he hadn't come along, things wouldn't be any different."

"You lie!" He took another wrathful step toward her, prompting her to retreat until the back of her knees came up against the bunk. "Next time, the son of a bitch won't be so damn lucky."

"What do you mean?" she demanded sharply, paling as a warning bell sounded in her brain. *Were his words an admission of guilt?*

"Figure it out for yourself." His mouth curled into a malevolent sneer before he suddenly turned and started back toward the doorway.

"Tate!" She impulsively gave chase, her heart thundering in her chest at the thought of what he might do. "Please, Tate. You've got to listen to reason."

"Why should I?" He stopped and rounded on her again. She was startled to glimpse real pain in his eyes.

"Because I—because I do care for you," she stam-

mered. There was a measure of truth in it. No matter
what he had done, no matter what he was threatening to
do, she couldn't banish all traces of the affection she
had once felt for him. Yet, she knew if a choice had to
be made, she wouldn't hesitate to do whatever it took to
protect Rand. *Whatever it took.*

"I'm no fool, Claire," he snapped, obviously uncon-
vinced.

"I know." She took a deep, steadying breath and once
again resisted the temptation to ask him if he was the
one who had shot Rand. Her instincts warned against it.
If his jealousy had provoked that ugly and drastic a response, then there was no telling what he might do next.
She shuddered at the thought of the guard who had
nearly been killed during the last train robbery. Yes,
Tate was capable of violence all right. . . .

"I won't pretend it's the way you want it to be," she
continued, fighting down a wave of nausea as she lifted
a hand to his arm and met his hot gaze unflinchingly.
"But I do care for you. And I'm asking you to forget
about Jake Parker."

"Are you tryin' to make a bargain with me?" he challenged mockingly.

"I'm trying to make you realize that seeking revenge
isn't going to bring us any closer." Her eyes held both
an entreaty and a steely earnestness when she vowed,
"If you try and hurt him, I'll never forgive you. And I
swear, I'll have nothing more to do with you. *Nothing.*"
She would do more than that, of course. She would
seek her own revenge. She would make him pay, even
if it took the rest of her life.

"Then I guess you've drawn the line real clear."

"Oh, Tate," she appealed, while sudden tears stung against her eyelids, "what's happened to you? You've always been so good to me, and to your brothers as well. Why are you set on destroying everything you've worked for?" For a moment, she forgot that he was a cold-blooded thief, forgot that he might have been the man who had tried to kill Rand. She shivered when his hand came up to close tightly upon hers.

"You're the only thing I want, Claire," he declared, his voice brimming with raw emotion now. "And if I can't have you, then nothing else matters. I'll do what I have to do."

His words struck an even deeper chord of fear in her heart. She snatched her hand away and clasped it to her throat.

"God help you," she whispered.

"I've made a pact with the devil. Didn't you know?" With a faint, humorless smile playing about his lips, he finally left.

She stared after him, feeling sick and frightened and enraged all at the same time. Although he had never admitted to anything, her suspicions were stronger than ever. Rand would be in danger until Tate was arrested . . . until Tate was either dead or behind bars. The prospect of that no longer brought anything more than a slight twinge of pity.

Whirling about, she dragged the mattress over to the stone fireplace and pushed it into the midst of the blaze. It didn't take long for it to burst into flames. When there was nothing left of it but a mass of glowing embers, she doused the fire, closed up the cabin, and rode back to the house in the gathering darkness.

She found Rand impatiently awaiting her return. Having decided not to tell him about her encounter with Tate until morning—there was no sense in troubling him with it now—she forced a smile to her lips and swept forward to relieve Harmony of her duties.

"Have you had your supper yet?" she asked the little girl.

Harmony nodded and rose from the chair she had drawn up beside the bed. Wolf, wagging his mammoth tail, pulled himself upright as well.

"Mama let me eat it up here with Mr. Parker. I'm not supposed to tell," she then confided, while flashing a mischievous look in Rand's direction, "but *he* ate some of it, too."

"Did he indeed?" replied Claire. She placed an arm about the child's shoulders and leaned closer to whisper conspiratorially, "I suppose we'll have to tell Dr. Harrelson, won't we? He might want to—"

"Where have you been?" Rand broke in to demand. Frowning, he folded his arms across his chest and subjected her to a hard, scrutinizing stare. It was clear that he suspected something.

"I told you, I had a few things to see to." She silently cursed the dull color staining her cheeks.

"What 'things'?"

"I think you should go on downstairs now," she remarked, calmly turning back to Harmony. She led her to the doorway and smiled again. "Thank you for your help."

"Is Mr. Parker going to sleep in your bed from now on?" Harmony queried in all innocence.

" 'Out of the mouths of babes,' " Rand quipped

softly, his eyes glowing when they met Claire's. Her color deepened.

"Why don't you take Wolf outside?" she suggested to the little girl. "It's a nice evening. Maybe the two of you should pay a visit to Sully over at the stock barn."

"Reverend Mueller says Sully's a character."

"Reverend Mueller is absolutely right."

"He's smart, all right," Harmony opined proudly. She threaded her fingers within the fur on the back of the dog's neck and propelled him along with her as she headed out of the room. "But not as smart as Will." Her parting words sent a shadow across Claire's face.

"Would you care to tell me now what the devil you've been up to?" Rand asked his wife once they were alone.

"Nothing. Nothing at all." She closed the door and wandered back toward the bed.

"Like hell. You—"

"I suppose Harmony kept you well entertained in my absence," she murmured, a brief, preoccupied smile tugging at the corners of her mouth.

"It won't work."

"What won't work?"

"Changing the subject." He watched as she reached up and began unbraiding her hair. "You were gone an awful long time."

"Was I?" Pulling the honey-gold locks free, she sat down in the chair beside him and folded her hands in her lap. "I didn't mean to be."

"Has Tate Jenner been by?"

"No," she answered truthfully. Her gaze falling, she

heaved a ragged sigh. "What if—if whoever tried to kill you tries again?"

"I'll have to make sure they don't succeed."

"Dear God, if only this were all over with," she said, her voice quavering.

"You left the ranch, didn't you?" He had his answer when her eyes flew back up to his face.

"How did you—?"

"Damn it, Claire! I told you to stay put!" Although the action made him wince, he raised both of his hands to her arms. "Where did you go?"

"To the line camp. I didn't think it would do any harm."

"And did it?" His handsome face thunderous, he tightened his grasp upon her. *"Did it?"*

"I spoke to Tate," she finally revealed. Blanching at the memory of the confrontation, she added, "He didn't actually admit to anything, but it was obvious he's set on revenge. Oh, Rand. You were right!" She swallowed a lump in her throat and felt the tears threatening to gather again. "He's not the man I thought he was."

"By heaven, did he hurt you?" Rand ground out.

"No!" she hastened to assure him. Alarmed at the savage gleam in his eyes, she shook her head for emphasis. "He only wanted to talk. I never let on that I suspected him, of course. Still, there was something about the way he behaved, something that made me almost certain he's the one who fired that shot at you."

"Are you sure you're all right?" After she had nodded mutely, he scowled and warned, "Defy me again, and I swear I'll—"

"For heaven's sake, I can't—"

"You can and will!" His fingers clenched about her arms until she cried out in protest.

"You're going to hurt your shoulder!"

"When are you going to learn to obey me?" he demanded, his gaze smoldering down into hers.

"When pigs fly, I suppose," she shot back. She was surprised when he suddenly released her and leaned back against the pillow.

"You are without a doubt the most bullheaded woman I've ever known." His tone brimmed with wry, loving amusement. "If this is what our marriage is going to be like, then God help me."

"You're free to light out anytime you want." They both knew she didn't mean a word of it.

"Free? Hell, sweetheart. You've got me roped and branded."

"I'm glad to hear you own up to it." Turning serious again, she appealed, "You won't take any more chances, will you, Rand? Tate seems to be getting awfully desperate." *I'll do what I have to do,* he had said. She shivered involuntarily and grasped at Rand's good arm. "Please, you've got to be careful."

"I'll be as careful as I know how."

"Is that supposed to be a comfort to me?"

"It is." The slow smile spreading across his face caused her to melt inside. "For the past six years, I never gave it a second thought. But now that I know you love me, I have every reason to keep myself alive."

"You haven't been doing a very good job of it lately," she observed archly, tossing a significant glance at his bandaged shoulder.

"I'm still here."

The look in his eyes, combined with the wonderful vibrancy of his tone, made her want to cast herself upon his chest and beg him to hold her tight. But she resisted the impulse. She stood and leaned forward to drop a light kiss upon his forehead, intending to return downstairs for a bath. He had other plans, however.

"Stay," he commanded, his hand closing gently yet firmly about her wrist.

"Don't you think you've had enough excitement for one day?" The light, teasing note in her voice belied the heat spreading throughout her body.

"Not by a long shot." He pulled her down beside him. This time, there would be no escape.

Ever mindful of his injury, she assisted him in liberating her soft, supple curves from her clothes. And when she joined him beneath the covers, she proceeded to drive him to utter distraction with her kisses and gentle, tantalizing caresses. For the first time, she took the initiative, boldly exploring his hard-muscled body until he gave a low groan and pulled her atop him with thoroughly masculine impatience. She smiled in mingled passion and triumph, and was more than willing to submit herself to his "retaliation." The victory, sweeter than ever before, belonged to them both.

Downstairs, meanwhile, another sort of romantic scenario was being played out.

For the second time in as many nights, Reverend Mueller had come to call. Sadie's heart leapt wildly at the sight of his approaching buggy. After she had greeted him with a warmly lit smile and the assurance that Jake Parker would make a full recovery, she led the way across to the porch swing and sat down.

"I have something I wish to tell you, dearest Sadie," said Thomas, taking his place beside her. His expression was quite solemn, and there was something in his manner that caused her to feel a sharp twinge of apprehension.

"What is it?"

"Today, I received a letter. Contained within its pages was the news that an old friend has passed away."

"Oh, Thomas. I—I'm sorry."

"As am I. Franklin had been unwell for a long time, but his death, nevertheless, came as a surprise. For the past several years, he had been serving as pastor to a congregation in El Paso." He paused for a moment and looked away before announcing, "I must travel there to pay my respects to his family."

"How long will you be gone?" The thought of a separation, however brief, made her spirits plummet.

"I will not be returning to Parmalee at all."

"Not returning?" she echoed in stunned disbelief. In the next instant, she felt as though her entire world had come crashing down about her. The color drained from her face. Her legs threatened to buckle beneath her when she stood and took an instinctive step toward the front door.

"No, no, my love. It is not as you think," Thomas insisted, his own heart aching at the sight of her distress. He rose and lifted his hands to her shoulders. "I have been offered Franklin's position. It is a much larger church than the one we have here. And I must confess, I had hoped to travel farther west before—"

"You're leaving," Sadie whispered brokenly, still reeling from the news. Dear God, was it possible that she had come this close to happiness, only to have it snatched away so cruelly? It seemed that she would go on paying for her sins the rest of her life. Lydia Cassidy and the other ladies of the town were right, she told herself in weary, anguished resignation. There was no escaping her past.

"I am leaving, yes," confirmed Thomas. "But only if you will go with me."

She looked up at him, her eyes growing round as saucers. He grasped her trembling hands with the strong warmth of his and smiled.

"I know this is all quite sudden. I know we had planned to wait, to enjoy a proper courtship, yet I cannot endure the thought of living elsewhere without you at my side." He released a sigh and shook his head. "I was afraid you would regard my decision as impetuous. It had been my intention to remain in Parmalee for at least a year or two. And I was convinced that, given time, your persecution would end and true affection take its place. If we leave now, it might well be said that we are simply running away."

"Yes. It might," she murmured. *What does it matter?* she reflected silently, her whole body flooding with joy. This good, kind, glorious man loved her and wanted her to be his wife. Together, they could make a fresh start. El Paso was a whole lifetime away from Parmalee.

"I prefer to think of it as an answered prayer," he remarked contentedly. "The Lord works in mysterious ways, does he not?"

"But what about Harmony?"

"She will come with us." His smile this time was appealingly crooked, and his eyes virtually danced. "Perhaps, my dearest Sadie, other men would be reluctant to bring a child along on a honeymoon, but I can assure you that I am not." His fingers tenderly cupped her chin before he stipulated, "Providing, of course, that you will grant me the honor of a private meeting once she is safely asleep each evening." He was enchanted by the sight of her rosy blush.

"Oh, Thomas. What—what will I tell Claire? It seems so unfair to up and leave her all of a sudden."

"I am certain that she will offer us her felicitations. She is a remarkable young woman, one who understands far more than you think."

"Is this really happening?" Sadie asked, lifting her hands to rest upon his chest. Her opal eyes shone softly up into the adoring, blue-green steadiness of his. "Maybe somebody should pinch me so I'll know it's real."

"I can think of a far more pleasurable way to convince you." He swept her close, his arms encircling her with a fierce possessiveness that both surprised and delighted her.

"Out here?" she gasped. Coloring guiltily, she cast a quick, worried look about.

"I believe the expression is, 'In front of God and everybody,' " he replied, his voice holding passion as well as laughter. She smiled and strained upward against him so that her lips were very near to his.

" 'In front of God and everybody,' " she repeated, her own voice low and sweetly seductive.

He needed no further encouragement. His mouth descended upon hers in a kiss so deep and intoxicating that they both yearned for the day when their whirlwind courtship reached its satisfying conclusion. They were still locked in the embrace when Harmony and Wolf came bounding up the front steps of the porch a few moments later.

"Mama, why are you kissing Reverend Mueller?"

With another guilty flush staining her cheeks, Sadie hastily disengaged herself from the arms of her betrothed and gazed down at her little daughter in a breathless fluster. Thomas appeared anything but repentant as he bent and lifted the child high.

"Your mother and I are going to be married, Harmony. Do you know what that means?"

"Uh-huh." She curled her hands about his neck and nodded. Her dark eyes were wide and guileless when she said, "It means you get to sleep in Mama's bed."

"Harmony!" exclaimed Sadie, her color deepening.

"That is correct," Thomas assured the six-year-old. He managed to suppress the smile that tugged at his lips. "But it also means that you will be my daughter now as well. The three of us are going to live together. We will be a family."

"Will we still live here at the ranch?"

"No. We will be journeying to a place called El Paso. I am told that it is a very lovely place indeed."

"All right. But I have to bring Wolf."

"We'll have to ask Miss Claire about that," Sadie cautioned. "He's her dog, after all."

"She won't mind," Harmony opined confidently. "Sully says Wolf's a good-for-nothing mongrel." She wriggled down out of Thomas's grasp and headed back across the moonlit yard, the big brown animal hot on her heels. "I'm going to tell Sully we're leaving!"

Sadie looked at the tall, blond-haired man beside her and smiled again. Glorieta had been the first real home she'd had in years; she would be sorry to go. But from now on, her home would be wherever Thomas was. The thought made her heart swell with the most profound happiness she had ever known. Just like Claire, she mused to herself in wonderment, she had been offered a second chance.

"You probably won't be given much of a good-bye when folks hear who it is you're marrying," she warned Thomas, though without a single trace of regret.

"I am far more interested in hello." He pulled her close once more.

"My mother isn't going to believe it when I tell her I've gone and caught myself a preacher."

"With you, my dearest love, I am only a man."

She had little cause to doubt it.

Chapter 14

True to his word, Rand was up and about the next day. He kissed away Claire's highly vocal objections, then took himself off to have a word with Micah after breakfast.

Claire heaved a sigh in his wake, reflecting with an ironic little smile that it was impossible to truly rein in a man like her husband. Her father, she recalled, had once warned her that Rand Logan would go wherever the wind blew him. She wondered what Samuel would say if he could see how things had turned out. No doubt, he would call her a damn fool for leaving herself wide open for a second heartbreak. But she couldn't help believing that, in time, he would see that the risk was well worth taking.

The morning passed in a pleasant whirl of preparations for Sadie's wedding, an event that would take place in only three days' time. While Claire professed herself reluctant to lose her two housemates, she was genuinely happy for them. The news of Sadie's impending marriage hadn't come as all that much of a surprise, of course; she had noticed the parson's attentiveness the first time she had taken Sadie and Harmony to church.

He had certainly been quick to rise to the pretty widow's defense that day. At least *some* good had sprung from the ordeal, she thought with an inward smile.

The sun was hanging almost directly overhead in the vast, cloudless expanse of the sky when she accompanied Harmony out onto the front porch for a much-needed respite from sorting and planning and packing. They emerged from the house just in time to observe Will Jenner reining his horse to a halt in the shade of the trees. He swung down from the saddle and approached them with a deceptively easy grin.

"What on earth are you doing here?" demanded Claire. Her gaze made a quick, encompassing sweep of the grounds. Most of the hands had ridden out at first light to check on the herd. Sully was somewhere about the ranch, as were Micah and Rand. *Rand.* She knew Will had come to see him.

"Well now, I'd call that a right fine welcome, Miss Claire," he drawled sardonically. Harmony was much more effusive in her greeting. She raced down the steps and launched herself at him, squealing with laughter when he caught her up in his arms. "Pretty soon, Little Bit, you'll be too big for me to carry."

"I'll never be that big," she promised him.

"Parker around?" he queried, looking to Claire. She glimpsed the troubled light in his eyes.

"The last I saw of him, he and Micah were working with the horses over at the corral." It was on the tip of her tongue to ask him if he had brought any more information about his brothers' plans, but she refrained from saying anything other than, "You're looking a bit tired. Maybe you'd care to come inside for a while before you leave." In truth, she *was* concerned about him. He was much too young to bear such an awful weight upon his shoulders. She could well imagine how torn he must feel at having to turn traitor against his own family.

"Thanks. I might just do that." He set Harmony on her feet and headed toward the corral. Claire watched as he disappeared around the corner of the stock barn.

"Do you think Reverend Mueller will let Will come to El Paso with us?" Harmony asked at a sudden thought.

"I'm afraid not." She settled a comforting, affectionate hand upon the child's shoulder and smiled softly. "I know you like Will an awful lot, but he . . . well, he's got his own life to lead."

"He's my friend!" Harmony proclaimed, with unexpected vehemence. She spun about and dashed away around the corner of the house, her gingham skirts flying up about her bare legs.

Claire heaved a sigh. Her own gaze clouded as it strayed back to the corral. She didn't have to wait long before Rand appeared. He closed the distance between them in long, purposeful strides, his blue eyes glinting coldly. She knew the moment she saw his face that something had happened.

"What is it?" she demanded, hurrying forward to meet him. Before he could answer, she asked, "There's going to be another robbery, isn't there?" Her throat constricted in sudden alarm when he nodded curtly. "Oh, Rand. I—"

"Don't leave the ranch, Claire. Sully will be here to keep an eye on things until I get back." He raised his hands to grip her arms and commanded, "Do as I say for once, and stay put." His tone was low and edged with steel, his features a grim mask of determination.

"What are you going to do?"

"Ride to Denton first. Malone and his two deputies are waiting to lend a hand." That would make six of them in all, he thought. Six against the three Jenners. On the surface, the odds certainly looked favorable enough, but Tate and his brothers would be armed and desperate. They wouldn't be of a mind to listen to reason.

"What about Will?" Claire asked, her voice scarcely more than a whisper.

"He and Micah are going with me."

"He could be wrong!" she pointed out in growing dread. "He was wrong once before, remember?"

"I remember. But that was because Tate changed the plans without his knowledge. I believe he's right this time. He's given us all the details we need. Tate's set on robbing the northbound train out of Dallas." He had already buckled on his holster. Claire's wide, apprehensive gaze flickered downward to the handle of his revolver when it briefly flashed in the sunlight. She swallowed hard and reached up to touch the thickness of the bandage beneath his blue cotton shirt.

"Your shoulder's not even healed yet. For heaven's sake, Rand. You can't—"

"I'll be fine." His mouth curved into a faint smile. "I told you, I've decided to keep myself alive."

"I'm coming with you," she declared, her eyes sparking at the idea. "If Tate sees me, there's a chance he'll back off, just like he did before."

"No." He shook his head and frowned down at her.

"The time has come to put an end to it, once and for all. It's my job, Claire. And by heaven, the last thing I need is to worry about your being in the middle of the whole damn mess!" He was not surprised to watch her bristle with proud indignation.

"So I'm supposed to sit here and do nothing while you—?"

"Exactly." He cut her off tersely. "I've got to go." Without another word, he swept her up against him and gave her a quick, hard kiss. She found herself released just as abruptly, and struggled to regain control of her breathing while he strode away.

"Rand!" she called after him, but to no avail. She watched through a haze of rising panic as he joined Micah and Will in front of the barn. It suddenly struck her that this could be the last time she saw him alive. A sharp pain knifed through her at the thought of the terrible danger he would be facing.

"*Rand!*" she cried again, gathering up her skirts and racing forward just as he and the other two men rode away. A sob rose in her throat, and she felt hot tears stinging against her eyelids.

"Leave 'im to heaven," advised Sully, coming up behind her. "He'll make it through all right."

"Oh, Sully. I—I couldn't bear it if anything happened to him," she choked out. For the first time in years, she turned and buried her face against the front of the old wrangler's shirt while the tears spilled over from her lashes. Sully held her, awkwardly in the beginning, then with the loving arms of a true friend.

"A good cry's not so bad sometimes," he said, his calloused, sun-darkened hand smoothing down along the thickness of her braided hair. "Hell, I've been known to bawl once or twice myself."

"You?" Claire murmured in disbelief. She raised her head and dabbed at her eyes with the handkerchief she drew from the pocket of her skirt.

"You needn't look so gol-durned surprised about it. I'm human, same as anyone else."

" 'Human's one thing, female's another,' " she put forth unevenly, imparting one of her father's bits of wisdom again. Her bright, worried gaze drifted toward the horizon where Rand had already disappeared. The awful waiting had begun. "You should get down on your knees and give thanks you're not a woman."

"I'm thankful, all right," he affirmed, with characteristic gruffness. "Every damn minute of the day."

She managed a weak smile before pivoting about and slowly walking back to the house. Her heart felt so heavy that she found it difficult to breathe. Still sorely tempted to defy Rand and ride hell-bent for leather after him—she might well have done so, if she hadn't been afraid that her interference would only make things worse—she climbed the steps of the porch and went inside to talk to Sadie.

The next hour crawled by at a snail's pace. She did her best to keep her mind occupied, but it was no use. All she could think about was Rand, and the fact that he would be facing Tate. Tate . . . the man who wanted him dead. She paled anew as his vow of revenge echoed within her brain.

It was nearly one o'clock when she stepped back into the kitchen with an armful of firewood. Alongside the table, Sadie knelt on the floor, fitting a new calico dress on Harmony. Mother and daughter exchanged a quick glance before Sadie pulled herself upright and set her pincushion on the table.

"He'll be all right, Claire," she offered comfortingly. "I've never known a man more capable of looking after himself."

"I just wish this day was at an end." Claire sighed. She stacked the firewood inside the stove and straightened to cast a preoccupied look out the window above the sink. "The hands ought to be getting back soon."

"It's certainly quiet around here with all the menfolk gone."

"Sully's here," Harmony said, correcting her mother. She squirmed restlessly while her mother unpinned the pieces of fabric and folded them away.

"Yes, Sully's here," said Claire, "though I haven't seen hide or hair of him for a while now." Visibly distracted, she dusted off her hands and started for the back door again. "I think I'll see if I can—"

"Wolf's barking," Harmony noted all of a sudden.

Claire tensed, her pulse leaping in spite of the fact that she told herself it couldn't be Rand. She hastened outside to the front porch. A powerful wave of disappointment crashed over her when she saw that no one was there. Nor was there any sign of riders in the distance. Her dull gaze fell to Wolf, who had been dozing beneath the swing after a recent meal. He had apparently been startled awake by something; probably nothing more than a dream, she mused with another sigh.

"You wouldn't have barked at Rand anyway, would you, old boy?" she murmured to the dog. He wagged his tail and settled himself back down upon the porch, only to spring to his feet and bark again in the next instant. "What on earth . . . ?"

Frowning in bemusement, she headed down the steps and across the yard to find Sully. Wolf stayed behind, still raising a ruckus even when Harmony finally ventured outside in an effort to quiet him.

"Sully?" Claire called out as she approached the stock barn. There was no answer.

Her frown deepened. Plagued by a sudden, sharp uneasiness, she pulled the barn doors open and slipped into the hay-scented coolness of the building. Her eyes widened in mingled shock and horror when they fell upon the prone body of Sully. He lay sprawled, face-down, near one of the stalls. A small pool of blood had already formed beneath his head.

"Dear God!" gasped Claire. Racing forward to drop to her knees beside him, she had done nothing more than check to make sure he was still breathing when a hand suddenly closed about her arm and yanked her to her feet.

"He's not dead," Tate Jenner assured her. His eyes burned relentlessly down into the startled luminescence of hers. "Not yet, anyway."

"*Tate!* What—what have you done?" she demanded in a choked voice, her head spinning as alarm gripped her.

"I'm clearing out. And you're coming with me."

"No!" She struggled within his grasp, unable to believe what was happening. "Let go of me! Have you lost your mind? What—?"

"I couldn't leave you behind, Claire!" His fingers clenched roughly about her arm; he jerked her against him with such brutal force that the breath was knocked from her body. "Parker won't have you," he vowed in a tone of deadly calm. "I should have finished him off when I had the chance."

"I *knew* it was you!" she spat at him. Her gaze filled with vengeful fury, and she muttered a curse as she lifted a hand to strike a hard, stinging blow across the clean-shaven smoothness of his cheek. "You cowardly bastard! You didn't even have the courage to face him like a real man!"

"I'll show you just how real a man I am!" he bit out. His arms clamping about her like a vise, he lowered his head and ground his mouth down upon hers in a punishing kiss. She felt bile rise in her throat; the taste of blood made her even more nauseous. With a strangled moan of rage, she brought her knee smashing into his groin. He stiffened in pain. And even though he raised his head and gave a blistering oath, his hand remained locked about her arm.

"I won't go with you, Tate," she cried, furiously striking out at him again. "You'll have to kill me first!"

"Like hell!" Without warning, he doubled his hand into a fist and sent it crashing upward against her chin. An unintelligible cry broke from her lips as darkness engulfed her . . .

She had no idea how much time had passed when she regained consciousness. Her eyelids fluttered open, her sleep-drugged gaze darting about the interior of the tumbledown shack in which she lay. The unfamiliarity of her surroundings made her throat constrict in panic.

"She's comin' around," Zeke Jenner announced to his two brothers.

Claire's eyes shot to where he stood surveying her from a few feet away. She sat bolt upright on the wooden bunk, only to wince as her head swam and her jaw throbbed painfully.

"Take it easy," cautioned Tate. He crossed the dirty, musty-smelling room and knelt on the floor beside her. "Don't move so fast."

"Where am I?" she demanded, her eyes venomously ablaze when they met his.

"Doesn't matter." Frowning, he rose to his feet and turned back to Zeke and Harmon. "Mount up," he ordered in a curt tone.

"You ain't leavin' her here, are you?" Zeke asked, with a nod at Claire.

"We sure as hell can't take her along!" Harmon protested. Zeke gave her a look that betrayed at least a small measure of unwillingness to involve her in the danger.

She was forced outside and up onto the back of a waiting horse. Tate bound her hands together with a length of rope, then tied the ends of the rope to the saddle horn so that she could not scramble down. She held herself stiffly erect when he mounted behind her.

"I'll hate you forever if you do this," she vowed, her low tone charged with emotion. "And as God is my witness, I'll see you in hell before I'll ever let you touch me again!"

"You'll regret those words," he rasped close to her ear. A tremor of dread coursed through her before he jerked on the reins. The horse beneath them galloped away from the shack. Zeke and Harmon followed close behind.

They headed southward across the sun-baked plains. Claire's mind raced to think of a way to escape. Her gaze swept the passing countryside, desperately searching for other riders, for any signs of civilization. If only someone could hear her cries for help . . . but she saw nothing. Nothing except the rolling, windswept prairie and the endless blue of the sky above. Closing her eyes, she sent a silent, anguished plea heavenward.

After traveling only a few miles they reached the railroad tracks. Zeke and Harmon immediately swung down to fetch the several large trees they had cut earlier. They began dragging them across the rails, forming a barrier they knew the train's engineer would try to avoid. Tate dismounted, loosened the edges of the rope from the saddle horn, and hauled Claire down beside him.

"Keep quiet and do as I say," he commanded brusquely.

"What are you planning to do?" she asked, though she already knew the answer.

"Bankroll our future." His smile was one of supreme, malevolent confidence.

"We haven't *got* a future," she shot back. She took a deep breath and tried another tactic. Her eyes softened, her voice coaxing. "Please, Tate. Don't go through with this. You'll only be risking the lives of innocent people. You'll be risking your brothers' and your own as well. Surely you must see how foolhardy—?"

"Foolhardy?" He gave a mocking laugh and boasted, "It might surprise you to know just how good we've gotten at this, Claire. We've pulled it off a dozen times before, both here and down south. No one's been killed yet."

"Perhaps not, but you've certainly come close," she pointed out, her eyes flashing anew. "And sooner or later, your luck is going to run out!" Rand's image rose in her mind again. She prayed that he and the others would arrive in time. But most of all, she prayed that he would come to no harm.

Tate said nothing more. He compressed his lips into a tight, thin line and seized her arm. She resisted as best she could while he propelled her along with him to the cover of trees nearby. He pushed her down onto her knees, holding her captive at his side while Zeke and Harmon secured the horses for a quick getaway. They settled in to wait while the warm, sage-scented breeze stirred the leaves all about them.

The minutes ticked by with nerve-racking unhaste. At long last, the faint sound of the train whistle pierced the air in the distance. Claire's whole body tensed, her blood drumming loudly in her ears. She had still scarcely given a thought to her own welfare. But her mind was filled with acute, terrifying visions of what could happen to Rand. *Please God, please keep him safe!*

"Zeke, stay put at the engine till I give you the signal," Tate reminded his brother.

"I still say Harmon ought to be the one—"

"Do as I tell you, dammit!"

Moments later, the train rounded the curve. Spying the pile of debris on the track just ahead, the engineer hurried to apply the brakes. There was an awful screeching of metal upon metal as sparks flew. The train's wheels ground to a halt.

Zeke and Harmon sprang from the trees, whipping their guns from their holsters. Tate yanked Claire upright once more.

"Cross me, and I'll start shootin' some of those innocent people you're so worried about," he threatened, his eyes burning with a sinister determination that made her blanch. She had no choice but to go along with him as he headed for the passenger car.

Zeke, meanwhile, raced to the front of the train and aimed his six-shooter at the engineer.

"Hands up!" he ordered. "Make a move, and I'll cut you in half!" He smiled when the engineer, a gray-haired veteran of more than one such disaster, raised his arms and stepped away from the controls. "Hold her steady, old man."

"I reckon he'll be doing that, all right." A familiar voice spoke behind him. Zeke suddenly felt the barrel of a revolver ramming into his back. Jerking his head about, he saw that it was Micah who had crept around from between the cars to catch him by surprise.

Harmon, meanwhile, had taken up a position only a few yards away. Too preoccupied to notice what had happened to Zeke, he stopped before the express car and shouted for the guard to open the door. There was no response. He cursed, his features turning ugly at the defiance.

"Open up, or I'll—"

The door finally slammed open. But it wasn't the guard who stood facing him with deadly calm. It was Sheriff Malone and his deputies.

"Throw down your gun!" said Malone. His badge glinted in the sunlight as he pointed the barrel of his rifle at Harmon. Flanked by the two armed men in his employ, he caught and held the younger man's fearful, belligerent gaze.

Harmon visibly wavered. His finger twitched on the trigger of his weapon.

"Don't be a fool, boy," the lawman warned softly.

"Damn your eyes!" Harmon shot back. But he knew he was beaten. And now that the moment had come, he realized that he didn't want to meet his Maker just yet. In spite of the pact he and his brothers had once made, life in any form was preferable to death.

Swearing again, he tossed his six-shooter to the ground and raised his arms in surrender.

That left only Tate.

Unaware that both of his brothers had been captured, he pulled Claire up the steps of the last car with him. He burst through the door, intent upon relieving the passengers of their valuables.

But there were no passengers. The car appeared to be completely empty.

"What the—?" he muttered, scowling in furious perplexity at the sight before him.

Suddenly he glimpsed movement out of the corner of his eye. He yanked Claire in front of him and backed into the corner near the doorway. Across the aisle, in the center of the car, a grim-faced Rand stood to confront him.

"*Rand!*" Claire said. She instinctively tried to step toward him, but her captor's arm tightened about her waist until she struggled for breath. She was clasped back against him with his gun jammed to her side. Her gaze was wide and terror-stricken.

"Rand?" Tate echoed harshly. The name was a familiar one. Rand ... Rand Logan. The man who had disappeared six years ago. *Claire's husband.* His eyes kindled with bitter fury as the truth dawned on him.

"Let her go, Jenner," ordered Rand. His own badge gleamed upon his chest. His fingers were sure and steady about the Colt .45 he held in his right hand. "There's no way out." Murderous, white-hot rage filled him as he looked at Claire's ashen face, but he forced himself not to make a move yet.

"Do as he says, Tate!"

Disregarding Rand's instructions to stay out of sight, Will emerged from around the corner of the doorway at the opposite end of the car. He started toward his brother.

"I had to tell them. It was the only—"

"What do you mean?" His brother cut him off.

"The Rangers made me do it, Tate! I had to tell them everything. But I only did it to keep you alive."

"Traitor!" snarled Tate. "Yellow-bellied traitor!" Angered beyond reason at the betrayal, he lifted his arm and fired his gun.

A strangled cry escaped Claire's lips when the shot rang out. She watched in horrified disbelief as Will crumpled to the floor. He clapped a hand to the wound in his chest, his expression one of boyish, pained confusion.

"Tate?" he murmured. "Tate, why ... ?" The boy grimaced before slipping into merciful unconsciousness.

"Dear God, you've gone mad!" whispered Claire. She squirmed within his bruising grasp again, but he held her before him like a shield.

"Give it up, Jenner," Rand directed, his tone more dangerously low and measured than before. His one thought was to protect Claire; he would not hesitate to sacrifice his own life if necessary. "You've got nowhere to run. There are four others with me." He began inching forward down the aisle now, ready to fire at any moment. This wasn't the first time he had been faced with a standoff. But it was the first time it had ever mattered so much. "Let her go, or you're a dead man."

"What are you waitin' for?" the other taunted. "Afraid you'll miss?"

"Claire isn't part of this. Hiding behind her skirts won't change anything." He continued to advance. "We know you and your brothers are responsible for the robberies. Let her go free, and we'll talk about a deal."

"Keep your deals!" With a contemptuous sneer, he backed into the doorway. "I should've put a bullet in your brain that night at the box social!"

"Tate, please!" Claire begged, a fresh wave of panic making her voice shrill. "Don't you see? *It's too late!*"

"Not for me." He dragged her outside to the steps and aimed his gun at Rand. "She's mine, Logan!"

"No!" screamed Claire.

"Drop it!" Micah suddenly enjoined from outside. He stood just below the steps, adding his own weapon to the standoff. His dark, solemn gaze never wavered from the other man's face.

Tate rounded on him. But instead of admitting defeat, he squeezed the trigger.

A second shot exploded in the air while the first missed its mark.

Claire staggered forward as Tate's grip upon her relaxed. She clutched at the doorframe for support and stared numbly down at the man whose lifeless body lay sprawled at her feet. Blood had already begun to trickle from a neat round bullet hole in his left temple.

She looked to Rand. His gun was still smoking.

The next thing she knew, he was gathering her close, his arms enveloping her with their powerful, loving warmth. She closed her eyes and rested gratefully within his embrace.

"Claire." He spoke her name in a hoarse whisper.

The nightmare was over.

PARIS WEDDING

Chapter 15

Three days later, there was a double wedding at the church in Parmalee.

Although Rand had been surprised by his wife's highly unusual request, he had consented to it just the same. *And* had been well rewarded for his acquiescence.

"This time, Rand Logan," Claire had proclaimed, with a captivating twinkle in her eyes, "I want you to marry me of your own free will. No shotgun in your back, and no running off afterward."

Sadie had proven only too willing to share the attention with the woman whose kindness and generosity had provided her with a second chance at love.

"You're the closest thing I've ever had to a sister, Claire," she had declared earnestly. "God willing, you'll find all the happiness you deserve with Mr. Logan."

And so it was that on a beautiful, starlit April evening, Sadie Bishop walked down the aisle on Micah's arm. A fully recovered Sully performed the same honor for Claire. Neither of the brides wore white, of course, but they both looked radiant in their simple homemade gowns. Harmony beamed a proud smile while leading the way. The grooms stood tall and handsome at the altar, their gazes warmly aglow as they waited to claim the women they loved.

A former seminary classmate of Thomas's had traveled all the way from Louisiana in order to preside over the ceremony. He gave silent thanks for the fact that his old friend had finally given up his bachelor existence. Never mind the talk he'd heard concerning Thomas's choice of a bride. One look at the way Thomas's eyes softened at the sight of the pretty, raven-haired widow, and he knew the right decision had been made.

The church was very nearly filled to capacity. Weddings, it was said, tended to bring out the best in people. Claire put it down to curiosity more than anything else. Curiosity—and a desire to see her "properly married" to the man who had abandoned her six years earlier. The news of her errant husband's return had kept the town buzzing for days. And now that it was known she would be joining the ranks of the respectable at long last, she received a bit more sympathy than before.

"It's about time Rand Logan faced up to his responsibilities," had been the incorrigible Lydia's assessment of the situation. "Heaven knows, you've suffered enough."

There would be no more suffering. Claire knew that with a certainty as Rand grasped her hand with the strong warmth of his and smiled down at her. She felt her heart stir wildly, just as it had done all those years ago.

" 'Dearly beloved, we are gathered here today . . .' "

* * *

The night had long since deepened by the time they got back to the ranch. Rand guided the buckboard to a halt beneath the trees and set the brake. Micah and the other hands offered the newlyweds another round of congratulations before taking themselves off to the bunkhouse. Sully remained behind.

"I'll see to the horses," he told Rand. His eyes were full of ironic humor when he added, "Guess you've got other things to do."

"Sully!" Claire protested, coloring in spite of the fact that she was a twice-over bride.

"Sullivan Greene, you and I are going to get along just fine," drawled Rand. He scooped Claire up in his arms and carried her inside the house. "Someday, Mrs. Logan," he promised, "we'll have a real honeymoon."

"We can have a real one right here at Glorieta." She released a sigh of utter contentment and entwined her arms lovingly about his neck.

"I've still got that hotel room in Denton."

"I know, but I—I'd rather stay here." Her eyes clouded at a sudden, painful memory.

The last time she had been in Denton was the day Tate had tried to robe the stagecoach. *Tate*. He was gone now. Zeke and Harmon were awaiting trial over in Dallas. And even though Will's physical wound was healing nicely, his eyes held a haunted look that revealed the damage done to his soul. In time, it was hoped, he would find forgiveness within himself.

"It's over, Claire," Rand assured her, his tone quiet and resonant. He set her on her feet in the lamplit bedroom. His hands slid up to close gently about her shoulders. "I've hung up my guns and turned in my badge."

"Yes, but I'm still afraid you'll miss—"

"I won't miss a damn thing." He pulled her close and gave her a long, splendidly intoxicating kiss. She moaned low in her throat, not the least bit inclined to stop him when he finally raised his head again and turned her about so that he could unfasten the buttons on the back of her gown.

"We finally put truth to the lie," she pronounced softly.

"What are you talking about?" A slight frown of bemusement creased his handsome brow, but he kept right on with what he was doing.

"Remember all those rumors I told you about, the ones that had everyone watching to see if I gained any weight after you'd gone?"

"I remember."

"Well, I suppose you could say, 'better late than never.'" She was smiling mischievously when he spun her back around to face him.

"Are you sure, Claire?" he asked, his deep blue eyes brimming with pleasure at the news.

"I'm sure." She raised her hands to his chest and smiled again. "Regular as clockwork, that's me. And now you've come back and thrown everything off-kilter."

"So I have." He grew serious for a moment, his strong, gentle fingers smoothing along the silken curve of her cheek. "You're happy about it, aren't you?"

"Yes," she was able to answer in complete honesty. "I'm happy."

"Well then, I guess I'll have to go a little easier on

you from here on out." The teasing note had come back to his voice.

"Don't you dare." Delighting in the sound of his low, vibrant chuckle, she curled her arms about his neck and swayed provocatively against him. "I got cheated out of a wedding night the first time around, Rand Logan. I'm not about to let it happen again."

"Damn straight," he murmured huskily. His mouth descended upon hers once more. All else was forgotten as they celebrated a love that had endured against all odds . . . a love that had found a new beginning.